THE MURDER OF HARRIET KROHN

On a wet and dreary night in early November, Charlo Torp, a former gambler who's only recently kicked the habit, makes his way through the slush to Harriet Krohn's apartment, flowers in hand. Certain that paying off his debt is the only path to starting a new life and winning his daughter's forgiveness, Charlo plans to rob the wealthy old woman's antique silver collection. What he doesn't expect is for her to put up a fight. The following morning Harriet is found dead, her antique silver missing, and the only clue Inspector Sejer and his team find in the apartment is an abandoned bouquet. Charlo should feel relieved, but he's heard of Sejer's amazing record — the detective has solved every case he's ever been assigned to . . .

THE MURDER OF HARRIET KROHN

KARIN FOSSUM

TRANSLATED FROM THE NORWEGIAN BY JAMES ANDERSON

LARGE
PRINT

First published in Great Britain 2014
by
Harvill Secker

First Isis Edition
published 2016
by arrangement with
Harvill Secker
Penguin Random House

A catalogue record for this book is available
from the British Library.

ISBN 978–1–78541–184–7 (hb)
ISBN 978–1–78541–190–8 (pb)

Published by
F. A. Thorpe (Publishing)
Anstey, Leicestershire

Set by Words & Graphics Ltd.
Anstey, Leicestershire
Printed and bound in Great Britain by
T. J. International Ltd., Padstow, Cornwall

This book is printed on acid-free paper

Dearest Julie,

Do you read my letters? I hope so, but I don't make any demands, I stay in the background. I've nothing to offer you and I know why you feel bitter. But I'm writing anyway — I am your father, after all. Writing has become a consolation, I find it soothing. You know how things stand, how I'm placed. Everyone's after me because I'm in debt, I feel like a hunted deer. I've no real friends any more, only lukewarm acquaintances. Do you remember Bjørnar Lind? He was my best friend, we'd known each other since we were boys, now he won't have anything to do with me. I owe him two hundred thousand kroner, and I don't know where I'm going to find that sort of money. I'm worried he'll put people on to me, worried about what they'll do if I can't pay. There are rumours that he's hiring someone to come after me. And you know what they do to people? They cut off their fingers with secateurs, I feel ill just thinking about it. Daily life is difficult. The dole isn't enough for necessities, it's impossible to keep up with bills and repayments.

If only there was light at the end of the tunnel! It's my fault all this has happened, and you mustn't worry about it, just look after yourself and be happy. Be young and fit and hopeful! But I am trying to deal with things in my own pathetic way. I have some initiative left even though I'm down on my knees. I've got plans. Dreams. I'm racking my brain frantically to find a solution. It spins and sifts and searches in all directions. When did we last see one another? It was on 27 May, do you remember? We argued. I was simply trying to describe how compulsive gambling is. The thrill of it, the addiction. You slammed the car door behind you, and I thought, I'll never see her again, no more chances for me. I drove home to Blomsgate with the feeling that I'd failed at everything. There must be a way out! Is it just that I can't find it? I stare into the future until I can't see anything any more, I pace to and fro in the house, I chew my lips until they bleed. I often think of your mother, I think of her with sadness and remorse. All the things she had to put up with as a result of my obsession. It was so much easier then, she took care of us and organised everything. She was a kind of corrective influence. I can't grasp that she's gone. Once a week I visit her grave, it's so sad. Often, I just want to fall to the ground, dig right down, lift off the lid and take her back. Yesterday, I bought a plant and placed it in front of her gravestone — an erica, the one with the mass of reddish-mauve flowers that can deal with almost any conditions, a bit like heather. I tend her grave, you know, I trim and weed and water. Sometimes I look for signs, to see if, perhaps, you've been hanging about there. Have you? Do you stand there crying all alone? I like the idea of acknowledging that death comes to everyone. Perhaps some just fade, sitting there withering away, like my mother. In my worst moments I've viewed death as a way out, I've still got my father's old revolver. Forgive this candour, you are not responsible for me. I won't live to be very old, I'm so tired already. Just think,

2

your grandmother is seventy-nine. But she just sits there immobile in her chair, only half alive. In a kind of slumber where nothing happens. But her features are still strong, like that prominent chin which you've inherited. As for me, I can't disappear in a doze, every cell within me vibrates. Blood courses through my body, my fingers quiver. At night I lie in the darkness listening, there are so many creaks and sighs in this old house, I don't get much sleep. Is it them? I think, has my final hour come? Today, I was at the Job Centre, but nobody wants a middle-aged man. And I've no decent references, either, nothing to show or boast about. Julie! I won't give up, even if I'm driven to drastic measures. I've spent every minute of every day searching for a solution. It all hinges on money I haven't got. Things I can't afford, plans I can't bring to fruition, debts I can't pay. Fear and shame are everywhere, in the terror of each ring at the doorbell, and in the long hours until sleep arrives, bringing the only solace the day affords. Unless, that is, I dream of ruin. Life can't go on like this, it's sapping my strength too much. This constant fear, this thudding heart. My own miserable face in the mirror, the knowledge that I destroyed everything. Just because of a flaw. A penchant for gambling, chance and luck.

I'm not asking you for forgiveness, only an iota of understanding. I'm on a different course now. Gambling is no longer a pleasure to me, I think I could walk past a fruit machine with my money safe in my pocket. But there's something about those flashing lights, it's a kind of intoxication. Time stands still in front of the machine, and I'm fully alive. I take possession of it, control it, challenge it, the machine greets me with its lights and music, draws me in, tempts me. And I surrender myself to it, float away, begin to dream. This may seem like weakness to you, but it's only half the truth. If you knew how desperate I am, how far I'm prepared to go for us to be in contact again. I've no one else but you. I feel I've been driven back to my last bastion and I don't know how things will end. I'm friendless, jobless and childless. No, not childless, I still cling to you, even though you don't need me, don't want me. Maybe you've seen me occasionally, sitting in the Honda outside your school, hidden amongst the vehicles in the car park. I watch you emerge from the building with a crowd of friends, see you healthy and laughing and fooling around. I see your magnificent red hair, like a cloud around your face. Do I have any place at all in your life? I don't know if I could bear it if you cut me adrift forever. To grow old alone with no ties to anyone. Of all the misfortunes that can befall us, loneliness is the worst. Not even having someone to weep with in this wretched world. You are the only thing I'm proud of in my life. But you look thin, Julie, are you eating enough? You must wrap up better, it's winter now. Mum would have said the same if she'd seen you with nothing around your neck. You always used to listen to her. Do you remember those happy days? When I still had my job at the car showroom. I was a good salesman, capable and reliable, and I remember the satisfaction of concluding each sale. The feeling of success, of being in the swing of things. Returning to you and Mum in the evenings, to the warmth and light. There's no light any more, my life is disappearing. While I write you feel so close. It's as if I'm holding your hand, I can't bear to let go. Listen to me! Think of me, let me feel that I'm part of your life! Are things all right with your flat, and at school? I dream of making some difference to you, of giving you what you want most of all. I

4

don't believe in miracles, but I believe one can change one's own destiny, it's just a matter of willpower and imagination. Of endurance and courage. I also believe it comes at a price. As things stand now, I'd give anything, I've nothing to lose. Dark, fearful days are all that lie before me.

CHAPTER
ONE

A man is walking through the darkness.

He is visible beneath the street lights for a few moments, then is swallowed up by shadow until he emerges again under the next light, as if his existence only flares up momentarily. That's how he experiences it, that's what his life is now. He comes to life and starts to glow, only to go out again, on and off like a hot, quivering fever. His fists are clenched in his pockets as he thrusts on through the darkness, but he arouses no interest. Nobody turns to look at him, he's an ordinary middle-aged man with thinning hair, and as he walks along he thinks, with something approaching amazement, that it's not visible from the outside. The thing I'm just about to do. How little people know. I'm moving in the midst of them, and look, they walk the streets immersed in their own affairs.

The faces coming towards him are expressionless. There's no happiness in them, no joy over life or the day, or the falling snowflakes. The life they own for just a brief span, and take for granted, glides past slowly as they dream of another life in another place. Of love, tenderness, all the things that human beings need. He walks on and on, he'd rather turn back, but he knows it's too late, he's come too far. He can barely comprehend how he's got to this point, but he pushes the thought away and allows himself to drift onwards, spurred by necessity and fear. He stares into the chasm that opens in front of him, it's bottomless. The leap scares him out of his wits, the leap is enticing. He curls his fingers inside his pockets, he's so fearful for them, he imagines the secateurs going through the thin skin, and the blood spurting from the stumps. He feels faint. He's unable to banish the image. He must get to a different place, even if the name of that place is disaster. He bears a huge shame, a miserable life, he can't take any more, he must act now. Occasionally, he raises his eyes and peers at the unsuspecting passers-by. They can't see all the horror that's slowly growing inside him. Is this really happening? Isn't the town a set, isn't this a film? The facades seem like papier mâché and everyone else like extras. No, this is real; he clenches his fists, feels the muscles tightening. He's on the move now, he gets ready, it's as if he's being propelled along a track.

His lower lip is cut, he doesn't know when it happened, there's the sweet tang of blood in his mouth, he thinks it tastes good. Later, when it's all over, people will grieve, cover their eyes and condemn. Even though he can explain. He knows he can explain, step by step, about the weary way, about the great abyss beneath him, if he's given time. If they'll only listen to his story. But people haven't got time, they've got their own tales of hard luck; oh, his burden is so heavy, he's so alone! Such are his thoughts as he walks along the street, with his hands deep in his pockets, and his face turned to the slushy pavement.

He's of medium height and powerfully built, and he's wearing a green parka. The parka has a hood, which is gradually filling with snow. His face is wide, his eyes grey and close-set, not a handsome man, and not all that shy, either. A high forehead, a wide jaw and a strong, unshaven chin. He's wearing decent boots, but the leather is worn and leaking water, his toes are numb. He hardly notices, there's so much to think about. No, he daren't think at the moment, he empties his mind, turning himself into a purely purposeful organism that doesn't look back. He must reach his goal now, not allow fear to intervene. It surrounds him, lying there like a colourless gas; he hardly dares draw breath. He passes a shop selling mirrors and catches a glimpse of his own face that makes him look away in horror. His face is so naked, his eyes deep in shadow. He keeps moving on, his figure strong and compact, his shoulders broad and round, and he walks with a resolute step. Each time his boots make contact with the pavement, the slush spurts in all directions with a sodden, slurping sound. Nothing can stop him. All the same, if I met someone now, he thinks, an old friend for example, we might make small talk or reminisce about the past. We might have a beer at The Dickens, and everything would be different. But no old friend appears. He has no friends, not any more, no work either; he's become reclusive, turned in on himself. He lives with fear and sorrow and worry. His world is small and mean. It's 7 November and sleet is falling. Great wet flakes. He lights a cigarette, inhales deeply, filling his lungs with smoke. It makes him cough, but he knows it will pass. Soon he catches sight of a Jet service station with its garish, neon-yellow signs. He gazes up at the large H&M posters. They cover the front of the block on his right. How strange, he thinks, that the buxom girl in the lacy underwear is naked on a bleak evening like this. She looks relaxed in spite of it all, though he is wet and chilled, but this is hardly something that troubles him. It's a fact he registers only vaguely, as if looking at himself from the outside. Soon he sees the door to the florist's. He slackens his pace at once. He makes his final approach peering furtively in through the shop window. He can't stop now, he's on that track, and before him is the plummeting slope that vanishes into darkness. At the same time he feels himself flinching, he feels shaken, he can't understand how it's happened, how he's come so close to the precipice. That before him lies a deceitful mission, a despicable purpose. Before *him*: good old Charlo. Charles Olav Torp. A perfectly ordinary man. A little unlucky perhaps, a little weak, but apart from that a thoroughly decent chap. Or is he a decent chap? He thinks he is, clenches his teeth and pushes at the heavy door. It opens inwards. He hears the sound of a bell. Its delicate tinkle disturbs him. He would prefer to arrive soundlessly, unnoticed and unheard.

He stands in the middle of the shop. Immediately the smell of the place assails him, sweet and stupefying. It's too much, for an instant he feels giddy and has to take

10

a sideways step to regain his balance. He hasn't eaten for a long time, did he forget? He can't remember any more. The day has passed in a fog, for him it's as if he's only now waking up on the edge of the abyss. His eyes take in the premises. It's like a mini-jungle of flowers and greenery, leaves and petals. He can make out artificial blooms and watering cans, plant food and leaf shine, wreaths of dried roses. An indescribable profusion of flowers. He reads their exotic names: chrysanthemum and erica, hibiscus and monstera. A young girl is standing behind the counter. She reminds him of his daughter Julie, but she isn't so beautiful because Julie is the loveliest, the best. His heart beats tenderly whenever he thinks of his daughter, but he also feels a gnawing pain, and his own betrayal hits him with its full horror.

He swallows and straightens and looks at the young girl once more; she's slender, her fair hair is in long plaits, and he notices her thin wrists, so amazingly pale and delicate. She's young, he thinks, and her bones are as pliable as a kitten's. She could probably do the splits or a backbend. Her skin is healthy and pink and almost unbelievably clear. Her eyes are lowered modestly. The floor is covered with flowers in blue and red plastic buckets. He can see roses, crimson and yellow, and other flowers whose names he doesn't know. He stands looking around diffidently with his hands in his pockets. For a moment he's overcome. He feels terribly exposed in the bright light, alone with this young girl who is still waiting. She's looking at him now, uncertain but receptive. She likes being there, likes her work, soon

11

the shop will close and she can go home to her little flat and a hot bath. Something nice to eat, perhaps, maybe something good on television. Or a long chat on the phone to a close friend. He doesn't know why, but he can tell that she's happy, that she's content with the way things are. Some people are content, he thinks, they must be or the world would stop, and the undergrowth would spring up and hide all traces of humanity. How beautiful, a bright green planet with no people, just a few grazing animals, and flapping, shrilling birds. The girl is thin, but she looks healthy. She probably eats only as much as she needs, he thinks, maybe she takes exercise and doesn't put on any weight. Or she's inherited the trait from a slim family.

He muses, kills time, feels that his heart is thumping tirelessly, and that his cheeks are hot, even though he's just been trudging the streets for an eternity, going round and round the town that's grey with sleet and mist. He stood on the river bank and stared down into the water, and considered that as a solution. To jump from the bank and allow himself to sink to the bottom. It would be quick, he thought, he'd see his life pass in front of his eyes. Inga Lill's illness, Julie's despair, his own sick mania for gambling. He pushes the thoughts away. It's all becoming real for him. What he'd pictured in his head for days and weeks, is now materialising. This is the first step. So harmless, so respectable, buying a bunch of flowers. The girl waits patiently, but she's becoming uneasy because he doesn't speak. She shifts her weight from one foot to the other, withdraws her hands then rests them on the counter once more.

Her fingers are adorned with thin rings and her nails are painted red. She pushes her plaits over her shoulders, they are as bright and shiny as nylon rope, but a moment later they've fallen forward again and are hanging over her breasts. And he knows that when she gets into bed at night and takes the bands off, her hair will be fluffy and full after the plaiting. How young these girls are, he thinks, how smooth, how translucent. They make him think of rice paper, porcelain and silk, they make him think of fragile glass. He can see her veins, a delicate network of green beneath the skin of her wrists. Life is pulsing there, with nutrition and oxygen and everything she needs to keep herself alive. He takes another deep breath. The light inside the shop, the powerful scent of roses and the cloying heat is almost overpowering. He sees stars. He feels his pulse rise and clenches his fists hard, he feels the nails pressing into his skin. Pain, he thinks, this is really happening. No, nothing has happened, not yet, but time is moving on, and sooner or later I'll get there. When I do, will it be awful? The girl behind the counter makes another attempt, she smiles pleasantly, but he doesn't return the smile. His face is immobile. He knows that he ought to smile, so that he'll seem like an ordinary customer, a man about to do something gratifying. Buy a bunch of flowers. But he's no ordinary customer and this is not enjoyable.

He approaches the counter hesitantly, his sturdy body moving with a rolling gait. He's uncertain about his voice as he hasn't used it for a while, so he puts some extra force behind it.

"I want a mixed bunch," he says, and the loudness of his own words makes him start. My feet are wet, he thinks, my boots aren't watertight. Cold perspiration is trickling down my back, but my cheeks are boiling hot. I'm not certain this is real. Shouldn't it feel different, shouldn't I feel more present within myself? I'm having so many strange thoughts. Am I losing control? No, I'm focused, I'm secure. I've made a plan and I'm going to stick to it. His chain of thought is interrupted by the girl speaking.

"Is it a special occasion?" she's asking.

The voice is sweet and childish, slightly put on; she's making herself sound younger than she is, protecting herself, so that he'll treat her gently. It's what women do, and he forgives her for it, but only because she's young. Grown-up women should behave like grown-ups, he can't abide the same affectation in older women, making the most of their reputation as the weaker sex, when they're really tough, resilient and clever, and more calculating than men. It makes him think of Inga Lill. She did it frequently, especially in the beginning. She would make her voice sugary sweet, ingratiating herself and hiding behind all that femininity. It made him feel boorish because he was simple and direct. Inga Lill, you're dead now, you don't know what's happening, and thank God for that. I'm losing the plot, he realises, I'm getting hung up on details; I must get to the point soon. How old is she? he asks himself, and studies the girl, could she be eighteen? She's older than Julie, who's sixteen. It doesn't matter, I don't know her, we won't ever see each other again. They've got so many customers here, and she'll remember hardly any of them because she's young and lives like all young girls, in a dream for much of the day, a dream of all the wonderful things in store for her.

She pulls up her sleeves and comes out to stand amongst the flowers.

Her jumper is tight-fitting and deep red; she's like a flower, a slender tulip, fresh, taut and vivid. Oh yes, it's a special occasion all right. Good God, if only she knew! But he doesn't want to speak, doesn't want to reveal more of himself than necessary. Buying flowers is a normal daily activity and can hardly be linked to the other thing he'll be doing later on. What is it he's about to do? Where will it end? He doesn't know. He's heading for the edge of the precipice to find a solution. A transition to something else. He looks round the place. The business has a good reputation. A large number of customers come in every day, he imagines a steady stream of people in and out. An infinite number of faces, an infinite number of orders, bouquets of many colours. He'll hardly stand out in his green parka. He's careful to lower his eyes, drawing the girl's attention away from himself. What blooms there are in the large buckets! He can barely believe they emerge from the damp, black earth. To earth shall you return, he thinks, and out of the earth come the flowers. Dandelions, or nettles. It's precisely the way it should be: death isn't as bad as its reputation, on that point he's quite decided. The girl waits patiently. She's a floral designer. She has professional pride. She's an artist with flowers. She can't just throw something together, any old mixture, it's all about creating a composition, about shape and colour and scent, she never makes two bouquets the same. She's got her own signature, but she needs something to get her started. A little inspiration, an idea. It's not forthcoming. Charlo is taciturn and uncooperative.

"For a lady?" she probes. She notes his unwillingness, she can't comprehend it, and it makes her feel uncomfortable. He seems disinterested, as if he's running an errand for someone, he seems awkward and nervy. He appears to be pouring sweat, his body swaying gently, his jaw clenched. Perhaps he's going to visit someone who's ill, she thinks. You never can tell.

Charlo nods without meeting her eyes. But then he begins to realise that if he's helpful and pliant, he'll be able to leave the shop sooner. He must clear his head now, he mustn't become preoccupied, he's got to see the plan through. My nerves, he thinks, are as taut as wires. He knew it would be this way. Once more he focuses on his objective.

"Yes," he says, "for a lady." Again his voice has too much of a bark about it, and on a sudden whim, which he feels is wise, he adds: "It's her birthday."

Relieved, the florist's assistant begins working. Everything falls into place and the slight frame gathers itself. The shoulders relax, the delicate fingers pick up a pair of tongs, she bends over the buckets and picks out the flowers, one by one. Her fingers hold the stalks so gently. She seems to have a plan, there's no more

16

hesitating, no uncertainty. Her eyes survey the buckets, it's a professional gaze, self-assured now. White lilies, blue anemones, sweet peas and roses. Slowly, a plump, pastel spray takes shape in her hands. She begins in the centre of the bunch with a lily, around which the other flowers cluster, nodding and dipping, but still held firm, each flower protecting and supporting the other; it's an art. He watches this, he becomes deeply fascinated and falls in love with what's being created, but shivers when he recalls that the flowers are to serve an evil purpose.

He stands waiting edgily. His heart is thudding hard under his parka, he wants to pacify it but can't, his heart won't listen to him any more. Oh, well, he thinks, let it beat as much as it wants, I've still got a mind, and that's working all right. I'm the one who decides, I'm the one who orders my body to do things. It's still my decision. He sighs, so heavily that she hears and glances up. She's wise to him, she knows that something's afoot, but she can't interpret the meaning of his behaviour. Instinctively, she retreats into her craft, the thing she knows. Arranging flowers. Charlo breathes easily again. Pull yourself together, says the voice inside him, nothing has happened, not yet. Nobody's got anything on you. You can still turn back, you can pull out and life will go on, go on until death. He throws quick glances at the bouquet, his thoughts wander far away again, he's only half there. He's a cipher, a nobody; now at last he wants to set himself free. Mentally he thinks he knows something about how the whole thing will come off. He's been through it again and again. He'll take charge of the moment, he'll direct all that takes place. There is no room for unforeseen circumstances, he brushes them hastily aside. He stares out of the window, sees that sleet is still falling fast. Tracks, he thinks, and feels in his pockets. He wants to check that he's remembered everything. He has; he's thought of the whole lot, he's thought about it for weeks. He's practised mentally, and sometimes, in his sleep, he's cried out in fear.

The bouquet grows.

The shop bell chimes brightly in the silence, and he starts. A woman enters dressed in a green coat with a black fur collar, her shoulders covered in sleet. She brushes it off with a hand in a beige-coloured glove and regards him with hard, painted eyes. She's weighing him up, isn't she? A sharp old trout who takes everything in, Charlo thinks. All the details, a personal trait that she may later be able to describe. But he has no personal traits, he's sure he hasn't, and he simmers down again. She leans over one of the buckets, draws out a rose and studies the stalk intently. He quickly turns his face away. The face that feels so large, as if it's hanging there, proclaiming itself like a pennant. He stands looking out at the sleet. It's most visible under the streetlights, a thick, greyish-white drift cutting across the darkness. He feels miserable. Because of his terrible destiny. I don't deserve this, he thinks, I'm a kind-hearted man. But dread destroys the soul. He's in the process of losing himself. The girl works on. Will she never be finished? The bouquet is big and becoming expensive. He thinks about the time that's passing, how he's standing in here exposed and susceptible. About how it could be dangerous for him. From now on everything will be dangerous. He's prepared for this fear. It's physical, but he can keep it at bay if he can control his breathing.

"The bouquet's two hundred and fifty kroner at the moment," the assistant says. She looks up at him, but just as quickly looks away, still uncertain because of his sullenness.

He nods and says: "That's fine." In a clumsy attempt at sociability, he adds, "It looks lovely."

She sends him a smile of relief. There is something nice about him after all, she thinks, and rejoices.

I ought to have chatted and smiled, Charlo thinks. Charmed her, because I can when I want to. Then she would have forgotten me with all the others.

"Will it be long before they're put in water?" she asks.

Now her voice is brighter, more open.

He stands there cogitating dumbly. Will they be put in water at all? He doesn't know. It's coming up to eight o'clock and he realises the shop will shut in a few minutes. He'll have to wait a while before setting his plan in motion. Until the traffic dies down in the streets. Until people have got home and he can wander past the houses unseen.

"About an hour or two," he replies, and watches as she packs the stems in damp tissue. She wraps them in cellophane, which crackles ominously, then in white paper.

19

Charlo has turned away once more, and when he turns back, he sees that she's putting the bouquet in a cone-shaped carrier bag. The bag has the words "Tina's Flowers" prominently printed on it in blue and red. He gets out his wallet to pay, his hands shaking slightly. The girl avoids looking at him and instead stares at his wallet, which is brown and tattered. Her young, alert eyes notice that the zip is broken, the leather is worn and the seams are gaping. She sees the small red-and-white sticker announcing that he's a blood donor. He pays, replaces his wallet and gives her a little smile. She smiles back, noticing that his left front tooth is chipped, and that he's never bothered to repair it. It makes his smile rather charming. Charlo glances quickly at the elderly woman who's waiting. The snow on her shoulders has melted, the wet patches shine in the light. She looks at the time, she's in a hurry and marches up to the counter. Her nose is sharp and red in her long, lean face. Deep creases at the corners of her mouth, blue bags under her eyes. He knows that he'll always remember this face. At last he can leave. The door bangs, the bell jingles.

The air outside seems strangely fresh. He walks through the streets carrying the bag. He's visible under a streetlight for a few seconds, gets swallowed up by darkness, only to become visible again under the next. The bag swings in his hand. All that trouble she went to over the bouquet, all that skill and experience, all to no purpose. The flowers are merely an entry ticket. That's how he'll get into the house.

And right into Harriet Krohn's kitchen.

20

CHAPTER
TWO

She lives in Fredboesgate, Hamsund.

It's a seventeen-kilometre drive. Harriet's house is one of a cluster of listed timber buildings dating from the middle of the nineteenth century, and is situated in a very quiet street. They are small, pretty wooden houses with beautifully framed windows. Most of the inhabitants are elderly, and most are well off. In summer, the frontages are decorated with flourishing window boxes full of geraniums, nasturtiums and marguerites. The house is only a few minutes away from the railway station; there are twelve houses in all, six on each side of the street. Harriet lives in number four. The house is lichen-green, the sills and bargeboards are painted yellow.

Charlo approaches Hamsund. It's still sleeting heavily, and he concentrates hard on keeping the car on the road, he doesn't want to end up in the ditch, not tonight. On the seat next to him is an old Husqvarna revolver, which isn't loaded. It's only for show, he thinks, she won't be uncooperative, she won't dare to be, she's elderly. He also has a pair of black leather gloves and a cotton bag for anything he finds of value. It is rolled up in his pocket. He's on the E134, driving by the river, which is surging along on his left, rough and black. He knows the river is full of salmon, but he's never bothered to fish. When he thinks about fishing, he remembers his boyhood. He remembers his father, who always wanted to go fishing, while he sat there getting bored, his rod dipping lethargically over the water. Fishing was too slow for him, too dull. This was something he never articulated, he didn't want to hurt his father, he didn't want to complain. I used to be a considerate boy then, he thinks. And what am I thinking about my father for, he's dead now and at peace. People pass away, just as I'll pass away, and that's good. It certainly is good, he decides, and squints at the road ahead.

The markings in the middle of the carriageway are only just visible, the sleet is settling like grey porridge on the tarmac, the windscreen wipers struggle with the slush. But the Honda doesn't let him down, the Honda is matchless and reliable. He's already worked out a good place to park. He'll do the last bit on foot, it's only a couple of hundred metres. There's an old, derelict hotel at Hamsund, and a car can be parked in the courtyard there, out of sight of the street. He's aware that the car could give him away, and that he must conceal it. He turns to the right and on to the R35, catches sight of Hamsund church, which is floodlit, and its gravestones. He passes an Opel showroom, a couple of shopping centres, and cruises slowly past the railway station on his right. It's a really elegant building, like a great layer cake covered with icing. How strange, he thinks, that his mind is running on cakes; everything seems odd this evening, as if he's playing a part in a film. There's hardly any traffic. People are indoors.

Now he sees the hotel, it's called The Fredly. A handsome white timber building with much fine ornamentation and dark, unseeing windows. He turns into the courtyard and parks; there are no other cars there. A notice on the wall facing him announces that unauthorised vehicles will be towed away, but he knows that no one will come here tonight, everyone is sheltering from the weather. Then he hears a noise. A sort of click and something ringing faintly, and he heaves himself round in his seat and looks through the windows. Is someone coming after all? Has someone seen the car? Again, he has an acute attack of nerves. I don't have to do this, he mumbles into the darkness. I'm not quite myself. Can't anybody stop me, isn't there another way? But nobody comes, and there is no other way. The voice within him is frail and attenuated.

He looks back on his life, how wretched it's been. Guilt and betrayal, weakness. Lies and deceit. Promises he hasn't kept. Has there been anything good about it? Inga Lill was good. Julie is the most precious thing he has. He tries to breathe evenly. He believes he's thought of everything, but he knows it's easy to overlook a detail, which could be crucial and might give him away later on. But this "give him away" doesn't seem so terrifying. It's in the future, and he hasn't arrived there yet, it's almost as if he doesn't believe in it. He's living for the moment, he's doing what he has to do and time is running out. That's what he'll say if they catch him. I had to do it, I saw no other solution, it was a matter of survival. He turns off the ignition. Sits in the car round the back of the abandoned hotel listening to the surrounding darkness. He hears his own breathing, it's rapid and rasping. He looks at his watch, the dial glows green in the darkness of the car's interior. He pulls the flowers out of the carrier bag and lays them in his lap. The bouquet is heavy, but otherwise nondescript, packed in white paper. What if she has visitors? he thinks. There are lots of things that could go wrong. But he doesn't believe Harriet Krohn has many visitors. He's studied her, followed her, listened in as she sat in the cafe with her best friend. She's a lonely old woman and will certainly hesitate to open her door. But I'm armed, he thinks, with these irresistible flowers and a World War II revolver; she'll have to do what I say. He pulls on his gloves and gets out of the car. Locks up. He pushes the revolver into the waistband of his trousers. Once again he listens, but he hears nothing, only the sound of his own boots splashing in the slush. If I can just get inside, he thinks, as he walks through the darkness, getting inside the house will be the trickiest bit. Old people are frightened of everything.

Harriet Krohn walks around her living room.

Her thin ankles carry her body's modest forty-nine kilos, her calves arched like bowed sticks. The veins are right under her skin and look like knotted branches, despite her thick stockings. This is her last day on earth, her last hour. She hears the ticking of the wall clock. The street outside is quiet. She sits down by the coffee

24

table and eats a slice of bread, spread with liver pâté. She has dressed the open sandwich with beetroot, she's fussy about what she eats. She has a cup of lightly sweetened tea with it. She tastes the fresh tang of the beetroot, it combines with the sweetness of the tea. Now she pauses. A grain of wholemeal from the bread has got stuck between two molars and is pressing like a wedge. She tries pushing one of her nails between the teeth to work it loose. It's no good, the nail is too thick. She needs a toothpick, but she'll finish eating first, then tidy up. There's nothing out of place in her home, everything is cleared away at once. She chews long and thoroughly because it's good for the digestion, and when she's finished she carries her cup and plate out to the kitchen, brushes the crumbs into the sink, rinses the cup. After that she fills a bowl with liquorice allsorts and places it on the table in the living room. It's mainly for decoration; she likes the colours.

It's too early to go to bed. It's only ten o'clock and she's bored. She must pass the evening somehow, and television doesn't interest her. She feels disgruntled. There's nothing to look forward to, nothing happy on the horizon. Only old age and a steadily increasing debility. Soon she'll be seventy-six, but she feels much more. She has plenty of family silver and a lot of money, but she hasn't the strength to use it, either on herself or others. She makes up her mind to write a letter. She's got a nephew in Germany with whom she keeps in touch. Writing a letter is pleasant, and she can use it to fill the remaining hour. She always goes to bed at eleven. She has an antique writing desk in the living room with a leaf that opens out, giving her a nice little working space. She glances out of the window, sees the heavy sleet. It's warm in the living room, she's got the heaters on full. Even though she's a tiny woman, she moves about with great effort. She was only thirteen when she was diagnosed with arthritis. Throughout her life she's battled to keep the disease at bay. But this is one of her better days: the pains can be much worse than they are this evening, 7 November. There are days when she just lies in bed moaning. Cursing her own fate which is so much worse than other people's. The bitterness makes her hot, she must get it out and down on paper.

She switches on the lamp next to the desk, it warms her left cheek. She can't see the man coming down the street. She's found a blank sheet of paper. She gets out her glasses and perches them on her nose, holds the pen over the paper. It's an almost spiritual moment for Harriet Asta Krohn. The white paper, pristine, all the things she wants to say. The pen won't stay still between her fingers, which are shaking with effort. But she knows from experience that as soon as it touches the paper, it will steady. Then she'll be in command of her muscles and manage to write in a fairly decent hand with thin, delicate loops. However, she knows too, that when she reaches the end her fingers will begin to tremble again, as the pain takes over. The grandfather clock ticks, Harriet's heart beats. And while it does, the blood circulates through her frail body; she's warm, she's replete. Then she feels the grain of wholemeal again, pressing. She'd forgotten her intention of finding a toothpick, but now she'll leave it. She thinks: I can do that later.

Charlo stands at the bottom of the front steps.

No one saw him go through the gate. Harriet is unaware of his proximity, even though he's only a few metres away. She's always lived alone, and much of her life has been spent in this house. She knows all its sounds, every creak of the old timber, the lilac that beats against the panes of the living room when the wind blows in the summer. The occasional mouse scurrying across the attic floor. The house is spartan. The rooms are small and hot, the furniture simple and carefully chosen, its colours and patterns blend together. There is little decoration, she doesn't waste money, she has no time for empty display.

Charlo climbs the steps. Harriet draws a deep breath and puts her pen to the paper, she writes "Dear". A gold bracelet on her wrist rattles on the writing surface. The letter gradually takes shape inside her head; she can hear her own voice within her, it's authoritative and flows lightly and easily, but her hand is much slower. In the midst of this tranquil interlude she's disturbed by the doorbell. A sudden, insistent note in the silence. She raises her head and listens in surprise, automatically glancing at the clock on the wall, as if the clock can tell her who's coming. Five past ten. It's well past the time for salesmen, and too late for her friend Mosse next door, she'd never call at ten in the evening. Unless it was something very out of the ordinary. Could that be it? Could something have happened? But then if it were Mosse, Harriet realises, she'd have phoned first, because she's considerate, and both of them are elderly. But the doorbell has rung and she sits in her chair with her pen in her hand, paralysed. She stares at the single word "Dear". Then she thinks, at least the door chain's on. But there's silence now, and she's perplexed. After all, it could just be children playing, excited by the sleet and running about the streets in search of mischief. To leave her chair and walk through the living room and all the way out to the hall would be an effort for her, she won't get up unless she has to. But the bell rings again, twice. The person at the door isn't going to give up. It's silly not to answer, she realises, she is a grown-up after all. Perhaps it's someone from the Women's Institute, they've got a habit of calling at any time.

She rises now, with difficulty, and walks with short, fumbling steps across the room. Again she feels the wholemeal grain wedged in her teeth. Now she's in the hall. Through the glass in the door she can make out a figure standing on the top step. A solid, black shadow. Again she hesitates. Who would turn up at this hour? She knows hardly anyone. First she undoes the lock, then she opens the door warily as far as the chain permits. There's a man in a green parka. He moves slightly so she can see him through the chink. Isn't there something familiar about him? She racks her brain but can't find him in the myriad faces stored there. He's holding a parcel up to his chest. She has no idea what it is. She stands staring at him through the crack as she waits for some explanation. Without realising it, her thin face has assumed a hostile and suspicious expression.

"Harriet Krohn?" the man asks.

The voice is friendly and light, as if the white snowflakes have made him merry, with their sudden Christmassy atmosphere at the beginning of November.

"Yes?" she says, and stares at the package, the little she can see of it through the gap between the door and the frame. How big it seems, how infinitely white.

"I've got a flower delivery," he says, beaming. Harriet is confused. Her birthday isn't for another month, and even when it comes, no one will send flowers.

"There must be a mistake," she stammers, still mystified. Has she ever been sent flowers before? Not that she can remember. That's suspicious in itself. But the flowers seem to whisper to her from within their white paper. Just imagine, flowers. Can it be? Has she forgotten something? Mentally, she ransacks the previous day, but comes up with nothing. The man waits patiently on the steps, it's snowing on his shoulders. The light above the door reveals the wet patches.

"I don't know who they're from," he says, "but someone's sent you flowers. I know I'm a bit late," he adds, "but I had such a long run today and I got stuck back there with the van in all that slush."

He rolls his eyes in exasperation.

Harriet still holds back. It's as if something is nagging at the corner of her consciousness. Clearly, she'll have to accept them. There must be a card inside, an explanation. But if she's to take the flowers, she'll have to undo the chain. She does so, her fingers clumsy, opening the door a bit wider. The man remains standing politely at the top of the steps. He doesn't advance, but is defensive, almost romantic, Harriet thinks, standing there with his flowers in the sleet. Her shoulders relax. She smiles and looks covetously at the white package.

"Well, this is nice," she manages to say. Again, something is tugging at her, trying to hold her back. She looks searchingly at the man, sees his teeth in the smiling face, they're shining white in the light from the lamp. One of them is damaged, she notices, but in a strange way it suits him.

"It is, isn't it," he says, and pulls something out of his pocket. A piece of folded paper.

"I'll have to trouble you for a signature," he says, "you'll have to sign for them."

Signing for a package sounds perfectly reasonable to her. But there's the sleet, it's so wet on the doorstep, so she takes the flowers, presses them to the front of her dress and steps back into the hallway.

"We'd better go inside," she says, "I can't write without something to lean on. And I can't write without my glasses, either."

She's quite flustered. She gives him a smile, it's not exactly heartfelt, but she thinks a little friendliness won't go amiss when he has to work in all this dreadful weather, while others stay at home in the warmth. He returns her smile, and again Harriet has the sensation that something is nudging her. However, her anxiety is suppressed by what is taking place. She feels the weight

30

of the flowers in her arms, it's a large bouquet. She feels suddenly important. It's high time, she muses. I've slaved all my life, I deserve a bit of attention. Could it be from one of the men over at the shopping centre, where she and Mosse have dinner occasionally? Could it be someone who frequents the cafe? Is it some secret admirer, dreaming his dreams? Could this be happening at her age? Her thoughts cause her to pat her hair. She turns her back on him and goes into the kitchen, Charlo follows her. His boots will leave wet marks on the lino, she thinks, I'll have to mop up after him, or I might slip and break my hip, and that mustn't happen, I've enough problems as it is. Things have been bad for a long time, but now something delightful has happened, she feels excited in a new way. How quickly and unexpectedly her ears can begin to burn. She goes to fetch her glasses, they're in the living room on the leaf of the desk.

"I'm sorry," she says again, "but I'm afraid I can't see a thing without my glasses."

Charlo nods, he's silent now, there's a sudden seriousness in his face, a paralysis, as if everything is congealing within him. He looks around the kitchen with rapid, secretive glances, but Harriet can't see them, she's on her way to the living room. Charlo waits with his thudding heart, it feels as if he has several hearts and that each is trying to beat faster than the next. On the floor by the kitchen unit is a bowl. It's as hot as hell in the kitchen; the heat courses through his cheeks. He knows what he has to do, but suddenly he feels bewildered. Harriet is shuffling across the floor.

He pulls himself together, gets himself back on that track, it's important to concentrate, to follow the plan he's worked out. Harriet returns with her glasses. She's wearing a plain green dress, her hair is unkempt. He doesn't want to look at her too closely, doesn't want to remember her face. She may be old, but her eyes are sharp. He realises that he's inside now, and soon he must get to work. He goes out quickly into the hall. Harriet sees him disappear but doesn't understand the significance of it. She hears a noise, a familiar click, and realises that he's locked the front door from the inside. She stands there staring after him in disbelief, she's dumbstruck; she can feel the grain of wholemeal no longer, there's the taste of blood in her mouth. He's locked the door, and now he's returning. He looks at her, a sideways glance. He has such a hounded expression, she thinks, so strange, and she sways slightly, leaning heavily on the kitchen table because she thinks she's going to faint. Her head feels boiling hot and there's a great rushing in her ears. Confused, she gazes down at the paper she's supposed to sign. It's blank. Harriet feels nauseous.

Suddenly she feels her meal repeating, the taste of pâté mixed with beetroot, and something else, acidic. Her cheeks prickle as the colour gradually leaves her face. Why doesn't he say something? He's just staring breathlessly at her. She opens her mouth to scream, but only a whimper emerges. Harriet is paralysed. She won't ask, she'll pretend nothing has happened, she fumbles for the package of flowers. If she unpacks the flowers, time will pass and her hands will have

32

something to do. She starts frantically tearing at the paper, feeling his eyes on her the whole time; if he'd just say something, explain. But he only stands there watching, like an unspoken threat. She needs something for the string and she keeps a pair of sharp scissors on a hook above the kitchen unit. It's several paces from where she's standing, but with a huge effort she pulls herself together and goes to the unit. It occurs to her that scissors are a weapon. But the idea of stabbing a living person with them is quite out of the question for her. She gets the scissors down and walks back to the table.

It's 7 November and it's snowing, it doesn't matter, it'll soon be over. She is thirsty, her tongue is dry as sandpaper in her mouth. She cuts the string and begins unwrapping the flowers. It's a big, well filled bouquet; she's never seen anything like it, never been given anything like it. She's lost control of her hands, they won't do what she wants at all, her arthritic fingers are like bent claws, the skin over her knuckles is smooth and shiny. These flowers, she thinks, they mean nothing at all; he wants something from the house, I see that now. I opened the door because I was greedy, and this is my punishment. She begins to sway again. She can feel nothing at all from her waist down, her legs are like posts. She opens a cupboard and finds a vase. Fills it with water and puts the flowers into it, pushes the arrangement towards the wall. The light above the unit catches the blue anemones. She wants to say a prayer but can't utter a word, and anyway she sees more clearly than ever that God doesn't exist. No God, no other people, only the empty street outside and her terrified breathing. Only the silent man who's behaving so oddly. She stands with her back to him and hears that he's drawing out a chair, as if he wants to settle down in her kitchen. She half turns and sees that he's sitting. He's buried his face in his black gloves, he's in despair about something and she doesn't know what. She stands there in perplexity, her heart fluttering.

The bouquet, oddly beautiful, pink, blue and white, fills the vase, it looks out of place on the shiny draining board, in her house with all its greys and browns. She crumples up the cellophane, she fumbles with the paper. Folds it in half and in quarters, until it's flat. As long as her hands have something to do, her heart will contract in ever-repeated spasms. This must be a dream, I'll wake up soon. She puts it all in the rubbish bin in the cupboard under the unit, doesn't dare bang the door, wants to make herself invisible. This isn't what I thought, she tells herself, he's a deeply disturbed man, and soon he'll explain. But he explains nothing. He gets up suddenly and composes himself, looks at her with tear-filled eyes, and Harriet thinks, he'll go now. Go now!

But he doesn't go. He opens his parka and begins to fumble about underneath it. His hand comes out holding a revolver.

She doesn't understand about the revolver. Parts of her consciousness are no longer working, everything turns black at the sight of the weapon, so she turns away and collapses over the worktop, letting go of everything, wet and warm down her thighs.

"Where's your silver? Jewellery? Cash? Quick!"

His voice barely holds, he feels like some farcical amateur and curses his cracking voice. He's squeaking like a mouse, he waves his revolver angrily. Harriet shakes her head distractedly, she doesn't want to part with anything, she doesn't want to move.

"Money," he says again. "Have you got any money?"

She makes no answer, she's standing with her back to him, pretending that none of this is happening. Charlo goes into the living room. There's a large, dark sideboard along the wall, he opens the drawers, they're full of silverware. He puts down his gun and begins to root around in the drawers. Harriet has turned now, she can see him rummaging about amongst her things, her family heirlooms. She can't bear it. Something starts smouldering deep within her, a prodigious feeling of injustice, because it's *her* silver, she's fond of it and it's worth a lot of money. Rage replaces fear. She follows him into the room and tugs at his shoulders, screaming hoarsely, her fury giving her unguessed-at strength. Charlo is thoroughly distracted, it's so quiet outside, people may hear. He hates being disturbed, this old woman is completely deranged, he pushes her away, but she doesn't stop. She charges at him again, her face is blotched with red. Charlo loses all reason. He's got to stop this screaming, he can't do anything, can't think clearly while she's standing there shrieking like this, so he grabs his revolver by the barrel, and lifts it like a hammer. Just one smack in the face, and she'll huddle into a corner and shut up. So that he can get on with what he's come for. Harriet sees the raised arm, she shuffles out to the kitchen, back to the worktop, still screeching, a long drawn-out wail of lament. He runs after her and hits her hard with the stock. The first blow finds a neck vertebra, it breaks with a dry click, and he thinks, Julie! Help me! Harriet sinks to the floor. Horrified, he sees that her body is jerking in appalling, cramp-like spasms. He can't bear her being like this, so he strikes again as hard as he can, strikes her head repeatedly. Suddenly a stream of blood wells up from her skull. He backs away in horror, gasping for air, looking at the thing lying on the floor; he thinks she's still moaning, there are still spasms in her legs, so he lashes out again, with even more force.

Then suddenly, weakness comes over him. The hand clutching the weapon is lowered. He wipes his forehead, gazes at the bloody butt. He gives his head a hard shake so that he can think. Because he knows that he must think now, he can't just let himself go. Deep down he realised this would happen. People don't part with their things without a struggle. She might be as covetous as him, mightn't she? He turns his back to the object on the floor, puts the weapon on the worktop, and feels in the pocket of his parka. He pulls out a cotton bag with a string closure. It's Julie's old gym bag that Inga Lill made. He returns to the sideboard in the living room. Now that all is quiet he works quickly and efficiently, he places knives and forks and spoons in the bag, there's a lot of silver, its value considerable. He opens a cupboard next to the sideboard, pulls the contents out, searching for money. When the sideboard is empty, he turns and looks around the living room.

He notices the letter that's been started lying on the leaf of the desk, notices the little bowl of sweets. For reasons he doesn't understand, he goes over to it and peers at the assortment. Automatically, he picks one he likes, the brown one with caramel and liquorice, and pops it into his mouth.

Then he goes into the kitchen. He doesn't look in Harriet's direction, she's just something dark in the corner of his eye, he's searching for a door that might open into a bedroom. It's at the back of the kitchen, hardly more than a boxroom. On the bedside table is a jewellery case. He digs into it with his gloved hand and puts the contents into his bag: brooches, rings, a bracelet and a string of pearls. And a large, heavy pocket watch that's certainly gold. He tears open the drawer of the bedside table; it's full of tablets, coins and hair clips. He opens a wardrobe and yanks the clothing out, he has a hunch that this is where she hides her money. That she likes having it close by when she's asleep. He finds a pink washing bag and opens the zip. Pleasure floods through him, for there it is, the money, a staggeringly fat wad. He stuffs it into the pocket of his parka, feeling tremendously elated.

He re-enters the kitchen. Harriet is lying like a slaughtered animal on the floor. She is so thin, and her body is strangely twisted. He sees her gold bracelet, but can't bear touching her. He's glad he can't see her face because right now his life is hideous: all that's been before, and what he's done now. He is repulsive, his tongue feels the missing corner of his front tooth as a nasty, sharp edge. He shoves the revolver under his parka, and takes a few paces to the side. Then he puts his foot in the wrong place, the heel of his boot goes into the puddle of blood and he slips, flails wildly trying to keep his balance. He stands for a few moments allowing his heart to calm down. Now he must go out amongst people again, so it's important to be self-possessed. Relaxed, assured and purposeful. He goes into the hallway, turns the lock, holds the door ajar, and stands listening. A shadow streaks across the floor, something black and noiseless. He starts. She's got a cat, he realises, it's been waiting outside, now it wants to come in to the warmth and light. He goes back in again to see what it will do. The cat stops and looks at the ruined body. It gives several long mews. Then it goes straight to its bowl to drink. He stands nonplussed, watching the cat. It raises its head and looks at him with yellow, half-closed eyes. How extraordinary, he thinks, that the cat is behaving as normal. He leaves the kitchen again, and the cat follows, he can't understand it. It sits on the steps watching him. He pulls the front door to, goes down the steps, the cat keeping pace with him like a shadow. He begins to walk towards the gate. There'll be no one about now, he thinks, I won't meet a soul, and if I do all they'll see is a silhouette in the snowy night. The cat follows him for a few metres, then it stops. Quickly he steps out on to the road.

He looks over his shoulder constantly as he wades off through the slush. But he doesn't see anyone, not a single person is out in Fredboesgate this evening. He sees television screens flickering blue in living rooms and silhouettes behind curtains. Everyone is minding their own business. He reaches the hotel and makes his way round to the courtyard, brushes the mushy snow off the windscreen. There are so many footprints everywhere, surely it wasn't like this when he arrived?

He gets into the car. Throws the bag with the silverware on the seat, and drops the bloody revolver on the floor. His right arm is weak, and he's pulled his shoulder. He rubs the tender spot, sits in the car panting, knowing that he must get away from Hamsund, but he sits there just the same. His heart is labouring, but he can't get it to ease down, it's pumping away at a terrific rate and he feels the heat rising to his head. He tries to breathe freely. Lays his head back, opens his mouth wide. Air down into my lungs, he thinks, air round my entire body. If he can only get out of Hamsund, if he can just get home, everything will be fine. My own home, he thinks despairingly, my own chair, my bed. The cool pillow against my face. The things that are mine, just as before. Can he do it? Can he manage to live with this? How could she carry on like that. She could have let him work away in peace and saved her own skin, couldn't she? Deep down he knows that this is where he was headed. He's known it all the time, it's lain there like a blot on his consciousness.

He leans back against the headrest and reflects. He's never quite fitted the pattern. And when he's looked at other people, he's always felt that they've been attached to the world in a totally different way. He's always had the feeling that he's ambivalent, remote. What's just occurred couldn't have been avoided. This acknowledgement is so dismal, he feels like the victim of something he doesn't understand. Something to do with fate. That the crime has lain in wait for him, trapped him like some pawn in a game, plotted by God or the devil, he doesn't know which. He shivers. He gets out his tobacco and rolls a cigarette, lights up and inhales deeply. Then he puts the Honda in gear and drives off.

She didn't survive that, he thinks, such a frail person, fragile and brittle as plaster. Soon he's passing the railway station. Thoughts whirl around his head, but his pulse is beginning to slow because he can't see anyone, and there's a cosy glow coming from the windows of Hamsund. The snow is falling soft and still. People are busy with other things, and he's getting away. All at once, he's aware of a shadow to his right, but he continues ploughing on, driving carefully on the slippery surface, it's his right of way. The shape is suddenly frighteningly close. Next moment there is a jolt, he hears the noise of metal crunching against metal, the bang is loud in the silence. He is thrown against the steering wheel and feels a blow to his chest. Then everything goes quiet and the silence is unreal. Confused, he peers through the windscreen and finds himself looking directly at another car. He is filled with cold terror. He remembers the revolver lying on the floor and what he's just done, remembers it as if for the first time. Suddenly he's wide awake, he's fallen from the track he was moving along, and into a tangled undergrowth of panic and fear. A young man is gazing at him from the other car, a pale face with frightened eyes and large, prominent ears. Charlo loses control. Without thinking, he gets out into the slush, crosses to the small white car and tears open the door. His body is shaking ominously, he flies off the handle, exploding like a firecracker. Everything that's pent up inside him spills out in a furious torrent. The boy seeks shelter from this storm, this vast stream of words; he holds on tight to his steering wheel, waits for things to settle down, but they don't settle down because all the floodgates inside Charlo have opened, and his fury is pouring out.

"I've got a claim form," the boy mumbles.

His arm moves towards the glove compartment, his thin hand is trembling. Charlo panics at the thought of a claim form. Documents to fill out, his signature at the bottom. He will be placing himself in Hamsund on the night in question, 7 November. He knows he can't do that. He's still leaning heavily on the doorframe and yelling into the car. His expletives become more personal, they erupt from him like white hot lava. He stops to draw breath. He thought he was empty, but more emerges, it's like vomit, he feels it in the pit of his stomach. Then his voice cracks and he begins to sob. He weeps over what he's left behind him on the floor, he weeps over Julie who won't see him. Then he's appalled at his own reaction. Only a madman acts like this, he thinks with alarm, and slams the door shut. He rushes back to the Honda.

CHAPTER
THREE

He can see no stars. Only a thick darkness.

Out of that darkness the snow drops quietly, this is the planet's ultimate night, it will never be light again, no sun will rise in the morning. So grisly was his recent act. He bows his head in despair. If he's being honest with himself, he thinks he's dreaming. Soon he'll wake up and groan with relief because it was only a nightmare. He switches on the courtesy light in the car, and looks down at himself. His parka is bloody. The collision must have been the hand of God, a sudden intervention to halt him in his flight and make him face justice.

The lights are on in Erlandson's house next door, and there, a shadow at the window. It's almost eleven o'clock, his right arm is trembling. He sits in the car smoking, can't tear himself away. Now and again he hears a hoarse groan, it's coming from him. He's killed Harriet Krohn, but all he can think about is the accident with the white car. He thinks it was a Toyota, a Yaris. The contretemps was inexcusable. His reaction unforgivable. Only a lunatic would have behaved like that. He takes a firm grip of himself, grabs hold of the bag of silverware and jewellery, the "Tina's Flowers" bag and the bloody revolver, gets out of the car and locks it.

His knees are weak. He bends close to the wing: a dent and the remains of some white paint. If only it were a bad dream, if only the wing were smooth and undamaged. Damn this weather, he thinks, damn this whole wretched existence that I can't cope with. Once again, he feels the need to cry, and some miserable sobs escape from him. He throws another glance at Erlandson's house, but there's no one at the window now.

He goes into his own house, slams the door behind him, drops the revolver and the bag on the floor. He throws off the parka, it lies in a heap. And there he remains, standing with eyes closed, leaning against the wall. He hears himself breathing and knows that he's alive, that the world is moving on. Even though he's sunk to the bottom, to the very depths of existence. There's a thudding at his temples, and the skin of his cheeks is prickling. He opens his eyes, sees his furniture and possessions. There's the photo of Inga Lill and Julie, he can't meet their gaze. He doubles up, starts tearing his hair, yanking so hard that his scalp hurts, that the tears come. He eases his shoulders, gets a firm grip of himself, sits down in his chair. The familiar, red chair. He lies back. Oh, he's so tired, so tired. He tries to force his breathing into an even rhythm, and succeeds. Just sit quietly now, breathe, rest.

Only after an eternity does he get up and cross the floor. He knows that he must meet himself in the mirror. Instead, he looks down and sees splashes of blood at the bottom of his trouser legs. Aghast, he kicks them off. He goes into the bathroom to shower, he imagines it will help, that perhaps he'll return to his old self. Can he ever be himself again? Didn't the door just slam and shut him away from everything; he imagined he heard a boom. He is standing quite naked in the garishly lit room. But then there's the mirror. Perhaps it's all hopeless if his eyes give him away as a killer.

He approaches the mirror with lowered head, again he closes his eyes. I know what I look like, he thinks, I don't need to make a big thing about it. He opens them again, looks straight ahead. His eyes are strange. His look is so distant, it reaches him from far away. Meditative, a little defensive. Is this really me? Am I alive? He steadies himself on the washbasin. This is too much for me, he thinks, I must calm down now, calm down, Charlo! He makes another attempt, lifts his head and looks at his reflection with a more forceful expression. That's better, he looks more collected. But there are those grey eyes, there's something about them. The irises seem metallic. He leans close to the mirror, looks at his own pupils. They're not completely round. His brow wrinkles in concern. Is it possible? Aren't all pupils round? He moves right up to the glass. They're cloudy at the edges, and elongated, like oval slits. But this is what I must look like, he thinks. I've never noticed it before, how strange, how horrible. It makes him start; then the goose pimples rise. He leans forward once more. No, they're definitely not round. It worries him enormously, he turns his back on the mirror. He stands there, unmoving, his naked body winter pale and hairy. Again he stops, freezes up, he can't budge. He tries talking sternly to himself, tries to tear free. He turns on the tap and stands under the jet of water. Then at last his mind moves on, and the hot water streams down. She's dead, he thinks, and it's my fault. But I couldn't help it, she was hysterical. She went for me like an angry terrier, I was caught off guard, I was frightened, I lost control. But I didn't want to do it, I didn't plan it, I've never been cold-blooded. Never. He wants the water to splash over him, warm and soothing. He stands there resting for a while. Steps out of the shower and puts on a dressing gown. Picks up the parka and retrieves the money from the pocket. His heart beats faster, there's a lot of money, a lot more than he'd hoped for. He settles in his chair with the wad of notes in his lap and starts counting. It's hard because his hands are shaking. His eyes grow large. The money is dry and smooth between his fingers, masses of thousand-krone notes. He counts them ten by ten, and places them on the table. Two hundred and twenty thousand.

He rushes across to the phone and stands with the roll of notes in his hand as he dials Bjørnar Lind's number. It's late, but he can't wait. He clutches the money tightly as he hears the ring tone in his ear. One ring, two rings, it seems to go on ringing for an eternity. But nobody answers. Frustrated as a child, he has to put down the phone without doing what he wanted. He places the money in the desk drawer. He goes into the kitchen and makes a coffee, pulls out a chair from the kitchen table, sits down and drinks the coffee with sugar in it. She's dead, and it's my fault. She's still lying there, it's night now, no one knows what's happened. He can't sit still, he's got a lot to do. He tries to move about slowly, it's important to maintain his composure. But he has no composure, his thoughts are working faster than his body.

Later, he stands at the utility sink and starts scrubbing the revolver with a nail brush. Lightly bloodstained water runs down the plughole. He fetches the rubber mat from the car and cleans it thoroughly. Finally he gets some bleach, squirting it directly from the bottle. He imagines this will remove all traces. His clothes must be thrown away, or perhaps he can burn them in the oven. He rushes about the house tidying, he hides the silverware and jewellery somewhere he thinks is safe. He bags up the bloody clothes and stuffs them into a cupboard together with the revolver. He wants to go to bed, but he's scared that he's forgotten something. He tramps from room to room, from the living room out to the kitchen, from the kitchen to the bathroom, a lost creature with aching eyes. He speaks severely to himself, attempts to take himself in hand. Nobody witnessed the collision, nobody saw him go to the house, nobody saw him leave it. Nobody except the cat with the yellow eyes.

At last, he goes to bed. He takes the money from the desk drawer and places it on his bedside table. If Lind's thugs come in the middle of the night, he has only to wave the cash and save his skin. Soon he'll be a man with no debts. He consoles himself with the thought, lies on his back and breathes out into the darkness. Lies staring at the ceiling. Frightened of falling asleep, scared to lie awake. This is what it feels like, he thinks, now I know what it feels like. I can live with this. I must live with it. My God, it'll be tough. He turns over to face the wall, packs the duvet tightly around him. I've got to sleep now, he thinks, I'm so tired. Must move on to my next day of unemployment, move on to the rest of my life. All the time he's listening in the dark. To make out if someone is at the door, or if there are footsteps outside the window. However, it's the collision that troubles him, and his own crazed reaction. That sudden bang and the shock through his body revisit him all night long.

Suddenly he's washed roughly ashore.

He feels the cool air on his face, he's abruptly and inescapably awake. It's like falling from a great height. The first thing he recalls is the accident. It hits him like a landslide, the thought of his own fury, and he moans as if in sudden pain. Remorselessly, it all comes back to him, in glimpses and fragments, her kitchen, the black cat. The actions, the images parade before him, in a line of rapid, fantastic tableaux. He lies quite still in bed while thoughts fly through his head, he wants to lie in the dark like this for ever, he wants to expunge the preceding day.

He moves his fingers carefully, the nice, whole fingers with their two gold rings. The day hasn't begun yet, he thinks, it won't begin until I open my eyes, I can switch the world on or off. He must gather his thoughts, introduce them one by one, sort through them. He knows he can't do it. Before him lies a mental storm, a blitz of ghastly images. The ugly green dress, the smashed skull. Eventually he opens his eyes. A little light is seeping in from behind the curtains. He sees the globe of the light fitting on the ceiling and follows the cable with his eyes, it's been routed along the wall and then down to the plug near the floor. He sees a little bit of a web in one corner and something dark that might be a spider.

I'm Charles Olav Torp, he thinks, it's so strange waking up in this heavy body. There are sounds outside, but the people making them know nothing, they think that today is a perfectly normal day. No one has noticed the trembling, but soon the ripples will expand and reach every respectable person. He conjures up a crowd in his mind's eye, and at that moment they turn to look at him, accusingly. He raises his right hand tentatively and holds it in front of his face. It's hairy and has thick nails. My hand, he thinks, and turns it, splays out his fingers, studies all the mechanics, thinks of the power in it, unleashed as soon as it gets a message from the brain. Strike her, now. Strike! Without a command, the hand would have hung limp at the end of his arm, and remained a good and loving hand. But he stood in Harriet's kitchen and gave his hand that command. No, it shot up of its own volition, he can't remember having shaped the thought, that he should strike her. Did he do that? His hand took on a life of its own and hit out without his wanting it to. His heavy flaccid hand. Isn't it the same hand he's always had? Isn't it larger than his left one? He raises his other hand to compare them. It

48

is larger, because he's right-handed; that's quite normal.

As he lies there staring at the spider, the minutes pass. He feels he's behind the curve and that he should get up and start his day. Get up now, it's over. Or is now the beginning? What awaits him in town? A continuous stream of people will observe him in the streets. What about the woman in the bakery where he usually buys his bread? Will she look at him with new eyes? He sits up slowly and places his feet on the floor. He's become so conscious of his right arm, the one that raised the revolver, he can't ignore it. Is it really much heavier than the left? He rubs his fingers together, there's a new and quite unbelievable sensitivity in his fingertips; he thinks he can feel the tiny grooves, the ones that form his fingerprint. He stands there with his heavy arm hanging, bent slightly forward, a bit limp. No, this is ridiculous, he thinks, stop this nonsense.

He grasps the bundle of money on the bedside table, walks slowly across the room, it feels as if his arm is hanging like a club from his shoulder, that even his gait has altered, that his walk is lopsided and bow-legged like an ape's. There is something the matter with his knees, they don't feel right. He stops suddenly and shudders. He can hear his heartbeat in his ears like an angry drumming. He freezes in that attitude, draws breath. In the stillness he hears a note, increasing in volume, he covers his ears, is afraid that everything that's going on inside his head may cause his skull to burst like some overripe fruit. He starts wondering if his brain might short-circuit if it has too much to do.

Because she's dead, and he's guilty. He thinks about all the electric impulses and imagines the sparks in his skull. Quite involuntarily, his knees give way, and he almost loses his balance. He saves himself in the nick of time, propping his body against the wall. He clutches the roll of notes. Turns towards the bed again, lets himself fall on to the sheets. Grabs despairingly for the duvet. Sleep now, must sleep, he thinks, must get away from all this horror. She was so angry! He wasn't prepared for her assault, he was naive. The first day is the worst, he thinks, the feeling will wear off, it'll become a habit. He hears the sound of his own breathing, as if it's coming from another man, a man lying next to him and breathing in his ear. The feeling is unpleasant, there's someone else in the room, someone who sees and listens and knows.

He creeps in towards the wall. He lies there tossing and turning, remembers that no one has seen him, that he's an insignificant person, that he's left no clues. He hasn't, has he? He digests this, the first little sprouting of hope; he's the one who'll get away with it, not everyone gets caught. Slowly, he gives the thought a chance, it's fragile, he's frightened of losing it, he concentrates hard, opens his eyes again, gazes at the wallpaper. Lilies, stripes. He puts the money to his nose and sniffs. Never has the smell of dry paper given him such blissful happiness.

He sits up slowly, then perches on the edge of the bed, pulls the curtains aside and looks out. He needs some everyday object to rest his eyes on, some assurance that the street out there is the same as ever. It has stopped snowing at last, and a line of cars is parked along the pavement. He looks closely at the cars, his face tense with the strain, a Mercedes, an Opel, a Ford. I'd better keep tabs on the cars outside, he decides, in case they're watching me. Why should they watch me? No one knows I was in Harriet's house. Once again he plants his feet on the floor, then summons all his willpower and walks slowly across the room. It's only a few steps to the bathroom, he'll seek shelter in there, under the hot water. Thaw his frozen body, become soft and supple once more. He drops the money on the kitchen table. Then everything closes down inside him again, he glances over his shoulder, but nobody is sitting in the living room looking back at him. He pulls off his pyjama bottoms, a little more clumsily than usual, he keeps on losing his balance. He thinks: relax now, get into the shower, Charlo. There's no cause for panic. She certainly won't have been found yet, people have lives to lead in Fredboesgate, they go to work as usual, the ones that have work to go to, the ones that aren't in the same sort of mess as I am.

Of course she's been found, a voice within him says.

No, it's much too soon, it's only nine o'clock.

Someone could have come to her door early. Presumably all hell has broken loose.

Don't get me worked up, it'll happen soon enough. I'm trying to keep calm.

You don't deserve to be calm. You're never going to feel calm again as long as you live. This is going to torture and trouble you every minute of the day, and when the time comes for you to die, you won't dare to let go because you'll be headed straight for hell.

He pushes the voices away. He moves in front of the mirror, unwilling and curious at one and the same time. Perhaps his pupils are round again, perhaps it was just his imagination. He leans forward and stares. No, in his opinion they're still elongated. He turns on the taps and stands under the hot water for a long time. Just shower now, he thinks, relax, forget. He moves towards the wall, feels the water running. He wants to become completely clean, it feels as if he could stand there until nightfall, washing everything away. Everything that's been, everything that's to come.

He glances down at himself. It's the same body as always, the stomach, the fairly sturdy thighs, the skin white from lack of sun. His chest is powerful, with a slight suggestion of breasts. Suddenly he feels very giddy and has to steady himself against the wall. He leans against the wet tiles, places a hand on his heart. He thinks there's a flickering in front of his eyes. Is it really possible that I went out there, he thinks, or is it just an evil dream? The collision leaves him in no doubt. The big crunch and the jolt through his body. He must tear himself free, get into the rut again, not ask questions, it's too late now, it's happened. He's got to think ahead, not dwell on the past. With his back to the mirror he dries himself. He guides the towel distractedly over his body, his spirit flounders, it's like treading water, he's afraid he'll drown in his own despair, his own fear.

He gets out clean clothes. Carefully buttons his shirt, does up his belt, goes to the mirror again, keeps himself under observation, as if searching for cracks. He thinks his face looks flat and immobile. Will he remember who he was? Will he remember his facial expressions? Can he find them when he needs them, so that people will recognise him, his smile, his laugh? When he does occasionally laugh.

He goes to the desk and dials Bjørnar Lind's number. Hopping from one foot to the other, bursting with the good news that he can pay his debt. But no one answers. He bites his lip, phones the local radio station where Bjørnar works, and finally gets through to a woman there. No, he's travelling on business, he'll be away for a while. She gives him a mobile number, he hangs up and then frantically taps in the digits. The person you're dialling is not available. Full of frustration he retreats to the kitchen. He takes the coffee tin out of the cupboard, fills the jug with water, flicks the switch, the light glows red.

Afterwards, he sits by the kitchen window slowly drinking his coffee. Halfway through the cup he has to fetch some sugar. It irritates him, this need for sugar, he never usually takes it. But it's only a trifle, he thinks; would anybody say, is there something up with Charlo? Is something troubling him because he's suddenly putting sugar in his coffee? He steals a sidelong glance at the radio, wants to switch it on, but hesitates. He doesn't know if he dares. What kind of words will they use? No, I'll do it later, he thinks, perhaps Harriet hasn't even been found yet, she doesn't get many visitors, and it's early in the day.

He looks around the kitchen. He's lived in this house for a long time, and yet in a strange way, he feels like a guest. This is day one, he needs to get acquainted all over again. The objects around him, the furniture, the ceiling light, they all seem familiar, but they're not his any more. It feels as if someone has cut his moorings, and that he's drifting in the room like a sorry shipwreck. He thinks: I'll never come home again. He stares out into the street, his gaze watchful. Just then a car appears, a large, dark car, it looks like an Audi. He follows it with his eyes, grips his coffee cup. He wonders why it's moving so slowly, as if the driver's looking for something, for him, perhaps; there's a momentary catch in his breast. It doesn't belong to any of his neighbours, he knows all the vehicles in the street. Erlandson drives an Opel, and Gram directly opposite has a Mazda. There, it's stopping, his heart pounds. Are they after him already? The courtesy light comes on, a man sits there leafing through something, a map maybe, or a book. Charlo stares with aching eyes.

He gets up and goes into the hallway. Takes out an old quilted jacket. He bends down and ties up his bootlaces, glancing occasionally at the door. Retrieves the bag of bloody clothes from the cupboard. For a long time he stands there psyching himself up. He's going outdoors, it's important to seem natural, relaxed, to stroll along. Move about, insignificant and grey, just as he's always done. He opens the door a crack. He wouldn't be able to face any of the neighbours, but the street is quiet. He walks the few steps to his car, notices the dent in the front wing. It makes him shudder. He unlocks the door with trembling fingers and throws the bag in. Oh, how that dent haunts him! He backs out into the street and changes into first gear. He wishes he had another car, a grey car. He feels that the Honda is giving off something, an angry red revealing glow.

CHAPTER
FOUR

Surely it's not possible that she's survived?

That she's crawled all the way into her living room on her elbows, and then phoned for help? That she's already reported and described him in the minutest detail? No, he says to himself, marshalling some common sense. That can't have happened!

He drives slowly down Blomsgate. In his head he's conducting an imaginary conversation with Lind, when he does finally answer his mobile.

Hi there, this is Charlo. Long time no see.

Silence at the other end. Then irritated grunts, and presumably rising suspicion.

What the hell are you ringing me for? You don't think I'll give you some more, do you? You've got some cheek!

That familiar, grouchy voice. Cold and reluctant.

Calm down, Bjørnar, this could be to your advantage.

Silence again, Lind is waiting. Charlo savours the moment, milks it, perhaps stands there with the roll of money in his hand, tapping the tabletop with it.

Well then, let's hear it. I haven't got all day.

Two hundred thousand in nice, clean crispies are here waiting for you. Come and get them. By all means bring your secateurs if you don't believe me.

Lind says nothing. The silence is charged with distrust.

And how have you managed that?

Charlo considers carefully.

Imagination, tenacity and courage.

He returns to himself again and watches out for traffic from his right. Just think how he almost fainted in the bathroom, that's never happened to him before. A sudden flickering in front of the eyes, a sensation of vanishing. Guilt. No, don't think about guilt, think about nice things. About Julie, who's young and healthy. He'd never have believed that Inga Lill could die of cancer, she was always so bright, so lively. Even now it's incomprehensible to him. The day she got the diagnosis, it was as if they'd both been struck by lightning. The car's a bit too hot, he switches off the fan, stares straight ahead at the snow-covered road. Don't give your thoughts free rein, collect them, take control of them, he thinks, and wants to concentrate. It's hard. Because Harriet Krohn is dead. He scratches his jaw, tries to think. It's a hundred to one that she's dead, she can't turn him in.

There's the brewery. Great stacks of red and yellow beer crates stand like high-rise buildings around the yard in front of the building, they resemble outsized Lego blocks. To be a child again and be able to play with a clear conscience, protected by adults. He loses himself in childhood reminiscences and remembers a particular day when he was walking back from school. It was winter and icy cold, the snow creaked under his boots. Just then he caught sight of something in a pile of snow close to his front door. A cat that had been run over. The cat was virtually turned inside out, its intestines were partly splayed out on the snow. It made him almost ecstatic, and inquisitive. He knew that his mother could see him from the window, but he couldn't help himself. He began prodding about amongst the cat's innards with a stick. It didn't move, he could prod as much as he liked, the cat was at peace. He was only seven, but he understood that much, and the stick worked frenetically amongst all the entrails, he couldn't get enough of it. After a few minutes his mother came out, she wanted to know what he was doing. From her reaction, he concluded that what he'd been doing was inexcusable. But he didn't think the cat was nasty. He was deeply fascinated. Pondering it now, he wonders if perhaps he's different, if other, normal children would have run away in disgust. Where did he get the idea of picking at the dead animal's remains? He thinks there's a meaning to everything, he analyses past events and searches for a flaw. If, that is, he has a flaw. No, he can't think of anything, he feels totally normal. Here's old Charlo. I'm perfectly normal, but I've killed.

He drives out along the main road, the houses get further apart. That car behind me, he thinks, and looks in the mirror, has been there a long time; a Renault, there's a man at the wheel, is he after me? Charlo can't get himself to relax. He feels exposed in the sharp winter light, he feels the car is making more noise than usual. He thinks all manner of strange things, it feels almost as if his cheeks are on fire. Nevertheless, it's a relief to be out amongst people, to be a natural part of the flow. Here, amongst the crowd, both good and bad, he feels anonymous. Gradually, the farms appear, and the apple orchards. He likes the landscape around here, the fields and spruce forests, the gently sloping wooded hills and the mountains. He likes the heavily pruned apple trees, decorative as Japanese letters in the bright snow. In May they will stand like buxom bridesmaids in white and pink. He glances at his watch, turns on the radio and listens. Maybe Harriet has been found by now, maybe someone has entered the house and a scream has pierced the stillness in the kitchen. He continually checks his mirror. He sees his own black pupils and thinks they've turned into slits now, like a goat's. No, he's imagining it, his imagination is playing tricks on him, he's under stress, after all. It's hardly surprising that he sees Japanese characters in the snow, or hears his own voice in his head.

Do you realise what you've done?

He grips the little knob on the gearstick, sits leaning forward and drives. Here's the familiar fanfare that signals it's time for the news, so he turns off on to the verge and stops. Chechen rebels have been caught on the Russian border, a suicide bomber has struck in Israel, flu vaccine has arrived. Nothing about the murder of Harriet Krohn. He bangs the steering wheel and turns the car back on to the road, he's frustrated almost to the point of despair. He wants to get it over with, the noise, the furore. Theoretically, she could lie there for days. They won't find anything, he thinks, I haven't left any traces. I was quick and pretty single-minded, even though I was agitated. He dwells on all the people who'll trample through her house, skilled, experienced people with limitless expertise. What sort of tiny fibres could he have carried in with him? Maybe one of his hairs fell out. Will they see his footprint in the blood and the pattern of his soles? He tries to breathe calmly. He's feeling hungry so he begins to look for a kiosk or petrol station where he can get something to eat.

Five minutes later he halts at a Shell garage. He sits in the car for a while hardly daring to go in. He runs his fingers through his hair, squints furtively through the windscreen; he can't see anyone. But at the end of the building he spies a large, green container. A rubbish skip. He reaches down and picks up the bag of bloody clothes. Then he grits his teeth, leaves the car and walks as coolly as he can to the skip, which has a lid. He looks over his shoulder, puts the bag in, covers it as best he can and bangs the lid shut. Then he goes into the shop. He wanders across to the counter and sees some large hot dogs browning on an electric grill. He chooses one with bacon and squeezes plenty of mustard on top. The young man who's serving watches him as he eats. He moves away, stops in front of the magazine rack and reads all the headlines. The crisply cooked skin crunches between his teeth, the mustard burns his tongue. He drinks half a bottle of Coke, says goodbye and goes out again. The food does him good.

Gradually, he relaxes. He drives on, studying the road signs and the traffic in his rear-view mirror. There's a Scorpio behind him, a green one. For all he knows the car might have plain clothes police in it. He doesn't seriously think it has, he's only considering the possibility, that they're all over the place, that they're looking for him, that they won't give up.

After half an hour he turns left at Møller's Riding Centre. He finds himself on a narrow, bumpy forest track, changes down into second, trying to drive carefully to spare the Honda. Soon he catches sight of the paddocks. Several horses are grazing the damp, half-frozen grass. Small patches of snow are lying here and there, it's still mild for November and the air is pleasant and clear. He sees low red-painted buildings, the riding ring, the stables, the parked cars and horseboxes. The place is idyllic, lying in a hollow in the landscape like so many toy blocks in a bowl, surrounded by gently undulating hills and forest. He glides into a free parking place. He needs to sit in the car for a bit first. It's still early in the day, only a couple of young girls are leading their horses for a ride across the fields. They'll plough through the flecks of snow together, screaming with pleasure. Again he thinks of Julie, he thinks of her with longing and hope, and dreams of what the future may hold. The girls don't even glance at him. He stays in the car. He watches the horses' rumps and their flicking tails, soon they're out of sight. Diffidently, he gets out of the car and stands for a while looking around, now he's there for all to see in his blue quilted jacket. But no one pays him any attention. He walks to the first stable. Opens the heavy door, and stands there listening to the noises within. He breathes in the strong tang of the animals. He hears the soft sound of horses chewing, a rhythmic munching; he recognizes the heady scent of dry hay, leather and horse muck. On his right is a bulletin board, he reads the messages and smiles.

"Please, tidy up after yourself!!" "Keep the area in front of your box swept." "Don't leave tack in the passage." "Keep the door shut, or the water will freeze!" It's all so familiar, so dear. With a kind of devotion he begins walking down the stable passage. Inside this building he's safe. This is a special space where no one can touch him. He is filled with emotions, smells and tranquillity, they permeate his body instantly. The great animals pay him no heed; undisturbed, they chomp on, tugging at the hay in long snatches, concentrating deeply on their food. A few sparrows circle beneath the roof, occasionally they land in the passage, find odd pieces of corn which they pounce on with energetic eagerness.

There are ten horses in all, he looks at each one with care. Two are ponies, they interest him less; a pony is, and remains, a pony and can never become a horse. He sees a very overweight Fjord horse, and a dapple grey he's not so keen on, partly because of its build, but also because it's thin. But he studies the other six with considerable interest. Walking up and down the passage, he reads the names on the box doors. Konstantin, born '92, owner: Grete Valen. Superman, born '96, owner: Line Grov. One of the horses stands out because of its impressive height, and also because of its colour. It's a bay. Charlo stops dead, and stands there staring. The bay is his favourite. The bay is the one he'll dream of, its deep, coppery colour shining in the light from the window. A pretty, arrow-shaped blaze on its forehead. A good, thick tail and a powerful neck. Its eyes are liquid and black, they observe him with stoic composure. Charlo holds out a hand and lets the horse sniff, its muzzle feels like fine, expensive velvet. He leans forward and blows into the horse's nostrils, he wants to implant his own smell. The horse is inquisitive, its ears tilt forward positively and its tail swishes from side to side. The horse really is big. Six hundred kilos, he guesses, with powerful legs and supple hindquarters. Definitely a dressage horse. It has the muscle mass typical of an animal which has done a lot of groundwork. It looks newly shod and well tended, its hooves are oiled and shiny. He stands there at the box door completely wrapped up in a daydream. There's no name on the door. But obviously someone owns the horse.

His musings are disturbed by the sound of the stable door slamming and footsteps approaching. Immediately he pulls himself together. Gets ready for a conversation. He looks down the passage and glimpses a young girl. She sends him a bashful glance, registers that she doesn't know him, and gets on with her task. He calls out a greeting and watches with interest, perhaps the bay is the very horse she's taking out. No, she's come for the Fjord horse. She places a halter over its head and leads it out into the passage, and ties it to a ring.

Then she disappears and returns almost immediately with a saddle. Charlo knows what a saddle weighs, but she's toting it on one arm as if it were a mere nothing, the horse's bridle is over the other. They've got muscles, these girls, after years on horseback, after forking tons of horse manure out of the box and down the hatch. Heavy, wet horse muck; stalwart, tough girls.

"Nice Fjord," he says, even though he doesn't mean it. It's been far too well fed, but is attractive despite that, champagne-coloured, with a pretty black-and-white mane. He likes Fjord horses very much, but not for riding. They're precise in dressage, but lack a certain elegance; the Fjord horse has got such short legs, he thinks, and looks at the girl. She places the saddle on the horse's back, tightens the girth with impressive strength and starts scraping out the hooves. Her trim bottom sticks up in the air, filling her tight riding breeches, and he looks at her rounded body and powerful thighs. That's how they ought to look, he thinks, buxom and bursting as ripe plums. But as always, whenever he looks at a young girl, he starts making comparisons with Julie. He never finds anyone to match her. Julie with her resolute chin and her mane of red hair. Julie with her firm, green eyes.

"What's his name?" Charlo asks, taking a few steps towards the girl, he's a friendly man. Even though he's just killed someone, even though he's just destroyed an old woman, he finds his voice again, he finds his good nature. He knows how to talk to people, and make conversation. It gives him an odd kind of pleasure that he can still interact with people as if nothing has happened.

Just then a cat slips in, followed by a Rottweiler puppy, it finds some hoof trimmings and begins to chew greedily.

"Champis," she replies, smiling shyly. Now that's apposite, he thinks, savouring the name.

"Would you know anything about the bay?" He looks over at the big horse. Its head is hanging over the door and it's chewing.

She pulls the Fjord horse's forelock over the browband, and arranges it perfectly.

"He belongs to Møller," she says, and goes to fetch a broom. She sweeps the passage clear of wood shavings and dung. She opens the hatch in the floor and sweeps it in with practised strokes.

"Møller?" Charlo enquires.

"The man who owns the riding centre."

Charlo nods. "I'm only having a look," he says in extenuation. "He's lovely. That's all I meant."

"Yes," she replies, and looks at him, curious now. "He's really lovely. But he's quite a handful."

"Have you ridden him?"

He moves closer to her, enjoying the conversation.

"Sort of." She replaces the broom. "He's a big animal and takes a lot of riding. But he knows a thing or two."

He nods, goes to the bay again, strokes his muzzle.

"D'you know what age he is?"

"Ten," she says. "A gelding."

She puts a riding helmet on. Then, finally, a high-visibility vest.

"And do they sell horses here?" he wants to know. She shrugs.

"Sometimes," she replies. "But you'll have to speak to Møller about that. He's feeding in the stable down there."

Charlo thanks her and goes out, walks down a steep slope, turns the corner and enters the lower stable. This houses ten animals, too. Several are small, fat Shetland ponies, hardly his favourite. Sweet, but unpredictable and as stubborn as mules, he thinks. But excellent for really young girls. At the far end is a couple of good-looking animals, a palomino, and a rather small piebald. Just then, a man appears in the door and catches sight of him. Something about the way he moves makes Charlo suspect that he's the owner. He's short and broad, with a wiry lock of dark hair hanging down over his brow. He continues his work without pausing, seems filled with a special serenity. He's at home here, amongst the animals.

"Are you the owner?" Charlo squirms slightly, he feels awkward.

"That's right."

He looks quickly at Charlo, but doesn't interrupt his work. The animals are more important, it's a matter of sticking to the feeding routines. His work is even and methodical. Just watching him gives Charlo a sense of peace. The man grabs a zinc pail from a shelf, then turns round and holds out his hand.

"Møller," he says nodding.

"Torp," says Charlo, and presses the hand. "Do you have horses for sale?" He tries to keep his voice light.

Møller scrutinises him more closely. Møller's eyes are dark and deep-set, but his gaze is firm. He's wearing a green oilskin jacket and long, lace-up leather boots.

"Occasionally."

The lock of dark hair falls across his brow. "Is that why you're here?" He works all the time he's talking. Charlo thrusts his hands into his pockets, wanting to hide an almost childish embarrassment. Eventually he gets the better of it.

"I've just come to look, mainly. But I am thinking about it. A bit later on. I was wondering what kind of money we'd be talking about."

Møller dips the pail into a sack of pellets and walks to the nearest box. His jacket crackles as he moves about, his boots smack against the cement. He empties a litre measure of feed into the manger, and the chubby pony dives in.

"I've sold horses for twenty thousand kroner," he says, "and I've sold them for a hundred and fifty thousand. It depends what you want."

Charlo watches Møller as he does the feeding. It looks like nice work, bringing food to the animals.

"Well, let's say I could manage something in between," he says. "But I've got to sell some things first, and that could take time. And I need a horse that knows a bit. I couldn't take a young horse that had to be trained right up from nothing."

"I know," he says, and digs into the pail of pellets.

"And preferably not a mare," Charlo adds.

"Bad experience?" Møller asks. He's not a terrifically accommodating man, his voice is a little terse, but he's not unfriendly, he's just sounding Charlo out.

"I'd probably go for a gelding," he says. "What about the bay in the stable up the way? I hear he belongs to you."

Møller glances at him.

"My daughter's riding him."

Charlo loses courage for an instant.

"Are you interested in him?" Møller asks in surprise. "He's large. Not many people dare to get up on that one."

Charlo shrugs defensively, attempting to curb his enthusiasm.

"Yes, he's large all right, but he makes an impression. But I've no idea what he's really made of. He's probably expensive. Good build. Lots of muscle."

"One metre eighty high," Møller says. He places the pail on the floor and wipes his brow with the sleeve of his jacket. His boots are caked with wood shavings and horse manure, and a thick black stubble forms shadows on his jowls.

"If I got an offer, I might possibly consider it," he says, and scrutinises Charlo more closely. He won't sell to just anybody. "He's a bit much for the girl, she's only thirteen. But we haven't found anything else for her, it's mainly so that he gets some exercise."

Charlo feels a flutter of excitement.

"Shall we go up and take a look?" Møller suggests. Charlo is surprised. He thanks him and stands there watching the man while he finishes his feeding. He parks the pail and the wheelbarrow in a corner and buttons up his jacket. Then he walks quickly out of the stable, and Charlo scoots after him. Two small girls, their legs sticking out, ride up on ponies, a couple of cars with trailers drive in, the riding centre is starting to hum with life. They go into the upper stable.

"I'll bring him into the passage," Møller says, "so you can see him better." Charlo nods gratefully, he feels a quiver of elation inside. He can't believe that he's standing in here, admiring a beautiful horse. That this man listens to him and takes him seriously. Møller ties the horse to the ring.

"This chap's pretty heavy to ride," he admits, and begins stroking the horse's neck. "But on the plus side he knows a lot. He's well trained, doing well in dressage and can clear one metre thirty. He's always been in good health. Even temperament. Strong-willed, but never any trouble. A fine, steady canter. He requires a lot of warming-up because he's large. But if he's given the time he needs, you've only got to give him the word and he'll go for hours."

Charlo listens enthralled, he believes every word that Møller says.

"What's his name?"

"Call Me Crazy."

"Didn't you say he had an even temperament?"

"Oh yes." Møller strokes the horse's muzzle. "He must have got the name before he was gelded," he chuckles.

"Breed?" Charlo asks.

69

"Holstein. Good pedigree. A dependable horse."

"He's beginning to sound expensive."

"I wouldn't take less than fifty thousand for him. That much I can say."

"Fifty?"

Charlo chews his lip, thinks of what he owes, thinks about the silver, tries to do a mental calculation. You can bargain with a horse's owner, he's sure of it. At any rate, down to forty-five. He thinks, he hopes. The horse is absolutely lovely, people would stop to look at him.

"Would you like me to saddle him so you can try him out?"

He shakes his head emphatically at this. "I hadn't given it a thought, I haven't ridden for years. But would it be annoying if I came out a couple of times to look at him? Could I take some photos?"

Møller nods his assent.

"Yes, just come along. The stables are open to the public. I can arrange for my daughter to put him through his paces in the ring, so you can see how he moves. If you're interested, that is. She wants something a bit smaller and lighter, I'm pretty sure she won't mind."

Charlo nods gratefully. "And another thing. What are your stabling costs? If I wanted to keep him here?"

Møller runs a hand under his nose.

"Three thousand eight hundred kroner. That includes mucking out weekdays. We put them into the paddock, and sometimes we can arrange for people to look after them."

"Well, that's what it costs then," Charlo says, engaged in febrile mental arithmetic yet again. But he can no longer make sense of the figures without paper.

He lays his hand on the horse's rump and feels the firm muscles. Runs his hand down its long, powerful leg. He looks closely at the pasterns, they look fine. Searches for the ribs. He can feel them, but not see them, and he knows that's how it should be.

"Ten years old, did you say?"

Møller nods. "I think ten is the best age. They're out of puberty, properly grown up and old age is a long time off. Satisfied?"

"Yes, thanks," says Charlo. He feels ecstatic. He's standing here with a stranger and a beautiful bay, and his voice is steady. Standing here in an old quilted jacket, with his nasty, slit-shaped pupils and no one notices them.

"Well, I'll go and have a think about it and come back to you," he says, and watches Møller leading the horse back to its box. Then he lays a horse blanket over its back and tightens the straps.

Charlo leaves the stable. He feels mildly intoxicated. He gets into his car, checks himself in the mirror, keeping his features under observation. Each time he looks again he sees that watchful expression. A man stares back at him, a man he has to get to know. It'll take time, he thinks, time is a great healer, just drive now, take it easy. He drives slowly down the forest track, and soon he's back on the main road. He stops off at a shopping centre to buy food. Takes a quick look at his watch, presses the button on the radio. Waits. A couple of minutes pass. There's the fanfare heralding the news. His heart beats faster again, because now it's broken, they're talking about the murder at Hamsund. A few words force their way in, stick in his memory. Particularly brutal. Elderly and alone. She probably let him in. Objects of value are missing from the house.

Charlo lays his forehead on the steering wheel, he listens, his entire body tense. Particularly brutal. Was it? He doesn't see it that way. He hit her until she lay still, and that took time. The woman was found by a neighbour. The police have some clues. They're encouraging people who were in the vicinity of Hamsund yesterday night to get in touch if they saw any suspicious vehicles near Fredboesgate.

The words seem to come from far away, he doesn't recognise himself, or the crime; it's become a case. As dry as all other cases, stripped of all drama. It's so strange, he thinks, it has nothing to do with me. Well it has if I let it, but I won't let it, I must push it away. I was in that room for only a few minutes, now I'm in another room, I've closed the door and locked it, and I'll never go back there.

The newsreader turns to politics. That was all it was, just a few seconds, before being jostled aside by other news. He turns off the radio and ponders. The police have some clues, but what could they be? Suspicious vehicles, he thinks next. Could one describe the collision and his uncontrolled outburst as suspicious? Obviously. A grown man doesn't lose his rag like that over a dent. Harriet Krohn, discovered now, and her house full of people, photographers and technicians.

Minute examination, tiny brushes, chemicals. With an effort he pulls himself together, gets out of the car and locks it. Walks away with his head down and his hands thrust deep into his pockets.

The shopping centre consists of four or five shops. He's just about to turn into the grocery store when he catches sight of something. A fruit machine. A Twin Runner with flashing lights. He stands staring at it. Automatically, he feels in his pockets for coins. His arm jerks, he sees all the glitter of the machine, its colours, the great pull it exerts. He's got a twenty-krone piece in his pocket. His fingers tighten around it. No, a voice inside him says, it's over now, finished. But his ears can hear the familiar sound of coins cascading into the tray, he's feeling lucky, this is his day. No! He turns his back on the machine and goes into the grocery store, strides off round the shelves. Call Me Crazy, he thinks. What a beauty.

He phones Bjørnar Lind again. Still no reply. Brimming with irritation he stands staring at the bundle of notes, it almost seems to be burning in the drawer. He wants to be rid of it, to get them off his back. In the evening, he settles down in front of the television to watch the news. Before it starts he's flustered and nervous, he rushes around the living room waiting, soon the bombshell will burst. He imagines that the murder will be the lead item of news, that the old woman will precede all international conflicts, and he's right. He strains forward in his chair, staring goggle-eyed. There is her house, and the street. He sees the technicians swarming everywhere in their white caps. He thinks of all the machinery that's been set in motion. They interview a policeman, he notices the name on the bottom left of his screen, Inspector Sejer. He notices the acute gaze, hears the deep, authoritative voice, sees the lion with its crown and axe on the man's shoulder. Charlo puts his hands in front of his eyes, he finds himself rocking backwards and forwards in his chair. He knows it will pass. So he finds it odd when they suddenly move on to other things, his own crime so quickly making way for the problems of the Middle East. He feels strangely devalued. It cost him so much, in terms of courage and dread and despair.

Then he remembers that there's something he's got to do. He goes down to the cellar and finds a large hammer, then comes back up and roots around in a drawer where he keeps his socks. He begins taking socks out and pulls them over the head of the hammer, carrying on until it has become a ball of material, both hard and soft at the same time. He picks it up, goes to the window and looks out. He can't see anyone in the street, so he slips out of the front door and approaches the Honda with the hammer, then wriggles under the car.

The ground is icy against his back. He feels along the dented wing, can't bear the ghastly mark, the reminder. He attempts to hammer the metal, but can't get a proper swing at it. He uses more strength, strikes again and again. If he could just remove this dent. It's dangerous for him, tell-tale. Occasionally he rests, with his eyes shut and his back on the gravel, he's wet and

74

cold, but he carries on beating as hard as he can. It's heavy work, it's wasted effort, he can't get at it, can't get enough force on the hammer. He'd like to give up, just lie there on the sodden ground until someone finds him and carts him off. He has to rest again, he can barely believe he's lying there thumping away in sheer desperation.

He tests the metal with his hand, feels that he's done a little good. Crawls back out to take a look. It's almost as bad as it was before. He can see the white streaks from the other car, and recalls that car paint can be identified and traced. He rushes indoors for a penknife, runs out again and begins scraping. He draws the knife blade across the metal, it makes a hard, screeching sound and he uncovers the matt layer beneath. Later on he can rub it down with sandpaper and buy some enamel paint, then the dent will be less obvious. There's nothing criminal about having a smash he thinks, and is grateful for the chance to buy something, do something and make the time pass. He keeps going until he's exhausted. The clean-scraped metal glints at him, but that's enough for the moment, he goes in and sits down to rest.

There is an alien emptiness in the house. A sort of echo in the room he hasn't noticed before, as if there's no furniture in it. He wants time to pass, he wants night to come. Then people will turn in, and nobody will think about him, search for him. He hears the ticking of the wall clock and the incessant thudding of his own heart. Now that the bombshell has exploded and everyone has heard about Harriet, why is it all so quiet?

Are they sitting whispering in corners? Dully, he chews his nail, tries to work out what he's feeling. A bad habit from the past reasserts itself, and he sits running his finger across his broken tooth.

CHAPTER
FIVE

He stands in the kitchen with one hand over his face. He feels the ridge of his nose and his dry lips, the wide chin which he knows so well, or used to know. He opens his fingers a crack and peers through them, taking in the room in small portions, its walls, its furniture. He sees his own feet. He feels his chest rise and understands so clearly the throbbing mass that is his body, tainted now, guilt is everywhere, in his right hand, in his head, in his heart. No, not in his heart, he never wanted this, never dreamt of being here. No human being ever does, they simply slide into perdition. He stands breathing silently, holding his face as if it's been reduced to a mask that will fall away if he lets go. Beneath there is only raw flesh and empty, black eye sockets. He feels his chest rise again. Although he doesn't deserve it, he'll get oxygen, he thinks, my heart is working in spite of everything, it doesn't fail even though I've done this terrible deed.

His goal is to wrench himself free from this mindset. He wants to go out and pick up the newspaper, but just then he catches sight of his neighbour, Erlandson, walking back from his car in his bluff, hearty manner. Charlo has no desire to talk to anyone, not now, he's feeling exposed. He can't assume the right expression, a thing that's never been difficult before. And it strikes him that from now on he'll have to relearn everything, daily tasks, meeting people, being the same person he's always been. But he isn't the same any more.

His next objective is to make himself some food, but he just stands there, struggling with his thoughts, locked inside a confined space. He feels an enormous need to pull himself free, to find more room. Here I am in the spotlight, he thinks, my cheeks are burning. I'm Charlo, the murderer. I'm standing in my own kitchen, leaning against the kitchen unit, and I could stand here till nightfall. Apathy protects me from all evil, no emotion can take hold while I stand here frozen. It all feels insurmountable, the next hour, tomorrow, the remainder of my life. Here I am, doing my small chores, no, I'm not doing anything, I'm standing paralysed, by the kitchen unit, my hand to my face, I can't bring myself to take it away. I imagine that the light will burn like acid. This will soon pass, it comes and goes, I know that, I must live with it.

He tries to lift his mind, to move to somewhere else, but it's quite an effort. My mother gave birth to me in 1963, he thinks, clutching at the images. I was a chubby baby, a nice child, a considerate boy, and later a pleasant young man, a good bloke as people used to say. Before I started gambling, before I borrowed money from all those people I never repaid. I met Inga Lill, we had Julie. But Inga Lill is dead now, and I can't manage alone. At the thought of Inga Lill he gets knotted up inside, he wipes an angry tear from his

78

cheek. Miserable, he holds his face once more, wanting to force his hand back down where it should be, to become the same man he used to know, the one who could look candidly at the world. He grits his teeth, feels the rough stubble rasping beneath his fingers.

His gaze wanders around the room and fixes on a picture that Julie did in her childhood. A mother and a father and a child, close together beneath a huge sun. That's not how it is any more, he thinks, I ruined it all and she hasn't forgiven me. He recalls the first time he saw her, a well formed infant fifty centimetres long. When she was a year old, Inga Lill started giving her porridge and she put on loads of weight and looked like a little pink doughnut. Six months later, when she began to walk, she slimmed down. At the age of five she began riding, and all the hard work soon showed as small, hard muscles, particularly in her thighs and upper arms; she had biceps like a boy's.

He clenches his fists. He thinks, if the police don't harass me, I'll hound myself, all the way to hell. He stares out of the window, bewildered, wishing the world were pristine, that 7 November had never been. His eyes move on. An old sea chest stands by the wall. He inherited it from his parents. Over the years it has been painted so many times that an unknown number of colours lie hidden beneath the present dark green. The chest functions as a seat, it's a roughly made piece of furniture, not especially elegant, but very spacious and solid. He used to sit on it as a child with dangling legs. Now the chest is full of footwear and other things.

Brushes and cloths, wax and shoe polish. And the bag containing Harriet's silver.

Charlo stares at the chest. He tears himself loose from the kitchen unit, crosses the room, raises the lid, roots amongst the boots and brushes, and lifts the bag out. A green and white check bag, with the initials "J.T." embroidered in red. It's heavier than he remembers. He tips the contents out on to the kitchen table, knives, forks and spoons. Cream jug and sugar bowl, candlesticks and vases. Because it's all tightly packed in sealed bags, the silver is as bright as new. Maybe Harriet collected it as a kind of investment. Maybe it was handed down to her by her mother or someone else. He pulls a knife out of the plastic and holds it up to the light. Checks the hallmark. There's not a scratch on the blade. He's not familiar with the pattern, but it looks old, and expensive. It's worth a lot presumably.

A fence, he thinks, the weak link, do I dare? Without someone to launder it, the silver is worthless. But, after all, a fence is in business, we must be able to trust one another. He should phone, he has a number in his wallet, but puts it off. He wants everything to settle down. No, things will never be calm again, he must battle this storm for the rest of his life, and he has no stays any more, it's as if he'll take off at any moment and fly away like an empty paper bag. His hands begin to shake. Another landslide is loosed inside him when he thinks back and remembers. He leans across the table, takes a few deep breaths. The things he took from her jewellery box have hardly any value: a string of pearls, imitation presumably, a couple of rings, a silver bracelet and some brooches, one an ugly old cameo. But the gold watch. He picks it up, weighs it in his hand. It's as heavy as lead. Fifty thousand at least, perhaps seventy or eighty. He stands there a long time looking at his spoils. He counts forks and knives and spoons, tries to calculate mentally. Then he packs the jewellery and silverware away in the bag and replaces it in the chest.

He goes to the kitchen unit and takes a loaf from the drawer, begins to slice it, focusing on the concrete thought that he needs food. A good grasp of the loaf in the left hand, the knife in the right. I must concentrate on this now, he thinks, I must act, do the little things. I must behave like the living. The fact that I've killed makes me feel different. Other people can't see it, I know that, and I can't reveal it, either. I must carry this from now on, and yet it doesn't feel like a weight. It's more like a blaze-mark, a notch. He imagines a notch cut into his heart, and that when he dies and they open him up, they will lean over his corpse and see the vile stigma. His heart, revealed. Disfigured. Ah! they'll think, that's how it is, he's carrying a burden of guilt! His hands begin to shake again, the knife ceases its motion in the bread. For a while he stands immobile, frozen in this position.

At last silence falls within him, and he cuts some slices of Jarlsberg and lays them on the bread. As he picks up his plate, he feels his body is behaving oddly, that it has no coordination, is unpleasantly slack. The feeling is reminiscent of when he was a teenager and growing too fast. His joints feel weak, his thoughts wander. As if the link between body and soul has been severed. Yes, he thinks, contact has been broken, my soul is drifting alone in a dark place with whispering voices, and my heart has a notch in it. With some effort he goes into the living room, seats himself in his comfortable chair, presses his knees together. Puts the plate on his lap. He bites into the crust, it's dry and hard. He hears the traffic outside, it comes as a relief, he's frightened of total silence, so much can grow out of it. From now on he thinks of other people as far removed from himself. It's not a guilty conscience that troubles him, nor the pangs of remorse. But a huge feeling of loneliness.

He phones Bjørnar Lind again and after the fourth ring it's answered. This is his great moment, this is what he's been waiting for and dreaming of.

"Hi there, this is Charlo. It's been a long time!"

Silence at the other end, just as he'd anticipated. And then an irritated, wheezing sound.

"You never stop trying, do you. The tap's been turned off, Charlo, you're not getting a single øre."

Charlo sits down in the chair at the desk and rests his elbows on the tabletop. He opens the drawer slowly and takes out the money, caressing the notes with his fingertips. The thin paper crackles.

"Whereabouts are you?" Charlo's voice is relaxed and low, he's in no hurry at all, he wants to draw the conversation out and enjoy it.

"I'm back home," Lind replies. "I've been in Sweden covering the harness racing. What have you got yourself into now?"

"Nothing. I don't need you for anything at all."

Again there's that wheezing sound at the other end of the line.

"So why are you ringing me, then?"

Lind's voice is hard and sullen, Charlo's head is as clear as crystal.

"There's something waiting for you here. I just wanted to let you know. You can come and get it anytime."

"Get what?" Lind asks. His voice still has a sceptical note, but now it's rising, sounding hopeful.

"Two hundred thousand," says Charlo. "All beautifully bundled up."

There's a long pause.

"Pull the other one!" says Lind in disbelief.

"You can drop that jokey tone," Charlo says, bridling. "And make sure your people stay away from me. I haven't had a proper night's sleep for months. Are you coming or not?"

Lind's tone becomes livelier.

"How did you manage it, Charlo?"

"That's none of your business."

"Have you completely lost the plot?"

"Don't you worry about me. Come over straight away so I can get this hell over and done with!"

He slams down the phone. He's swelling with pride, he's on top of the world. He packs the money in a large envelope, and settles down to wait. He glances out of the window and notices that the sun is about to penetrate the layer of cloud. He clutches the envelope. In less than fifteen minutes he spies Lind's Chrysler cruising past in the street. He sits calmly, waiting for the doorbell. The moment is indescribable. The sound peals through the whole house. He rises languidly, strolls across the room and opens the door slowly.

Lind, tall and lanky, stands there with his hands in his pockets looking at him.

"Well, Charlo, things on the move, are they?"

Charlo folds his arms. Looks up at the sky.

"I think it's going to clear up," he says nodding. Lind catches sight of the envelope.

"Is there anything I need to know?"

"Not a thing," Charlo says evenly. "Take the money and keep your mouth shut, that's all I ask."

"What about a little gratitude for the loan?"

"Yes, thank you so much." He holds out the envelope and bows exaggeratedly like a courtier. "Make sure that people know I've paid."

"What do you mean?"

"You know perfectly well. I've heard the rumours."

Lind opens the envelope and begins counting, the notes are in bundles of ten.

"My, this looks good."

A grin of satisfaction spreads across his face.

"Naturally. I'm an honest man. And I'm done with every kind of gambling."

Lind gives him a tight-lipped smile. "I won't believe that until I've seen it. But, if you've really kicked the habit, good luck to you."

Lind nods curtly and walks to his car. Charlo stands watching him leave. Now the sun breaks through in earnest as the car slips out into the road, and everything is gilded and bright. His head is completely quiet. He goes inside and opens a window, he weighs next to nothing, he floats through the rooms. There's twenty thousand kroner left in the drawer, that's enough for some small bills. Could that be birdsong he hears through the open window? Perhaps not now in November, but outside someone is whistling, cheerily.

The scraped wing seems to leap out at him when he goes to his car. He drives to an auto accessories shop and goes to the shelf of enamels. He tries to find a shade of red that matches the Honda, but can't decide. Shakes the aerosol he's holding, hears the pea rattling about inside it. Which is best? he wonders, one that's too light, or one that's too dark? And what shade of red does he actually require? Plum red, scarlet, he doesn't quite know, he hesitates. He decides on the lighter shade. At the counter he notices the newspapers and buys two different titles. On the front of *Dagbladet* is a photo of a large bunch of flowers, what a strange front cover, he thinks. There's something about it that's familiar, it rings a bell. He picks up the newspaper in horror.

Did you make this bouquet?

Instantly, he feels his face stiffen. He can't believe his eyes. Panicking, he scrabbles in his wallet for money, snatches up the papers and the aerosol and rushes out to his car. Slams the door hard. His heart pounds wildly, they're already on his tail. No, that can't be right. But the flowers, what does that mean? He reads the article rapidly.

Look carefully at this bouquet, which was found in murder victim Harriet Krohn's house at Hamsund. The flowers have obviously been arranged by a professional and were absolutely fresh when the body was found. The police assume that the bouquet was put together by one of the town's florists, and hope that the person who made this particular bouquet will remember it, and possibly also the purchaser. Detectives are unwilling to say more about the significance of these flowers. The bouquet consists of one white lily, blue anemones, sweet peas and roses. If you think it's familiar, please get in touch with the police immediately.

He lets the newspaper fall. Horrified, he stares through the window. I didn't realise they had so much imagination, he thinks despairingly, a bunch of flowers on the worktop, why did they attach so much importance to it? He thinks about the young girl at the florist's and he feels a nasty jolt pass through him, because, for some reason, he's certain she remembers him. No. It's not possible, she couldn't give a precise description, I look so ordinary, he thinks, so anonymous. But the blood rushes to his head, and when a car pulls up beside him, he ducks down as if he's searching for something. Perhaps, he thinks, it would be better if I stayed indoors until this blows over.

He puts the car in gear and drives off. The can of spray paint rolls about on the floor; his brain is working feverishly. He conjures up the florist's assistant to see how much he can remember. Concentrates, narrows his eyes. She rises in his mind in all her youthful beauty, her fair plaits and red jumper. Her hands, her mouth. The rings on her fingers, her sugary way of speaking. He parks outside the house and goes in. Seats himself at the kitchen table and rests his chin on his hands.

Why should she remember me?

Because you were nervous. Because you had a special glint in your eye.

That's silly. I was silent and sullen, maybe, but otherwise perfectly anonymous.

Everyone has a distinctive feature. She's quick witted, young and sharp, she's taken everything in. And it's obvious she'll recognise the bouquet, she's an artist.

But it was right at the end of the day. She must have been tired.

Don't kid yourself. It's only a question of time, and they'll be at your door, Charlo. In a murder case they never give up.

He rubs his eyes hard and thinks of Julie. Perhaps she's doing her homework now. He can see her quite clearly, that mane of red hair cascading down her back, her face deeply concentrated on her books. What's that car driving past? A grey Volvo, he's seen it before. No, it's only his imagination, besides this one's green. They don't know who he is. They don't know where he lives or what he's done. He leans forward across the table. Listens in the silence. There's a gentle hum. In the evening he turns off all the lights, people will think he's gone away. I'm lonely, he thinks, but I'm out of debt. The darkness protects and soothes him, broken only by the blue flicker of the television screen.

Uneasiness is there the whole time.

This resentment, this bustle inside his head, disturbs him. He constantly returns to his childhood. The images are so bright and uncomplicated, he enjoys being there, he gradually calms down, remembers his mother, remembers how caring she was and her deep, warm laughter. And his father with his broad shoulders. How did I turn out so weak? he wonders, but in the same instant recalls his crime, that he has killed. What strength he needed, what courage he had to summon to ring Harriet's doorbell. That he could get himself off his knees and do so much violence. He, who'd never laid a finger on anyone. He remembers her thin face, contorted with rage and fear. And his own fear drove him on, through the series of heavy blows. Panic pushed him over the edge and gave him strength. No, he wants to return to his childhood again, childhood has become a refuge. The present is unbearable, he thinks of nothing except his crime, and the collision. It all sticks fast in his mind.

Every time he eats, the food swells in his mouth. He steals a glance at his hands. Haven't they turned darker? Has he always had such red hands? He closes them, opens them again, thinks of all the links between head and hand. The millions of impulses that make his hands open and close, make his legs walk. What about his heart, he thinks, does that play a part? No, the seat of wickedness is in the head. He clasps his head with his hands and squeezes. Inside here, he thinks, dropping his chin to his chest, inside here it was growing without my knowledge. From the start I was weak, and weakness can be genetic. But Mum is strong, he realises, and Dad was a decent, hard-working man. He stands at the window looking at all the innocent people. Their hearts are pure. He moves away and goes to the kitchen instead. He's become a haunter of dark corners. I've taken a life, he thinks. And what's left of my own must be lived in the shadows, alone. I'm paying a high price. Will I ever be able to look people in the eye? Then, with a great effort, he pulls himself together. One important thing remains. He gets his wallet and fishes out a small card with a telephone number. A fence who won't ask questions. Merely an intermediary, a man he'll never meet again. It's a case of sink or swim. We're in the same line of business, he thinks, this fence and me, and there's no avoiding it. He stands with his back to the window and dials the number.

CHAPTER
SIX

They're to meet at the railway station, at the far end of the long-stay car park. Charlo's heart is pounding. He gets out the silverware and the gold watch and places it in a bag. The jewellery is worth very little and no one would give anything for it, so it remains in Julie's gym bag at the bottom of the chest. He halts in front of the mirror, and looks at the face he must now reveal. His nose seems to be sticking out, and his ears are burning. Exposing himself like this is abhorrent, but he has no choice. He forces his face to relax because the muscles round his eyes and mouth have a tendency to twitch in a creepy, revealing manner.

He puts the bag in the car and sets off. He constantly checks his mirror, it's become a habit. He crosses the bridge. At the railway station he turns to the left, his gaze raking the parked cars, and right at the far end he sees a man leaning up against a BMW. The man watches Charlo's Honda, and comes over as soon as he's parked. Charlo hardly dares look at him. He sits in the car with his head lowered and waits for the other to take the initiative. And he does. The man taps on the window and looks in. He's surprisingly young, just a stripling, but shrewd enough for all that. A gangly bloke with a long, blond mop of hair and listless gestures. He asks no questions, they avoid making eye contact, they're there to do business. He gets into Charlo's Honda. The silver makes an impression, as does the gold watch. Charlo holds his breath as the man studies the hallmarks, he's got a loupe with him, he's left nothing to chance. He pulls out a pocket calculator and begins to add up. Charlo waits patiently. He doesn't want to haggle, or try to force the price, he just wants to get it over with.

"The watch is engraved," he says and looks sceptically at Charlo.

"But you'll melt it down, won't you?"

The man weighs the watch in his hand, screws up his eyes for an instant, it's obvious he's tempted. Then, finally, it disappears into his pocket and Charlo breathes more easily.

"I'm only a middleman," says Charlo. He ventures a smile. The young man sneers, displaying yellow teeth.

"That's what they all say."

Charlo lowers his head again, feeling a bit naive. The fence continues to study the silver. He appears to have all the time in the world and doesn't seem to be nervous at all.

"I think it's antique," Charlo says, "a pattern that's maybe gone out of production. What do you think? I only mention it because it affects the price. Doesn't it?"

Still no reply. The man is holding a fork, examining the design. Charlo looks over his shoulder, but few people are about and everything's quiet. The man delves into the bag once more, he works on imperturbably. Now he's got to the candlesticks, he weighs them in his hand.

"You can take these back home with you," he says, "they're only silver plate."

"Silver plate? I'd rather not. I mean, surely you've got more contacts than me. Can't you just get rid of them?"

The other shrugs and taps his calculator with agile fingers. Charlo looks down at his hands and wrings them hard. A small eternity seems to pass. The man adds, weighs, examines, he's got an acute, appraising eye.

Then, finally, he comes to his decision. He looks down at the display, catches Charlo's eye and announces authoritatively.

"Forty thousand for the lot."

Charlo sits there gawping.

"Forty?" he stammers. "But the watch alone is worth seventy for sure. Perhaps even eighty."

"In the shops, yes. This isn't a shop."

"No, no, I realise that."

"I've got to take my cut, of course, you realise that. And then I'm taking a risk, you've got to pay for that as well."

"Naturally." Charlo nods mechanically. He'd hoped to make fifty or sixty, but he daren't push it. The man has the money in his inside pocket, he begins counting it out.

"I'll throw in the bag as well," Charlo says.

Once more he attempts a smile, it isn't reciprocated. He feels tense and needs to lighten the mood. It's a relief to be rid of the silver, all he wants is his money. He gets it. He counts it, and nods that it's right.

The fence opens the door, sets one foot on the ground, and sends him a sharp glance.

"We need each other, so keep your mouth shut."

Charlo nods and returns his gaze. The man goes off to his own vehicle, revs up the engine and drives off. His car disappears. Charlo puts the money in his left inside pocket, close to his heart. Now at last he can do business.

The bay will greet him with great, dark eyes, and ears laid amicably forward. Perhaps a small whinny of pleasure. It will lower its big head and lick his salty fingers, nuzzle his jacket a bit. He sets out for the riding centre and slows down as soon as he approaches the paddocks. He parks his car and jogs over to the stable and enters. He walks to the last box and stops dead. It's empty.

He stands there staring, stunned. Has someone beaten him to it? No, that's impossible, the bay was for him! Just then he hears the door slam, and shortly after Møller comes up, his riding boots thumping the cement.

"My girl is working out in the ring," he says, "now's your chance to see what the horse can do."

Charlo breathes a sigh of relief. Møller stops in front of him, legs astride, manly in his green jacket.

"Are you still interested?"

"Absolutely," Charlo says, nodding. "But what about your daughter? What does she think?"

"It's fine by her." He stands square and looks intently at Charlo. "If you can manage forty thousand, we've got a deal." Charlo looks at him wide-eyed, his thoughts whirling around his head. Forty thousand. He can manage that. His heart pounds. He nods smiling broadly.

"I'll go and take a look."

"Do that," Møller says. "She's not bothered about people watching her, she's used to it, and she's good."

Ah, but not *that* good, Charlo thinks. He opens the heavy stable door again and trudges down to the riding ring. The wide door is open. He walks in slowly and immediately catches sight of the bay. His heart leaps. A teenage girl is sitting on the horse, appropriately dressed in white breeches and black polo-neck sweater. She gives him a quick look and then concentrates on the horse again. Charlo finds a seat. She steers the horse to the wall where a sound system has been installed, he can see her rooting on the shelf for a CD. She wants to show what she can do. The horse stands patiently. She finds what she's looking for, reaches up and inserts the CD, then grips the reins again. A second later music fills the great space. At first he can't recognise it, the opening is unfamiliar to him, but then the drums come in and a choir of festive voices. It's Vangelis' "Conquest of Paradise". It's certainly loud enough, the music fills the entire ring, which he estimates must be getting on for two thousand square metres. He feels the music centring on his breastbone, it numbs and suffuses him, makes him surrender completely. His eyes are wet, he's got goose pimples.

94

The girl puts the horse into a walk. Charlo takes in the sight as his pulse pounds at his temples. She's riding with short, tight reins and tiny commands. A girl of fifty kilos is directing a horse weighing six hundred. She's doing it with imperceptible tickles of her whip on the horse's hindquarters, shifting her body weight almost indiscernibly from side to side, or backwards and forwards, and with small jerks on the reins. The horse can do most things. It takes small steps, it trots on the spot, does pirouettes and traverses and lead changes. Its transitions are superb. It trots the length of the ring, it does a collected working canter, then suddenly switches into an extended canter, foam frothing around the bit. Wood shavings swirl about the shiny hooves, it doesn't take long before the horse is damp with sweat and glowing like clean copper. Yes, you're good, he says to himself about the young girl. You're light on the reins, and you've got good contact, but you don't ride the whole horse, he thinks, you don't take its hindquarters with you. All at once she comes towards him. Her gaze is completely devoid of fear.

"Are you the man who's going to buy Crazy?"

She has a pretty, round face beneath the black helmet. Boots with long spurs, elegant black leather gloves.

"You don't like the idea, maybe? Of selling him?"

He regards her nervously. Why should she want to part with this beautiful specimen of horseflesh? He is filled with anxiety as he squints up at her. She shrugs nonchalantly. The horse has lowered its head, and is nibbling its forelegs.

"As long as I get another one, I'm not bothered," she says simply. "I've changed horses several times already. I'd like an Arab, they're lighter."

She stares at him as she speaks, stares at his legs and at his hands, and glances rapidly and inquisitively into his eyes. She's one of those bright, tough girls, presumably a fearless rider.

"Will you be doing dressage?" she asks. And he thinks, I don't look much like a rider, it's hardly surprising she's asking. Before he has time to reply, she says: "Or will you be jumping? He's a good jumper. One metre thirty, very sensitive to the reins and he'll jump a long way, too."

"No," Charlo finally says, looking at the horse all the time. "My bones are about as brittle as dry twigs, I think I'd better keep my feet on the ground."

She unfastens the chinstrap of her helmet.

"You'd never buy a car without giving it a test drive," she teases.

He smiles bashfully, shakes his head, feeling a little embarrassed. It's been a long time since he was on a horse, but he's tempted all the same.

"I'm not exactly dressed for it," he parries, he feels incredibly clumsy next to this girl: an ungainly grown man like him, with a belly and thinning hair. Wearing a lumpy old quilted jacket.

She slips resolutely off the horse's back and hands him the reins. Charlo takes off his jacket. Stands hesitating for a moment. What's he getting into, where will it end? In the sawdust perhaps, head first. A broken neck. Or cracked ribs.

"Do you need a whip?" she asks full of blue-eyed innocence. Charlo shakes his head.

"I'll ride him at a gentle trot, that should do."

"Now that he's well warmed up," she says, "he'll move easily. He favours the left," she adds, "in case you're interested." Her gaze is insistent, she wants to play.

Charlo gulps. He puts his foot in the stirrup, gathers the reins in his left hand, and grips the saddle with his right. Silently, he counts to three, then pushes off hard and swings himself up.

"I'm afraid he's in for a shock," Charlo says, "I probably weigh twice as much as you."

"That's nothing to Crazy," she smiles. "Come on, let's see!"

She's enjoying herself like the child she is. He sets off at a walk, tries to keep his back straight, tries to relax. The horse's movements are big, Charlo bobs away, the horse's body is warm between his thighs. He does one circuit at a walk, leans forward a bit and digs his heels in. The horse immediately changes into a nice, easy trot. He feels hot, his cheeks are burning. He trots round three times, then stops in front of the girl.

"And now, do two circuits at the canter," she says eagerly. She's playing instructor, her voice is full of authority.

Charlo wavers. He strokes the horse's neck, feels the thick arteries under its skin, he feels so important sitting there. As if he's in the right place, in control at last. The horse will do what he asks, he is its master, he feels that. But cantering?

"Just ride him in a volte, then he'll do a nice circle, and he's got a very easy canter. Come on!"

He does half a circuit at a walk and goes into a trot. He hasn't lost his former skills, and can ride with a certain elegance. But when it comes to cantering, he's not sure. He doesn't want to land in the sawdust, he's not young any more, not supple like the girl on the ground. She's watching with excitement. But then, I'm already living dangerously, he thinks, and sits well down in the saddle, kicks his right heel into the horse's flank, once, then once more, and suddenly the horse alters his rhythm, his movements are drawn-out, undulating. I'm cantering, he thinks exultantly, and nothing matters, when you're on horseback the rest of the world fades away. The girl has started clapping her hands, Charlo is pouring sweat now, he's concentrating hard, letting himself be carried away, while the mane billows, and the hooves beat the ground in a regular rhythm. He feels like the wind, like a wave breaking, in that special joy of being one with the horse, round and round in great circles. Then, suddenly, he feels weak and tired. He eases down to a trot, and then to a walk. He halts, pats the horse's neck.

"Wonderful," he says wiping the sweat from his brow.

She nods proudly. Charlo slides down the horse's flank and lands gently.

"But can you let him go? Are you sure?"

She smiles indulgently. "I don't want to keep riding the same horse for years, I like changing. Will you buy him?"

"Yes. I've just spoken to your dad, and we've agreed. Can I ask you something?"

She nods.

"Can I take a couple of photos of him? Would you hold him?"

She comes over and takes the reins. Charlo gets his camera out of his pocket, raises it to his eye and gets them in the frame.

The horse has raised its head as if wanting to pose. Loveliest horse in the world, thinks Charlo, and clicks the shutter.

CHAPTER
SEVEN

"Daddy!"

Julie squeezes his fingers, her hand is hot and clammy.

"Can I ride on that horse? Can I ride on it now? Straight away? Will you help me?"

She goes on and on tugging at his hand, imploring him with her green eyes, standing there fizzing. She's about to explode like a firework. They're at the stables for the first time, and her gaze has lit on a white pony. He smiles and squeezes back, looks down the passage for an adult.

"Maybe," he says, "but I must ask someone first. We can't just ride off, because someone owns it."

"Who's the person who owns it? Can you ask now? Can I ride on it now?" She's quivering with anticipation, and stroking the pony's neck the whole time. Her eyes have that special lustre, as if she's found gold. He looks at the rotund Shetland pony and down at five-year-old Julie who's wearing a red snow suit and has stout boots on her feet. She's thrown her fleece-lined mitts on the floor. She's his, she's his dearest possession. Satisfying all her wishes is the very mainspring of his life.

100

He tells her to wait, goes along the passage, and then down to the ring where an instructor is busy with a group of children. They're bumping along on mounts large and small, all hot in the face and concentrating hard.

"That white Shetland pony," he says, looking at the instructor with a plea in his eyes, "could we saddle it up and have a go? I've got my small daughter with me, she's beside herself with excitement."

The instructor is wearing a set of blue thermal overalls and a warm hat with earflaps; she turns from her charges and looks at him.

"Has she ridden before?"

"No," says Charlo, "but I have. We can manage on our own, we don't need any help."

Suddenly, she looks away from him and shouts across the large ring. "Form a volte, girls, don't ride so close together!"

Charlo glances up towards the stable, then back at her again. Thinks about Julie waiting in the box, he can't bear to disappoint her.

"Just five minutes," he implores, "I can saddle up and do everything. Perhaps she could have lessons here. Could she? She's five. What would it cost?"

She smiles, studying him. "A hundred and fifty kroner an hour. Once a week. His saddle is hanging in the tack room, on the peg marked Snowball."

He thanks her and rushes back. Julie is standing with her arms round the pony's neck.

"Come on," he says, "we've got permission! We'll go and get his saddle. But we'll have to keep to the edge of the riding ring because there's a lesson going on there, lots of riders, and we mustn't get in the way."

She jumps up and down, clapping her hands.

"And you've got to do what I tell you," he orders.

She nods. She follows him out to the tack room and watches as he lifts the saddle down, her cheeks red with anticipation. He examines her boots to see if they've got proper heels. They have. He carries the saddle out and leads the pony into the passage, Julie stands watching. She strokes the pony incessantly, she pulls its tail, unable to restrain herself. He struggles a bit with the bridle, but gradually he remembers, gets it on and tightens the straps. He glances down at Julie's legs and shortens the stirrups. There are some riding helmets on pegs, he finds one that fits and puts it on her head.

"Off we go, then," he says "but watch your feet, he's heavy."

"I want to lead him," Julie says, she's turbocharged, this is an enthusiasm he's never seen before.

"No," Charlo says, "Daddy's got to help you the first time, we don't know how friendly he is. Not all ponies are friendly," he says looking serious.

She glares at him, fiercely. Of course the pony's friendly, the pony will do whatever she wants, she's sure of it. A certain resoluteness has come over her, a single-mindedness, as if someone has flicked a switch. He sees this and understands, he was a child himself once. He's hung about stables, and he knows what obsession is. They arrive at the ring. Charlo leads the pony in, finds a spot away from the others and lifts Julie up. She grasps the reins, her eyes light up.

"Now," he instructs, "feet in the stirrups. Sit well back and lift your chin. Fine," he says, pulling at the bridle, and the pony moves off immediately with short, waddling steps. Julie holds the reins tight, her body begins to sway. She's turned dumb, her look is far away, and she no longer notices Charlo, it's as if she's somewhere else. The pony ambles along with its head down, they walk in a tight circle, round and round in the ring. Julie looks about proudly, to see if the others can see her, see how grand she is. Now and again she takes the reins in one hand so that she can stroke the pony's neck. Charlo feels a huge sense of satisfaction because he's given her joy. He isn't prepared for what follows. They keep this up for twenty minutes or so, until he begins to look at the clock in the knowledge that Inga Lill is waiting with the dinner.

"Well, Julie, we'll have to stop now. That was fun, wasn't it?" She doesn't answer, or nod, just purses her lips. She stares firmly ahead.

"Again," she says, clinging on hard. He does another circuit. Wants to be extra generous and does one more after that.

"Now," he tries again, "that's enough, it's getting late." She clenches her hands in front of her, won't release the reins.

"Don't want to go home," she says sullenly, there is an almost fanatical look in her eyes. "I want to do more riding. Go round again. Lots of times."

Charlo smiles to himself. But at the same time he must be an adult, she's got to listen to him, they can't stay here till nightfall.

"Julie," he begins, "we can come back another time. Maybe you can start lessons with the others. Wouldn't that be nice? But now we've got to go home and have dinner."

"Not hungry," she says emphatically. "I want more riding." He reaches out for her gently and lovingly, but she twists out of his grasp, pushes him away with one hand. Suddenly, she digs her heels into the pony's sides, and it begins to trip along at a good rate. Charlo jogs along beside it.

"Easy now, Julie," he gasps. "We can't go on all night. If you think this is fun, we can come here again, but now we've got to go." She tightens her grip on the reins again, looks over his head.

"He's not tired at all, he wants to go on. I know he wants to go on!"

Charlo is completely at a loss. She's strong-willed and has shut him out, she's at one with this plump, white creature which walks patiently round and round.

"Maybe Mum's frightened about us," he essays, trying to meet her eyes, but she won't look at him.

"I want to go round some more times," she declares with an authority he would never have believed possible. She clings to the pony, she's made it hers. Again, he starts walking round, thinking about what he's set in motion.

"Tomorrow," he says, and looks at her, imploringly now, "tomorrow we'll come back again. I'll speak to the riding teacher, and perhaps you can have lessons on him. Once a week. It's expensive, but I'll talk to Mum about it."

104

She's not listening, she's stroking the pony, her body is undulating, he notices that she's got excellent balance, that she feels at home. Then he stops suddenly, halting the pony and making his voice stern.

"We're going now, Julie, that's enough."

Sternness doesn't come naturally to him, and she calls his bluff, knows that he doesn't mean it, and pushes on with the pony. She's as impenetrable as a brick wall. She's lost her heart to Snowball, he's her first great love, rules and regulations no longer apply. Charlo runs his hand through his hair and sighs. Just then he has an idea.

"You can ride up to the stable," he says, "that'll be a little ride in the open air."

Reluctantly, she allows herself to be led away, but the idea of leaving the pony is too much for her. He leads her out, hooves slap against asphalt. Julie straightens her back, a look of sadness in her eyes. The golden interlude is over, she can hardly bear it.

"Tomorrow's another day," he says "and before that we need a bit of sleep. You're really good, you've got a natural talent, I'll boast about you to Mum, and then she'll say yes. Won't she? Aren't you pleased about that?" They've arrived at the stable door. Julie isn't pleased, her lower lip is sticking well out. Then it starts to quiver.

"There," he says, "just slide down, I'll catch you." But she doesn't slide down. She just sits there clamped to the reins. He stretches and clasps her round the waist, and begins to pull. She clutches the pony's mane and holds tight, he pulls harder. The pony begins to shift from one foot to the other.

"Julie," he begs feebly, "you've got to be a big girl now and not be silly, I can't take any more." Eventually, she allows herself to be lifted down, her body stiff and stubborn, but she's still holding the reins.

"You can lead him in," says Charlo, and she leads the fat pony down the passage and into his box.

"Now he needs a bit of grooming," Charlo explains, "because he's been working hard. First we've got to take off all his tack, and then we've got to find a brush. We've got to clean out his hooves and stroke him a bit."

Julie runs to the tack room and returns with a brush, she begins grooming as hard as she can, until her hair is damp with sweat. Charlo puts everything back in its place, washes the bit in hot water; he has the strange feeling that he's seeing the start of something big. Something that will take over. He sees a bag of dry bread in a corner, takes a piece out and hands it to Julie. He shows her how to hold it. The pony wolfs it down in record time. Then she stands loitering at the box door, she can't stop stroking the white muzzle. He can't get her to come away. She holds on to the bars tightly and resists him.

That was the start of it.

Her passion for horses resembled his own passion for gambling. A constant, burning ache within him. That, from then on, all thoughts were directed at one thing: satisfying a craving. He saw it take hold of her, that spark that would never be extinguished. He thinks of this as he walks along Blomsgate, on his way to buy the papers. He passes the veterinary surgery and the bakery, sees a woman walking towards him. He glances quickly at her and notices the distance between them. This frontier, he thinks, between me and everyone else. The feeling of being in another country with a strange language, the feeling of living on completely different terms to other people. It's hard.

He enters the shop, chooses three different newspapers from the rack and pays. He sticks them under his arm and walks back again. And then, just as he's striding down the road, something happens to one of his legs. It jerks as if a spasm has passed through it, then it gives way beneath him, his left knee fails and he pitches helplessly forward and falls flat on his face. He strikes the ground chin first, and it scrapes along the pavement, his skin burning and stinging. The papers fly everywhere.

He lies there for a moment struggling, looks back, dazed, to find out if he tripped, but he can't see anything. He wants to get up, but he's hesitant. He doesn't know if his knee will take his weight. He's totally confused, he sees people coming down the street towards him and feels a complete twerp. Perhaps they think he's drunk. At last he crawls to his feet again. Gingerly, he tests his left knee, unsure if it'll take the strain. He bends down for his newspapers. A man comes up offering help, Charlo brushes the arm of his jacket and waves him away. He puts the papers back together again, they're wet. His chin aches and stings. He looks down at himself in surprise, can't comprehend what's happened. His knee feels weak, but it just about carries him.

He walks on cautiously. To collapse like that, as if he were some old man. It was as if he'd been struck by lightning. Could there be something wrong with him? No, there's nothing the matter, his health has always been good. He used to get colds as a child, and just recently he's begun to think he might need glasses because his eyesight occasionally seems weak, it's something that comes and goes. But apart from that, excellent health, he's always taken it for granted. He squeezes the newspapers under his arm. The fall worries him, a dawning anxiety, but he banishes it, enters the house and sits down in a chair.

For a long time he sits there contemplating, searching for the answer. Perhaps he slipped on a patch of ice. But he knows it's too mild for that, there's only slush. Could it have been a banana skin? No, his knee gave way, it lost strength without warning. He dismisses the incident. There are limits to how much time he can spend thinking about it. As if people don't fall occasionally: they trip, they slip, they have poor coordination, it's no big deal. But his chin is stinging badly. He opens the first newspaper. Initially, he doesn't see anything about the Hamsund case. He's looking forward to the big silence, to the day it's no longer talked about and everyone's forgotten it. He opens the second paper. He leafs through it slowly, there's lots of sport, which doesn't interest him. Suddenly, he catches sight of a photo. He recognises

108

the man straight away, he's the one leading the Hamsund case. Charlo reads the brief article.

In connection with their ongoing inquiries into the murder of Harriet Krohn at Hamsund on 7 November, the police would like to hear from a man who was involved in a road traffic accident. The accident occurred at about ten-thirty p.m., only a short distance from the murdered woman's house. Inspector Konrad Sejer says that, for reasons that remain unclear, the man refused to fill in a claim form. Sejer has emphasised that this person is not regarded as a suspect in the investigation.

Horrified, he lowers the newspaper. Runs his hand over his tender chin. The collision, he thinks, it's got me. What he has most feared is now becoming a reality. The Toyota, his outburst, they've registered it. They're searching for his car. Perhaps they've already found him, perhaps they're watching him, waiting for the right moment. He sits there with a hand in front of his mouth, his eyes round. Quickly, he glances out of the window, gripped by a dawning sense of panic. As if they didn't know how to find him, as if they weren't experts and couldn't take in all the details: clearly he's grossly underestimated them, now it's just a question of time. He places a hand over his heart because it's beating so hard. No, they're only trying it on, checking every avenue, and he's not a suspect. But he can't come forward. And that's clearly suspicious as well.

He sits there despondently. And then there's the problem of his knee. Again, he has an insidious doubt, he goes to the bathroom and pulls his trousers down. The knee looks perfectly normal, he compares it with the right one. I just wasn't concentrating, he thinks, I tripped over my own feet and fell, it's nothing to worry about. But he knows this isn't true, there's that little voice of protest inside him, fretting on about weakness in his joints. He doesn't want to hear it, he pulls his trousers up and goes to the mirror. The graze on his chin is nothing. He can't even be bothered to put a plaster on it.

He goes back and reads the third newspaper. There is a photograph of Sejer in this one as well, taken in profile, a man with pronounced features and short-cropped, grey hair. The same story about the accident at Hamsund. "We're simply forming a picture of all the traffic in the area," Sejer explains, "so it would be useful to make contact with the man who collided with a Toyota Yaris at the junction near the railway station on the evening of 7 November. Since he was in the area where the murder occurred, he may have witnessed things of importance."

"Do we know what make of car this man was driving?" the journalist asks. The question is printed in bold type.

"We have reason to believe he was driving a red Honda Accord."

Charlo goes to the window and stares out into the street. What about his neighbour Erlandson? He reads the papers, too. Maybe he's seen the dent in the car's wing, it's quite possible. Erlandson's so inquisitive, he likes standing at his window staring out. For a moment he's overwhelmed with fear. They're on the trail of a red Honda. His legs won't carry him any more. Isn't there a grey Volvo parked down there? It looks familiar. All these troubles that are crowding in, they wouldn't exist if Inga Lill were still around.

What do I really look like, have I got any distinguishing features? Thinning hair and a green parka, the youth in the Toyota won't remember more than that because I was behaving so badly, he wouldn't have noted any details. At least not my car registration. Well, perhaps a bit of it. Then they'll check and eliminate. They'll come to the house and ask questions, I'll get nervous. My gaze will waver, I'll contradict myself. No, I won't, I'm in control. It's a matter of concentration. He clenches his fists and opens them again, leans on the window sill. Some people escape punishment. Just keep quiet!

CHAPTER
EIGHT

Inga Lill is frying fish on the stove, it smells good. Charlo helps Julie off with her clothes. There are layers and layers of them, and in the middle he finally unwraps a hot little girl with skinny arms and legs. She pulls herself free and storms into the kitchen, bursting to relate all that's happened.

"Where in the name of goodness have you both been?" Inga Lill asks, wiping the sweat from her brow. It's warm in the kitchen and she's sweltering.

"I've rode a pony," Julie says. She's hopping up and down, her red hair bouncing.

"Ridden a pony?" says Inga Lill dismayed.

Charlo dives in. "We've been to the riding centre, and they let her have a go," he says. "Just a couple of circuits."

"A couple of circuits? Have you seen the time?"

"I'm learning riding there," Julie says, "Daddy said I could." She plumps down on a chair and puts her elbows on the table. Inga Lill pushes them off again. Then she scoops the pieces of fish out of the frying pan and places them on a dish.

"We'll have to talk about that," she says. "It's bound to cost a lot of money."

Charlo goes over to her, glances at Julie and winks.

"There isn't much to talk about," he says, "believe me."

He gives his wife a meaningful look, nods in the direction of Julie's red head, rolling his eyes, to convey what he's recently witnessed. But Inga Lill hasn't witnessed it, her shoulders tense with reluctance. She puts the dish on the table and drains the potatoes.

"They have so many accidents," she murmurs quietly, so that Julie won't hear.

"You let her cycle by the road," he says, "that's worse."

"But she wears a helmet," says Inga Lill.

"She does on horseback, too," he retorts. They look at one another. Julie hangs on her mother's expression.

"I want to ride," she says emphatically, staring down at the table and holding her fork ready for the food.

"Wash your hands," says Charlo. "You've been in the stables. Come on, we'll go to the bathroom." He helps her get the water the right temperature, and they stand there close together soaping their hands, their eyes meeting in the mirror.

"I want to go again tomorrow," she says defiantly, rubbing her hands so the lather flies. Charlo dries them with a towel.

"Julie," he says, "it's one lesson a week. We can't afford more than that."

"I can brush," she says decidedly and takes the towel from him, "and I can go there and stroke him, and comb his tail and things. I can give him bread and carrots."

They return to Inga Lill who's sitting ready at the table.

"You need so much equipment for riding," she says anxiously. "Boots, helmet, high-visibility vest, things like that."

"She can borrow all she needs," Charlo ripostes, "and she can ride in the boots she's got, they've got decent heels. She can borrow a helmet, too. Maybe we'll have to buy a riding whip, they cost about thirty kroner. Yes, and then a pair of good gloves. That's all."

Inga Lill falls silent and starts eating. Julie keeps her under observation, keeps peeking in Charlo's direction, things are moving too slowly for her. But Charlo is playing the long game, he knows Inga Lill, knows that she needs time.

"Julie mustn't suffer because of your anxiety," he says between mouthfuls. "Supposing she wanted to do Alpine skiing. Lots of injuries there. Supposing she wanted to do handball, that's really rough. Supposing she decides one day that she wants to start diving."

Inga Lill sends him a sideways look. "Well, I suppose, if she just rides in a circle and doesn't start jumping. If she doesn't ride out in traffic, but stays indoors and only rides when there's a teacher there, that's probably not so risky."

Charlo bites his lip. "Of course she must start jumping, that's what makes it fun. But they begin with a pole on the ground. They start from the bottom."

"I shan't come," she says, "I won't sit there watching, my nerves won't stand it."

Charlo smiles. "But mine will," he says. "Your daughter's tough, Inga Lill, she's got plenty of guts. She's must be allowed to go her own way. Ballet's never going to be her thing." He catches himself as he says it. "Dancing is actually the toughest thing you can choose, it's a constant battle with pain. I'm glad you're not going to be a ballet dancer, Julie," he laughs.

She giggles over her fish, revelling in this father who's organising everything for her.

"But she'll have to join the Riders' Club. It's obligatory, to do with insurance and all that."

Inga Lill sighs heavily.

"You should be pleased," says Charlo, "you've got a daughter who wants to do something. Just look what the other girls get up to when they're older. Hanging about in the evenings outside the service station looking for boys. It's better for her to be in the stables, at least she'll be doing something meaningful."

Eventually, she manages a valiant smile and surrenders. Julie wolfs down large quantities of food, she's already preparing for her new future as a rider.

"You'll have to shovel horse manure," Charlo cautions her, "and it's very hard work."

She nods eagerly, looking forward to shovelling horse manure, looking forward to the whole rest of her life, now that it's just beginning. He smiles gratefully at Inga Lill. She looks tired. She was ill even then, but none of them knew it.

The hours in the stable are what bring him and Julie so close together. They share everything, the joy and the

115

drudgery, the laughter and the tears. They set off in the evenings in all sorts of weather, the heat of summer, the storms of autumn, and the frosts of winter. On the coldest days the harness is so stiff that it's almost impossible to bend the straps. But Julie keeps warm. Three circuits of the ring, and she throws off her jacket. She grows and starts jumping, and the jumps gradually get higher. Charlo's heart races each time she flies over, he feels a mixture of fear and triumph. Sixty centimetres, a metre, one metre twenty. Goodbye to Snowball the pony, and on to a big horse, a gelding called Mephisto. It's serious now, the passion never cools. It fills the days and nights. And always those green eyes on his, insistent.

"I want my own horse."

"We can't afford it, Julie."

"Then I'll save for it myself," she says, "I'll get a job."

He nods his encouragement, thinks it's good she's got dreams and he knows she's got willpower.

"And maybe I'll get some money for my confirmation. I can use that."

"Yes," he says. "We'll manage it."

She clutches his jacket, holds him fast.

"Is that a promise, Dad?"

He looks at her and nods. "Yes, it's a promise."

The memory of it makes him shudder. She saved twenty thousand kroner, and he gambled the money away behind her back. Another memory returns. He's in the shop with Julie, Inga Lill has sent him out to get some groceries. On the way he stops at a fruit machine, rummages in his pocket and finds a ten-krone bit and

116

sticks it into the slot. Julie watches him sceptically, she sees the symbols spinning in the windows, some coins clatter into the dish. Hearing the noise, people turn and look at them.

"Fun, isn't it?" he says and smiles, pushing in another ten-krone bit. The machine begins its whirring. Charlo is full of childish pleasure. More coins clatter into the dish.

"Mum isn't very happy about all this," Julie says with doubt in her voice. "Every time you see one of these machines you've got to feed it."

"It goes to a good cause," he says, inserting another coin. "And anyway, I do win sometimes."

"Can't we go home, I'm hungry."

"Ready soon. I've got a bit of money left."

She gives a sigh of resignation and puts her hands on her hips. She's the best girl in the world, but can she get bad tempered. He plays with all the money he's won, shrugs his shoulders and follows her out. It's this he's remembering now. That he turns his back on the machine and leaves, but he can still feel it tugging at him, as if there's a cord fixed to his back. He wants to return, he wants to stand there in the light and play until it's night, there's a yearning within him, a hunger. In front of the machine the world shrinks, it narrows to a tunnel, it's just him and the coins, the sounds and the lights. He forgets that Inga Lill is sick and, when the money rattles out, it's as if a torrent is coursing through him.

He's promised to take Julie to Øvrevoll.

117

"Europe's most beautiful racecourse," he says and looks at her with excitement. Inga Lill listens with a stern countenance.

"You're not to gamble there," she says firmly, and Charlo laughs out loud. For goodness' sake, gambling couldn't be further from his mind, they're going to take in the superb horses, look at the people, that's all. Have a soft drink in the sunshine, enjoy themselves. Because he thinks he's in control.

Fruit machines were the first, small rise in temperature, soon to develop into a fever which gripped him day and night. It made him happy, it brought him despair. He's pleased Inga Lill doesn't know what's happening now, that she died when he was still an honest man. Was he ever honest? Wasn't there something rotten at the core of him the whole time, and now he's wilting? Isn't that why his knees are weak? Then he's there again, in Harriet's kitchen, he sees her back, close to the kitchen unit, a few wisps of grey hair about her ears, and he hits her as hard as he can, hits her as the thunder booms in his ears. Dazed, he rushes to the window, stands staring out, gripping the sill hard. Again he has that sensation of weakness. It only last a few seconds, then he's strong again. He tears himself away and sits down at his desk, gets out the phone book. He turns to the Yellow Pages and looks for a vet.

She's a slender woman, vaguely boyish, with a thick fringe and freckles on her nose, a worn pair of jeans and a windcheater with a cord at the waist. She moves her head about a lot as she speaks, is keen and enthusiastic, her hair dancing about her face. She drives up in an estate car and lifts her heavy case out, walks ahead into the stable. Charlo follows her. On the case's lid he reads the inscription: "A horse is the lady's best friend."

"Well," she says, looking at the bay, "he's a grand looking chap."

Charlo nods proudly, Møller agrees. He stands, arms folded, watching Charlo and the vet like a hawk. He's well prepared, he's vouching for the horse, but now the expert has taken over and he must defer to her. He puts a halter on Crazy and leads him out into the passage.

His hooves give a hollow ring as he treads the concrete. The horse is going to be minutely examined. The horse is going to be checked and tested. She runs through all his joints and muscle groups. She checks his symmetry, eyes, ears and mouth. She rasps his teeth. She examines his pasterns and discovers a swelling, Møller says he was born with it, that it isn't pathological. She leads the horse outside and runs with him in the snow, then she gets Møller to run with him. She says he trots perfectly. She asks for his vaccination card, and Møller produces it from his pocket. She gives the horse a worming dose, forces his great mouth open, sprays the yellowish-white stuff in, snaps his jaws shut and holds them.

She asks questions about his feeding routine, previous injuries and illnesses. She asks to see his pedigree, which is excellent. Call Me Crazy out of Pericles and Adora Z. Born and raised at a stud in the Netherlands, sent to Denmark, then taken to Norway

119

by ship in 2001. Road safe, experienced competitor and obedient as a child. Cooperative getting in and out of a horsebox, easy to shoe. At last she smiles broadly, and gives him a good pat on the neck. She whispers to Charlo: "How much is he asking?"

"Forty thousand."

Her smile widens even more. She's got a large gap between her front teeth.

"He's a snip."

Charlo has the money in his inside pocket. Blood money, it strikes him suddenly, but nobody knows. Nobody knows, nobody saw him, it was dark on the evening of 7 November, and people stayed indoors. He pays the vet seven hundred kroner, thanks her for her help and accompanies Møller to his office on the floor above the boxes. It's dim and snug beneath the coved ceiling, with a special smell of horses and painted wood. They are going to sign a contract, it's an important moment. Charlo is as excited as a child. He sits down in a chair, and watches Møller fetch a fat sheaf of documents. The horse has had two previous owners, he hands the whole lot over to Charlo to study. Charlo takes the money out of his wallet, tells Møller to count it, which he does while Charlo reads. And as he sits in the comfy office and looks around, at cups and rosettes and pictures of horses, an idea comes to him. He glances furtively at Møller who's writing the contract of sale. Should he chance it? It can't do any harm, he can only say no.

"You wouldn't happen to have any work going here?" he says, and regrets it immediately because Møller is looking at him in surprise. Suddenly, Charlo feels like a beggar.

"Well," he says, drawing his answer out, "I've run this place for years without much help. So not a job as such," he pauses. "I'm not quite sure, not a full-time job, at any rate."

"But part-time, perhaps?" Charlo says. He smiles, wants to maintain an easy tone.

"Well, I do sometimes feel I need a handyman," Møller admits, "and there's a lot of mucking out with twenty horses. There's jobs in the ring, repairs and such like. Are you good with your hands?"

Charlo nods energetically.

"I've got an HGV licence," he adds. "If that's any good. I'm looking for work, and have been for some time. Time hangs heavy, you know." Møller nods and understands. He pushes the contract over to Charlo.

"We may be able to come up with something," he says. "Let me think it over. If you don't mind starting with small stuff, at least to begin with. Here, you need to fill the rest out. The horse's new owner and your signature." Charlo picks up the pen and signs. On the dotted line marked owner he writes: Julie Torp.

He's seated in his chair with a beer, looking at the contract. It's on the table in front of him, a golden piece of paper. When he picks it up and reads it, his hands shake. He can hardly believe it, that he'll be making amends at last. As he drinks, he dreams, beautiful images of Julie on the horse. But there's also a knot of uncertainty inside him. He's afraid she may slam the door in his face, turn him away before he's had the chance to speak. The cost was high, but everything has a price, and sometimes you have to pay with blood.

He thinks about his heart, he can still see the notch in it, but now it's covered in grey scar tissue. Everyone bears scars, he thinks, both inside and out. He settles back in his chair, doesn't want either the radio or television on because now he can take the silence, it spreads through the room and puts him at his ease. But it's still fragile; he concentrates on sitting perfectly quietly, breathing deeply and rhythmically. Again he sees Julie, his thoughts have travelled back. She's placing one foot in the stirrup and swinging herself up on to Mephisto. He holds her jacket, she always gets so hot, and her riding teacher comes across to him, holding something out.

"The last four lessons haven't been paid," she says, handing him the invoice. He claps his hand to his forehead, says, Christ, I must have forgotten. Julie keeps her eye on him, she sees what's happening and drives the horse away, disappears. He takes out his wallet, it's empty. It's the shame he remembers most of all, because this happens time and time again, because money flows from his wallet and into fruit machines in a constant stream, it's as if he's haemorrhaging money. Charlo shuts the images out, he wants to see something different, something nice.

But what comes to his mind is Inga Lill's funeral. The organ, the whispering voices, and Julie squeezing his hand so hard that he thinks she'll crush it. How are we going to manage now? he thinks, because Inga Lill has always been the corrective influence in his life. Now she's gone, it's as if he's lifting off and losing his last contact with the ground.

He returns from his daydream and looks about the room. He's back on track now, he's got himself some work, and he'll really slog at it. He'll put every ounce of effort into the years he's got left, he will serve his time. In his own way. He stares out into the street. Some cars are parked along the pavement, he studies them carefully, he's got it into his head that the grey Volvo is after him. He can't see the Volvo at the moment, and all the cars are empty. I'll be forever looking over my shoulder, he thinks, unless the case is time-barred. That mightn't be for decades, perhaps I won't even live that long. But it would be nice to experience that day. He supposes that time-barring is almost the same as forgiveness. OK, what you did that night at Hamsund was terrible, but we won't bother you any more, there are other important cases pending. That's how he imagines it will be. He looks at his watch and wonders if Julie has gone to bed. Maybe she's lying there with a book, turning the pages, unaware of all the things that are about to happen.

CHAPTER
NINE

Next day he counts the hours and minutes and seconds.

It's eleven o'clock, the long break, and Julie will be eating her packed lunch, she thinks it's just an ordinary day with maths and English and gym. She doesn't know that I've finally done something for her, for us. She doesn't know what I went through for her, and for our future. He paces from room to room waiting, chain-smoking, nervous and jittery. Outside, the sunshine is hazy, and when at last he goes to his car, he treads on frozen leaves, they crunch loudly in the silence. Everything is so bright and sharp and cold. He's becoming reacquainted with himself. After feeling like a stranger in front of the mirror for so long, he feels more relaxed. It's taken time, but time has come to his aid in the form of the rising hope that perhaps he'll get away with it. Some people do escape.

He thinks about this as he drives to Julie's. He feels like some love-sick teenager going to ask a girl out. She lives in a house in Oscarsgate, where a number of sixth-form college students have bedsits. They share a kitchen and bathroom, and Julie has a grant so that she can pay her own way. He parks by the pavement and stays in the car for a moment. He gazes up at her window. Does he dare go in? Julie is so strong, so emphatic. So bitter about everything that's happened. He gets out of the car and locks it. Counts the stairs going up. He hears the sound of music playing softly behind her door, but no voices. He stands there with his arms dangling, stands there with his sore heart, dressed in old corduroy trousers and a thick, checked shirt. At last he gives his right hand the command to knock at the door. Immediately the music becomes fainter. There she is in the doorway. Her green eyes darken with surprise, then they narrow, and she turns quickly away from him. She doesn't shut the door, but stands there, silent, her shoulders tense.

"Julie," he asks, "can I come in? I've got something important to show you."

How thin she is, he thinks as he says it. It's good Inga Lill can't see her.

There's no sign of curiosity in her posture. He can't see her face, he's looking at the back of her red head.

"Something important," he says again, and takes a step forward. Opens his arms clumsily. Simultaneously he's overwhelmed, it's a long time since she was so close, he could reach out and touch her. He doesn't, he stands there and waits.

"Well, then?" she says at last.

Her voice is curt, Charlo holds his breath. He knows that he'll have to humble himself, he's prepared for her to sling bitter recriminations in his face. She begins to walk across the room, he follows her hesitantly. He catches sight of a bed, a desk and a television set.

Pictures on the wall: Snowball and Mephisto, and several of Johnny Depp. A floor lamp with a pink shade, which sheds a warm, romantic light. Various items of clothing litter the floor, she begins picking them up, almost mechanically, her expression hard. He stands in the middle of the room studying her, looking at her surly back. Her jaw is working angrily. Despite this, he feels the bond between them, it's still there, and that's why her cheek is twitching. He wants to ask if he can sit down, but doesn't know where to begin. But he imagines how, when he's explained his errand, her eyes will quickly light up as they used to, as he remembers them, green and twinkling.

"It's been a long time since we saw each other," he says to her back.

She continues her aimless tidying, moving things, keeping her hands busy. He feels a bit desperate, crosses to her bed and sits down. He's on her home ground now, he has to tread warily. But he feels strong, too. He's come with good intentions, he's come to make it up to her, for his betrayal.

She goes to the desk, takes a seat there, watching him. Then she covers her face with her hands. It's deathly still in the room. Charlo can't say anything, she is the one who's initiated the silence and how long it should last. He sits and lets himself be tortured as he awaits the signal, a word, a look. So that he can move on. But there is no signal. He realises that he's an adult, he gathers up his courage and speaks.

"You haven't wanted to see me. And I've respected that. I've had nothing to offer you, only a miserable life."

She remains silent.

"But now it's all different," he says, looking at her intently. "I've got a new life. I've stopped gambling at last."

She takes her hands away from her face and looks at him.

"You said that before."

Her voice is flat. But then, suddenly: "What have you done to your chin?"

He places a finger on the scratch, and gives a shrug of embarrassment.

"Oh," he says lightly, "that was just an accident. It's only a cut."

She rises and takes a few steps, coming closer. Her gaze is so direct that it burns.

"What do you want here?"

He attempts a smile, he's eager and wants to explain.

"Have you been drinking?" she asks. "Is that how you got the graze?"

He shakes his head emphatically.

"Don't worry about me," he says looking at her, he feels his heart swell, for she's beautiful standing there, with her green eyes.

"I don't go out drinking. I've finished with that sort of thing."

She doesn't believe him, she gives him a sidelong glance, her eyes still narrow.

"Julie," he says, "tell me how things are going. Are you getting on well at school?"

She stares out of the window, at the town's roofs. Her jaw is jutting out, he's seen it do that so many times before. So much wells up inside him; her mouth, which she's inherited from Inga Lill is wide and generous, her narrow shoulders, her long neck. That she is his, that they should be together.

"Have you come here after all that's happened to ask that? About how things are going at school?"

He tenses up inside. He doesn't like the tone of her voice.

"You must forgive my clumsiness," he says, "I'm not a clever man. But I have actually come about something, I haven't arrived empty-handed."

Involuntarily her eyes move to his hands.

"Yes, everything's fine. I'm thinking of going to veterinary college."

Her voice is at once defiant and proud. Charlo's cheeks get all hot. My daughter, the vet, he thinks. I'm blessed with this beautiful, sensible girl, who'll maybe take me back. She must take me back!

"But," he says, feeling his secret aching to come out, "what do you do in your spare time? Have you got time for anything besides homework?"

She pouts at him, stands there picking at her nails, which are short and unpainted.

"Yes," she says at last, grudgingly, "I read a bit. Go to the cinema now and again, with friends, a whole load of us."

He leans forward, wanting to catch her, wanting to see her pupils dilate and turn black when he tells everything.

"You've got some spare time, then?"

She doesn't understand what he's driving at. She sizes him up and turns defensive.

"Yes," she says tentatively, "I suppose so."

The voice is less unwilling now, but it isn't soft like it used to be when she was happy and completely relaxed with him.

"What about stamina?" he asks. "Have you got plenty of that, too?"

She can't follow his drift, but she is listening now, her mouth half open.

"You've become so thin," he says, "there was much more of you before."

She looks down at herself.

"That's because I don't ride any more," she replies.

"But those muscles will come back quickly enough if you start again, won't they?" He rummages in his jacket pocket, quivering with excitement. Feels the photograph between his fingers. "Because this chap's strong," he says holding out the picture.

For a moment she stands there transfixed, staring. Then she moves right up to him. She takes the picture, examines it and shakes her head. Unable to understand what he means or what he's telling her.

"Who's that girl?" she asks, looking at Møller's daughter.

"That's the previous owner," he says, "but now the horse has been sold. It was sold yesterday, in fact. After a thorough veterinary examination." He gets ready to drop his bombshell. "And the new owner is someone I know, too. Her name is Julie Torp."

She stares at the photo again, can't take it in. Her face is still deadpan.

"You're having me on," she says weakly. But he notices her eyes begin to shine. Even so, she holds back. She knows him too well.

"I'm not having you on," Charlo says, turning his palms up to show that they're clean. Then he remembers that they definitely aren't clean, and lets them fall again. "But I quite understand that you need some proof," he says, and reaches into his inside pocket, takes out the contract of purchase and holds it out. She takes the document and reads it, wide-eyed. Reads it several times, looks at the picture again. Stands there with these two things. Her voice is needle-thin.

"Call Me Crazy? You've really bought him?"

Charlo laughs: "Yes, I've really bought him. The money's been handed over. He's stabled at Møller's Riding Centre. A Holstein," he says, "six hundred kilos. You'll have quite a job on your hands, I promise you."

She drops on to the chair by the desk, leans across its top. She caresses the photo between her fingers and shakes her head once more. She remains like this for a long time. Even now she won't show her pleasure, she doesn't dare, she doubts.

"But how did you manage it?" she asks, and stares at him in disbelief.

Charlo sits up and prepares, and then delivers the carefully constructed and highly plausible account he's concocted.

"The thing is that your grandmother had a lot of family silver," he says. "She gave it to me as an advance on her estate. You know, how old people begin tidying things up at the end of their lives. And, of course, she wasn't getting any pleasure from it in the nursing home. Oh, I know I should have saved it for you, and for future generations. But your life is now, and I wanted so much to make amends. So I got a good price for it. I've paid off my debts, I've put all that nonsense behind me now, I've got work, too, a little job at the stables."

"Family silver?"

"Valuable old cutlery," he tells her, "a pattern that's gone out of production, quite sought after. But, Julie, don't mention it to Grandma when you're there, she's so muddled, and I don't want to run the risk of her regretting it all and demanding to have the silver back again."

She nods, glances at the photo again.

"But you owed two hundred thousand. Was the silver worth that much?"

"Yes. There was a gold watch as well. Candlesticks and that sort of thing. So it was just enough."

"Call Me Crazy?"

"He's as gentle as a lamb. Don't let the name frighten you."

She clutches the picture. She's still dumbfounded, and keeps glancing at him, wants to check that he's being truthful.

"Julie," he begins, "you've no idea how lovely he is, you can't see his colour properly in the photo. I took it in the ring, you know, and there wasn't enough light."

At this something subsides in her, some of the suspicion and doubt.

"Have you ridden him?" she asks suddenly.

"Just briefly." He smiles at the memory.

"Did you give him a canter?"

"Yes, I rode in a volte," he answers. "But I didn't dare try a jump."

"Cowardy custard," she teases. She gets off her chair and goes over to him, sits down beside him on the edge of the bed. And they sit there close together. Charlo can smell the scent of shampoo on her hair, he'd like to give her a big hug, but he doesn't.

"When can we go and look at him?" she asks.

"As soon as you've finished your homework," he jokes.

She leaps up and starts turning out her cupboards.

"D'you read my letters?"

"Yes."

He sits on her bed with his hands clasped in his lap. She's suddenly in a great hurry, and he recognises that old enthusiasm, which he hasn't seen for so long. She's looking for some riding breeches, you know, the checked ones, she says, d'you remember them? It's a delight to sit here like this watching her, all sorts of things come flying out of the cupboard. Sweaters, blouses, underwear, at last she finds the breeches. She yanks off her jeans and puts the breeches on.

"They're a bit big perhaps, but I haven't got any others."

"You'll soon grow into them again," he says, "just you wait. I've bought you a monster, I hope you realise that?"

She laughs at him and dives into another cupboard for her riding boots.

"The leather's scuffed and dry, they need some polish, I'll do it later."

She pulls them on. Stands in the middle of the room in her checked breeches with their leather reinforced seat, and stares down at the long boots.

"It's been so long since I've worn this stuff," she comments, looking at him.

Charlo is dumb with admiration. Now he recognises his own Julie again. He's no longer alone, he's got a family like other people. She stands before him, ready. They walk into the street together.

"Dad," she says, "you've pranged the car."

Charlo lowers his eyes to the asphalt for a moment, thinking of all the things he must be careful about.

"Yes," he says, "it was some numbskull who didn't know when to give way."

"You've been trying to repair it," she declares. "That's the worst repair I've ever seen. Why didn't you take it to a garage? If it was someone else's fault, didn't he have to pay?"

Charlo gets into the front seat, mulling it over.

"I got the damage assessed and the money paid out," he lies, "but I used it for something else. Something more important."

She gets in, accepting his explanation, finds a scrunchie in her pocket and gathers her hair at the nape of her neck. He can see her hot breath inside the dark car. I've got her, he thinks, now it's a case of not losing her, I mustn't make mistakes.

"Dad," Julie says suddenly. "You know what I'd like to do? Before we go to the stables?"

He changes gear and drives down the street, while he waits for her wish, which he will naturally fulfil, that's what he'll do from now on. It'll be his mission for the remainder of his life.

"I'd like to visit Mum."

He nods in complete agreement.

"We'll do that," he says emphatically, "we'll go at once. Is it long since you were there last?"

"I don't find it all that easy," she says quietly.

No, Charlo ponders, visiting the dead doesn't provide much sense of peace; he always has a feeling of helplessness when he stands by the headstone, a feeling of being superfluous. But now there are the two of them. He turns in by the church. They walk between the graves, silent, a shyness has interposed itself between them. Then they arrive, stand hushed with bowed heads. They each read her name: "Inga Lill Torp". The grave doesn't need much tending in early December. Charlo notices that the erica is frozen, its reddish-mauve has turned to brown.

"Anyway, the gravestone's nice," Julie says, and he nods, thinks that he made the right choice.

"Next time we'll bring a candle," he says.

They stand a while thinking their own thoughts, then they shake off the solemnity and return to the car.

"Are you excited?"

She nods and blows on her hands, then for a joke, pinches her own arm. Again, Charlo has to laugh. It's heartfelt laughter from deep within him as if he's slightly drunk. He turns the car and joins the main road. They are still slightly shy in each other's company, but, Charlo thinks, that doesn't matter, that'll pass, we need time.

"We ought to have brought a bag of carrots," she says.

He nods. "There's a shop not far from the stables, we can stop there. Of course we must have carrots."

They buy carrots and a couple of Cokes. Out of habit, Charlo looks at the newspaper headlines while he's at the checkout, but Harriet Krohn has been forgotten. He imagines her file buried in a drawer, because there are so many other killings, so much else to spend time on than an old woman from Hamsund. But he knows it isn't true. The investigation will be plodding along, and they're presumably working behind the scenes. He pushes these thoughts away, they drive the last bit to the stables, park the car and emerge into the cold air. Julie has gone quiet.

"Well," Charlo says, "here we are. Let's get into the warm."

He plucks up courage and puts an arm around her shoulder. He opens the heavy door. Just then, a black cat darts out, and Charlo jumps. The cat brings back memories. For one mad second he imagines it's the same cat, and that it's following him. He shakes off the eerie thought and points down the passage.

"The last box on the left."

Julie walks up to the bars. Charlo stands next to her and watches. The hairs on the back of his neck rise.

★   ★   ★

She had just been born.

Lying trembling on Inga Lill's stomach, naked and curled up like a pink frog. A velvety down covered her head. I'll never forget this moment, Charlo thought. It etched itself into every cell of his body, suffused every part of him. It's the same with this moment. Julie standing next to Crazy, cradling his great, heavy head and stroking him gently on the muzzle. The horse lets himself be stroked, closes his eyes now and again, looks sleepy. Then she must feel him all over, his ears, his mane. She runs her hand down his legs, looks at the powerful hooves. Rises again and looks the horse in the eyes. Her voice, when she speaks, is soft.

"Want to go for a run, boy?"

Charlo is drawn back, to that first time she sat on Snowball and couldn't be dislodged. He reminds her about that now, and she gives him a broad smile. He helps her saddle up, and together they walk down to the ring. Charlo lays a rug over the horse's hindquarters. She mounts, puts the horse into a walk and disappears down the long side.

"Bye, Dad," she says. "See you in a couple of hours!"

Charlo is so moved that he stands there staring, breathless. Joy leaps in his breast. This is his doing. He's sacrificed himself for this. He shakes his head in astonishment, and looks round for a chair. Finds one, and begins rolling a cigarette. He lights it, inhales greedily. He follows Julie with his eyes.

His thoughts begin to wander again. It's bad luck that they're already searching for a red Honda, maybe he needn't be too concerned about it, but still, it's worrying. He crosses his legs and shivers a little, it's quite cold in the ring and he hasn't got a lot on. That knee giving way under him is a bit suspicious. It's not easy to relax, not easy to concentrate on what's happening in front of his eyes. He should be happy, satisfied, now that he's reached his goal. The horse is moving at a free walk, with its head up and slack reins. I'd like to sit here for years and watch Julie and Crazy. I don't ask any more of life. I just want to be left in peace. Don't I deserve that? I've gone so far and sacrificed so much. He feels chilly and shuffles his feet, but notices that Julie is riding towards him. She lifts the rug off the horse and hands it to him.

"Here, you poor, frozen old man," she says, laughing.

She looks so buoyant, she's shining like a beacon, her hair is exactly the same colour as the horse, they are a pair. Charlo packs the rug around himself, Julie puts Crazy into a trot. There, he thinks, there goes my daughter. Riding her own horse. He's large, certainly, but really he's just the right size. Her main interest is dressage, she's quite good at it too, I reckon she'll improve a lot now that she's got her own horse. But she jumps as well, one metre twenty, pretty good for a sixteen-year-old. It's a Holstein. I've always had a weakness for bays. I'm absolutely certain that those two will make their mark.

Møller comes into the ring. He stops next to Charlo, thrusts his hands in his pockets and tilts his head in acknowledgement.

"Well," he says, "they make a fine pair. Going well?"

Charlo nods. "I think they've hit it off. It happened so quickly, too. The horse does what she asks, there's no doubt about that. His traverses are lovely. So very precise, when you consider his size, and he's got long legs, too. It all looks very promising." He pauses. "Are you ready to put me to work?"

"Yes, I am actually," Møller says, and kicks laddishly at the sawdust. "Now that you're available, I've lined up various things. I've bought some new mangers which have got to go up, and the windows in the stables need to be better insulated. The water has a tendency to freeze in winter, we've had to carry in buckets of water before now. In the summer, I might get some painting done, including the fence around the outside ring, and the stables. Maybe the garages, too, they're blistered, especially on the west side."

Charlo nods enthusiastically.

"Let's make a start," Møller says, "then we'll see how many hours it comes to. It's difficult to say anything about your wages now, but I'm sure we'll come to an agreement." He stands there a bit longer, watching Julie, now she's reining back very elegantly, the horse steps back correctly with straight legs and lowered head.

"Well I never," Møller says shaking his head. Charlo is soon warm beneath the rug. Julie rides for two hours, until her fringe is damp and the horse is sweating.

CHAPTER
TEN

It's morning, he's up early.

The kitchen table has become his observation post, he sits by the window eating, keeping an eye on the passing cars. He sees a Ford and shortly afterwards a Volkswagen Beetle. He puts two spoonfuls of sugar in his coffee and marvels at this new habit acquired so late in life, but it does him good. A taxi drives past, it's for hire. The bread is stale, he leaves the crusts, they're hard and hurt his gums. Buying bread for one is impossible, he thinks. Inga Lill was always so clever about that, she'd cut up the entire loaf and then pack the slices individually in a container. The container went in the freezer. She'd thaw them in the toaster, and then she always had fresh bread. Dear Inga Lill. It isn't easy. But things are going better now, I'm in a different place. I'll do the right things from now on, I promise. I want Julie to feel proud. I want her to point me out to others and say, that's my father. Cool, isn't he?

He clears up after his modest meal. Afterwards he poses in front of the mirror. He relaxes his shoulders, sticks his chin out, notices that he's lost three or four kilos, that his face is sharper, it suits him. It was from his father that he inherited his wide jaw and his long, straight nose. His shirt is blue and grey, the colours go with his eyes. One thing at a time, he thinks, live for the minute. Do all the little things that decent people do. Life is made up of details. Have a proper breakfast, choose something to go on the bread, Gouda and marmalade are his favourites. Shower and shave, get out clean clothes. Run a comb through his thinning hair. Go out and get things done. He puts his quilted jacket on and goes to the car. He avoids looking at the dent because each time he does he's filled with a huge despair.

He drives off down Blomsgate then takes the bridge over to the east side of town. He parks outside the Job Centre. This district is a planning nightmare, where lovely old timber houses have been annihilated by new commercial buildings, without any plan, or any system at all. But this is his neighbourhood, where he grew up. Its untidy character is close to his heart.

He puts twenty kroner into a parking meter, enters the building and takes a ticket. Number fifty-eight. Forty-nine is being attended to at the counter. He glances at the people who are ahead of him. You can see it straight away. These men are unemployed. They're on Social Security. They've lost their self-respect, there's no hope in their eyes. They read brochures listlessly and avoid looking at one another. This is going to end now, Charlo thinks, I don't want to be one of them, I want to be part of society, I'm a young man with strong arms and sense enough. It's important to him now to do things right.

He finds a vacant chair, straightens his back. Here am I, he thinks, Charles Olav Torp, covered in my own crime, clothed from head to foot in that terrible deed. It's so strange that they can't see it, that it doesn't stink, or shine out. Can he atone for his misdemeanour by behaving well for the rest of his life? Not as regards the justice system, but in terms of the great, eternal reckoning? If there is such a thing. Sometimes he does sense something larger. As he did in Harriet's kitchen, when he felt someone else take control, he'd assumed a role that was intended for him. He waits half an hour. A tall, lanky man is being served. He's never killed anyone, Charlo thinks, there's something natural about the way he leans on the counter, a spontaneity he himself has lost. Just as guilt is manifest in people's faces, so innocence is visible as a kind of unpretentiousness.

He rolls the ticket in his hand and thinks about Harriet Krohn. A picture immediately springs to his mind. There she is, still lying on her kitchen floor with her face in a pool of blood. Even though the rational part of his brain tells him that, obviously, she's been taken away. People will have arranged a grave, he thinks. Her beneficiaries. An idea takes shape in his head. At last, number fifty-eight comes up on the display above the counter. He goes over and leans forward. The woman is about his own age, thin and short-haired and with a small, pointed chin. Her glasses are modern, without frames, and have very small lenses. Behind the spectacles he sees a pair of turquoise-coloured eyes. They regard him without enthusiasm.

141

"I've just come to sort things out a bit," Charlo says, his voice loud and clear. If the others can hear what he's saying, that's fine by him, he's an example they'd do well to follow. "The point is that I'm in receipt of Unemployment Benefit. Have been for two years."

She waits for him to continue. Her pupils are completely round, he notices, and life hasn't been kind to her, her irises are flecked. He believes in such things. That life's pain and despair leave their stain in the eyes. Only children have completely clear eyes, without any marks or discoloration.

"But now I've found a job. At a riding centre. As a handyman. It's not much, not to start with, I'll have to show them what I can do and make myself indispensable, and then perhaps there'll be more work in time. That's the plan, anyway. What do you think?" he says, smiling at her.

"Yes," she replies, "that sounds like a good tactic." She smiles back, a quick smile. Asks him for his name and ID number.

She's the type who needs thawing out, it's unmistakable. Certain people won't open up unless you work on them a bit, and he's good at that. Used to be good. He props his elbows on the counter, rests his chin in his hands, ensures eye contact.

"But it's only a small job," he says, "I can't live off it. I assume you'll reduce my benefit, but I can't say exactly what I'll earn. Not yet. Because I've only just begun. Or rather, I'm actually starting today."

"Then we'll have to see how things develop," she says, and searches her screen.

142

It's not easy to hide from the authorities, one keystroke and she has all his personal details. Born 1963, address: Blomsgate 20.

"Have you any idea about your pay?"

"There's talk of a part-time job. But we haven't discussed an hourly rate."

She taps away, peering through her glasses.

"You'll have to inform the Social Security office. The only thing I can suggest is that you bring your wage slips in here," she says looking at him.

"I could send them by post."

"That'll do fine."

She makes the necessary notes. Charlo waits patiently.

"I thought I ought to say something," he says, "I don't want problems later on. With the authorities. For fiddling and so forth."

"I quite agree. We find out about all that anyway. Plenty of people try it on."

"Don't know how they dare," he says calmly, holding her turquoise gaze.

Then he walks tall through the Job Centre and out.

Now, with his golden mission accomplished, he sets out for a drive. Randomly at first, around the streets. He looks at people and buildings, he wants to make the time go. So that it will be afternoon, so that he can fetch Julie. He looks at the town's glitter, enjoys all the lights, the reflections in the river, the headlights coming towards him, white, yellow or bluish. A Freia chocolate advertisement, a clock on a wall, it's half past nine. He ends up in Elvegata and follows it into the tunnel and out on to the E134. He follows the road without thinking. Finally, it clicks. He's driving towards Hamsund. The river is on his left, black and cold and swift, its restless power troubles him. It flows on, unstoppable, the way his life is ploughing on to the moment he fears most. The unavoidable moment of truth. There's so much to be frightened of. Young people have such quick minds, their sight and hearing are good, they pick up everything, every detail. Like the young girl in the florist's, so trim, so slender in her red jumper, he can't forget her, and maybe she can't forget him, either. His silence, his reluctance, his old green parka. He dismisses the thoughts, glances up at the sky. It's a fine day. He's finally on an even keel, he's behaving respectably now, nobody will be able to pin anything on him, not murder, not social-security fraud.

He drives to Hamsund church. The graveyard lies quiet and deserted, picturesquely covered in snow, and with a special, frosty beauty. He parks, stands for a while looking around, drawing the fresh air into his lungs. The milky sunshine makes everything glitter like diamonds. Slowly, he starts walking amongst the graves. It's possible that she only has a wooden cross, he thinks, because it takes time to choose the right stone, and time to get it ready, it must be carved and polished and engraved. He looks over his shoulder continually, but he can't see anyone, it's too early in the day. He searches around for a long time. Now and then he stops to admire the white church, it's medieval and recently restored, perhaps the finest in the county. He hunts systematically, reading all the names and pondering all the destinies. Occasionally, he finds a young person's grave, then he stops and muses, saddened by the thought of the short life. Four years old, thirteen years old. It makes him think of Julie, and what it would be like to lose her, but it's beyond his imagination. Julie is so healthy and vital, nothing can touch her.

He's been looking for half an hour when suddenly he finds himself in front of her grave. Harriet Asta Krohn is lying here, right below his feet. I could have brought some flowers, he realises, it would have been the decent thing to do, another mark in the reckoning. But I didn't think that far, I only considered the new image I could take away with me. An old woman in a beautiful coffin, her hands clasped on her breast. Not the horrible one from the kitchen which has tortured me for weeks, that twisted, ravaged body, the unattractive green dress. He tries to corner his emotions. That her life ended in such a manner, how it was all his doing. He can't quite link them, the images that flash through his head, of the revolver butt in her skull, of her collapsing and turning into this wooden cross. Is it really true?

He stands before her grave a long time, holding himself straight, thinking the whole thing through. Trying to put a defence together. You got in my way, you scared me with all your screeching, and it didn't take much, either, you were old. As brittle as a reed. Afterwards, I was in shock. This has marked me for life, you know, it's not just something I can forget. But the fact is, I have a daughter, and I have to be there for her, all the rest of my life. So I can't dwell on this tragedy. It

145

mustn't be allowed to destroy me, it's bad enough as it is. Things are still fragile between Julie and me, we've a long way to go. So if it were up to me, Harriet, I would stifle the memory of you from now on. I can see that everything here is nice, it's neat and tidy, and presumably you'll soon be getting a handsome headstone. Harriet Asta Krohn. A fine name, with a good ring to it. I'm working out your age, you were almost seventy-six. A respectable age, I probably won't live that long. Maybe it's of little comfort, but you reached your average life expectancy.

He bows his head and feels at peace, standing with clasped hands and enjoying the sensation of calm that finally settles on him. He can put this calamity behind him now, and move on. At last, he really is moving on. Suddenly, he's aware of a noise behind him, a sort of crackling.

"Wasn't it terrible?"

He starts at the sound of the voice, turns and finds himself staring at a woman. His mouth opens in surprise. She's standing on the path behind him with a carrier bag in her hand. Brown coat, black bootees and a small crocheted cap, which resembles an old tea cosy. Beneath the cap he glimpses some snow-white curls.

He mumbles a flustered reply, something unintelligible.

"I'll never rest easy unless they're caught. I live in the house next to hers, number 6 Fredboesgate. Are you a relative, by any chance?"

She moves closer. "I don't remember you from the funeral. But that's hardly surprising, I wasn't at all myself that day."

146

She falls silent now, and examines him closely. Charlo is dumbstruck. His first impulse is to flee, but something holds him back. He must keep cool, so he listens to what she's saying and clenches his fists in his pockets.

"Mosse Maier," she says, stretching out a brown-gloved hand. He takes it automatically, squeezes it carefully. "I was the one who found her. I noticed the lights on in her house at three in the morning, and that frightened me. So I got up and looked through the window. At first I wanted to phone and find out if everything was all right, but I couldn't bring myself to do it. I've thought since how cowardly that was. But I'm elderly and live alone, I hadn't the courage."

Charlo listens and nods, her outpouring holds him there, he can't bring himself to leave.

"But when I got up at seven the lights were still on. That was really strange, too, because Harriet never got up before nine. She had arthritis, you know. Lots of aches and pains. I hung back for as long as I could, but eventually I went over. Her front door was unlocked, and then I found her in the kitchen. And that was a sight I shall never forget, I can tell you. They hadn't just hit her, they'd beaten her to a pulp."

The carrier bag crackles in her hand again, he suspects she has a plant in it.

"I didn't know her," he puts in, turning towards the grave once more. "I was just passing."

"Ah, I see. I thought you were her nephew, she's got a nephew who lives abroad and she used to talk about him a lot. But it's terrible, isn't it?"

He nods again, searching for some escape route, but she hasn't finished yet, she holds him there. Fragile she may be, but her eyes are blue and intense.

"The worst thing is that one gets so scared."

She walks the final few steps to the grave and scrabbles about in her bag. Her hand emerges with a small, green wreath. "Everything's been ruined. I don't sleep well at night any more. For some reason it's good to come here. It calms me down. Now at least she's at peace."

She bends with some difficulty, places the wreath in front of the cross. "And the police have been a great comfort. They ring and ask how things are going. And drop in now and again. I can tell you one thing, they won't give up on this case. Those responsible will be found."

"Were there several of them?" he asks, looking at her intently.

"Well, I wouldn't know anything about that. But the way her house looked, it wouldn't surprise me. The strange thing is that she seems to have opened the door herself. Harriet uses a door chain, she's most particular about it. But they probably spun some good story, in any case she let them into her house. I'd like to know how it was done. If there's one thing I've learnt from all this, it's that you can't trust anybody."

He nods again, takes a couple of steps, wanting to go off and get away.

"Oh, I'm sorry to have burdened you with all this. But I thought you were a relative, as I said."

148

"I was just passing by," he says, "but I remember the case, of course I do. It was in all the papers. This is a beautiful spot, by the way. This church and churchyard. One of the loveliest I've seen."

He talks away, but his cheeks are burning red, he can't stop them. He runs his hand through his hair, finally stammers something about the weather, that it's delightful walking in the churchyard.

"Yes," she says, "this is where we'll end up. It's like coming home. But life is too difficult to comprehend sometimes. How things like this can happen."

"There's a reason for everything," Charlo says, and glances down at the wreath.

She shakes her white head. "Not for this. This is pure madness."

He's filled with an uncontrollable desire to explain to her. That he's most definitely not mad, that he's as much a human being as she is. It's almost bursting out of him, there's a rushing inside his head. But her eyes have become searching, as if she can see him clearly now. Her blue gaze is acute enough, it's obvious she's coming to her own conclusions. The meeting disturbs him just as the collision did. He gives her a curt nod and disappears as fast as he can, hurries back to his car. He sits inside it, worrying. It troubles him deeply that she discovered him there, by the grave.

There she is!

Julie's running towards him, he sees her straight away, her red hair stands out in the crowd of youngsters. There's a new spring in her step. She chucks her bag in the back seat and jumps in, the car rocks on its suspension. She's hot and breathless. Now he's able to relax again, he's concentrating on Julie. He's still uncertain about his new role, whether now, at last, he can be Dad again. Does she really want to spend time with him? She fastens her seat-belt, glances at him from the side. Her voice is lively and cheerful.

"Did you remember the carrots for Crazy?"

He smiles and says yes, he has remembered the carrots.

Charlo puts the car in gear and thinks, here we are, my daughter and I, driving together, we're friends. This is what I've always yearned for. I took drastic measures, but I got to where I wanted to be. Again, he corrects himself. This is not where he wanted to be, he only wanted Julie. Have I got her now? he wonders, will she remain with me for ever?

"What are you thinking about?" Julie asks.

Charlo considers. He wants to be honest. Build up a good relationship without any deceit or illusion.

"I'm thinking about the things I'm frightened of," he says. "What I'm most frightened of at the moment."

"And that is?" she wants to know. Her smile is lurking just below the surface, there isn't a cloud in her sky, she doesn't want to be serious.

He blurts out the answer. "My health."

"Oh?" She looks at him in surprise. "But you're always in good health."

"Yes," he says quickly, "but I'm a smoker. We don't live as long as other people, you know."

He gives way to a car on his right.

150

"Each and every cigarette harms me," he announces dramatically.

She laughs her trilling laugh again, it fills the car. She gets out a scrunchie and gathers her hair at the nape of her neck. He looks at her slender throat, the graceful way she holds her head, the bridge of her nose, beautifully arched. This is his own flesh and blood, this is something he has a right to, hasn't he? He was willing to kill for this. No, he wasn't willing, it was just that there was no other way. What about the old woman in the churchyard, what's she thinking now? What the hell's wrong with my knees? No, he doesn't want to start thinking about that, there are enough things troubling him, plaguing him. His thoughts run in circles while his hands rest on the steering wheel, while his heart pumps blood. He has turned his own destiny around, and his crime strikes him as daring and cowardly in equal measure. That he was prepared to go so far for another human being, that he could no longer stomach being a victim.

"Sometimes there's a flickering in front of my eyes," he confesses.

"Really?" She studies his profile and he meets her gaze.

"Can you see anything in them? Sometimes I think they look strange."

He stops at a red traffic light, and seeks her eyes. She looks hard.

"Strange, how?"

"There's something about the pupils. They look odd."

She leans forward a little and examines him carefully. Then she begins to giggle.

151

"Go on! They're completely normal."

He blinks several times with relief.

"It's good to be free," he says, and puts the car in gear again.

She turns to look at him.

"What do you mean? Free?"

"That I don't owe money any more, I don't gamble. The other day I walked past a Twin Runner and didn't even touch the money in my pocket."

"Was it hard?" she asks teasingly.

"Yes," he says seriously. "You don't understand these things, but it was hard, it cost me a lot. But afterwards it felt good. A victory over myself."

"We're on an even keel," she announces, and looks at the road again, her green eyes shining. He nods. He needs a cigarette, but doesn't want to subject her to the smoke and goes without.

"And you?" he asks looking at her. "What are you most scared of?"

She shakes her head in resignation. "I think that's a silly question, under the circumstances. I'm frightened of losing Crazy. I want to be where we are now, for ever."

Charlo nods in agreement.

"We can both drink to that," he says contentedly.

He's more relaxed now because, with Julie at his side, he feels protected, and he can't imagine anything bad coming to ruin it because what they have together is great. After all, I'm a caring person, he thinks, and what's growing up between us is precious. But his crime is inconceivable, it was a false step.

"What will you do while I'm riding?" asks Julie.

152

"I'm going to put up some mangers," he answers. "They're blue. That really worries me."

She laughs at him. "Why?"

"The stables are red, and the box doors are brown. The mangers ought to be black. Or possibly green. It's a matter of aesthetics. Møller can't see it, he knows about horses, but not about colours."

"He's obviously bought the ones he could afford," Julie remarks matter-of-factly. "I bet the blue ones were the cheapest."

Charlo gives a deep sigh. "Yes," he says, "it's the bottom line that counts. I know all about that."

A silence falls between them, and Charlo can't think of anything to fill it. He concentrates on his driving, and listening to Julie breathing next to him, catches the scent of the mild soap that fills the car's interior. It's enough just to sit next to her, it's good to be two against the rest of the world. But he always has to think before he opens his mouth. Consider what's safe. He attempts to recall the time when he could simply talk off the cuff, quickly, without thinking, say anything that came into his head. The time before he began to gamble, when everything was easy between him and Inga Lill. He tries to imagine an interrogation. He's seen plenty on television. He believes he'd get through one, simply because he'd have to, if he didn't want to lose what he's finally gained. That cost him blood. At the same time, he envisages the legal system as a mill, grinding incessantly, and that sooner or later he'll be picked up. But that's for later, he thinks, for now I'm sitting here with Julie, she's quiet in the seat next to him, looking forward to the work. I've given her what she desired. That's all I wanted.

"What was it like for you when things were at their worst?" he asks, throwing her a look. "I mean, as regards the gambling."

She thinks about it, lowers her head.

"Well," she says, "it was so embarrassing. You were always parked in front of those fruit machines. And everyone could see you. A grown man standing there playing like that, completely hooked. I didn't understand it. The people in my class saw you too, standing there, day after day, shoving money in. Mum often used to send me out to fetch you. Because you never came home from the shops. And when you finally did come, you hadn't got what she'd asked for. You'd always gambled away most of the money."

He's silent, letting it sink in. He feels an ache of shame within him.

"But the worst time," she continues, "was when we went to Øvrevoll. And the people you rubbed shoulders with there. And the money I'd saved. The way it suddenly disappeared."

Charlo clears his throat. "Can I say something really daft?" he pleads.

She makes no reply, just waits.

"My earnest desire was to double that money. I felt so lucky that day, it's impossible to describe. A certainty that the winnings were there, that they were waiting for me. That's how it is sometimes. I could hardly believe it when I lost. Julie," he says intently. "It's an illness."

154

She nods again, not wanting to be serious, looks at him, smiling warily. "But what if you have a relapse?"

He shakes his head emphatically.

"It won't happen. I'm certain of it."

"But how can you be so sure?" she says, wanting more assurance, more security.

"I'm in a different place now," he says. "And I'm not looking back."

His great fear is that the horses will panic when he starts the drill. He looks at the huge animals doubtfully, thinks of all that bone and muscle and all the things that could happen. Those thin, delicate legs.

"It's just a matter of getting on with it," Møller says. "Sometimes they rear and jostle, and make a real mess. But I can't empty the stable, Charlo, we'll have to take what comes."

He takes his courage in both hands. He's marked out where the manger is to go, the old one has been taken down. He makes no comment about the colour. It's quiet in the stable, he can hear his own breathing and his thumping heart. Then he starts the drill. It doesn't make much noise before it touches the wall, then it drones through the entire building. The horses listen with pricked ears. Nothing happens. He stops, has a rest, looks down the passage. Møller stands, legs apart, and signals that he can continue.

"They're calm because I'm standing here," he explains, "I can stay until you're done. When Julie's finished riding, you can do the wood shavings in the ring, it's mucky now. The tractor's in the outbuilding with the key in the ignition."

Charlo carries on working, and hangs up the four mangers. The bright blue colour clashes with the rest of the interior, just as he'd imagined it would. It irritates him, green would have looked lovely. Afterwards he decides to clean out the box for Julie, he wants to be useful. He gets hold of a wheelbarrow and shavings fork; it's plastic and some of the tines are broken, but he works hard and manages it. The muck is heavy, he sieves the wood shavings through the tines, shovels until he's hot, fills up the wheelbarrow, empties it down the hatch. He fetches fresh shavings, and gives it two barrowsful. When he's finished the box is pleasant and dry. He goes down to look at the tractor. It's a John Deere. He gets in and turns the ignition key, feeling like a small boy. He walks into the ring to look at Julie. He borrows the yellow blanket, sits down in a chair. He'd like to sit like this for ever, watching the two of them at work. Things are good now, Inga Lill, he thinks. We've found each other again, now we'll always be together. He notices that Julie is practising reining back. She does it over and over again, sitting back hard in the saddle, firm touch on the reins, spurring gently. He never tires of watching them.

Will she have dinner with him?

With a smile, she agrees. She covers Crazy with a horse blanket, gives him carrots, kisses him on the muzzle. Afterwards she hangs around in front of his box, she can hardly tear herself away.

156

"Well," says Charlo. "He'll still be here tomorrow."

Julie goes out to the car with him, they visit the shop and Charlo gets some frozen lasagne. Then they drive to Blomsgate, and Charlo thinks, I can't bear to be alone again. While Julie's with me I forget about other things. Unpleasant things. Surely, I deserve someone. Perhaps there is some justice in this world after all, and I'm no good on my own.

They stamp the snow from their feet on the doormat. Julie pulls off her riding boots, Charlo sets about making the food. Julie isn't often at his house. She moves about the living room, studying the pictures on the walls and standing at the window looking out.

"Why did you lose your job?" she asks all of a sudden.

Charlo drops what he has in his hands.

"I thought Mum had told you," he says in an undertone.

"No. For your information, she used to protect you, in spite of everything."

He can feel his heart again, racing beneath his shirt. He has no choice but to come out with it. Her gaze is enquiring, she's practically an adult, he thinks, and she has got rights.

"I misappropriated money," he says finally. "A small amount, but they discovered it."

Julie doesn't look surprised. Just very serious.

"I was lucky," Charlo continues and begins slicing bread. "They never reported me. But I was sacked on the spot. It was humiliating," he adds, "and I'd lost so much of my pride already. It was worse for Mum. I thought it was going to kill her."

"It did, too," Julie says tersely. She regards him keenly.

The knife slips out of Charlo's hand. He gulps.

"Mum died of leukaemia," he says, "they couldn't do anything."

"Sorry." She looks down at the floor, she's folded her arms.

"I haven't got much to be proud of," Charlo says, getting two plates out of the cupboard, "but I am proud of you. You've a perfect right to ask questions. I'll answer them as best I can."

He opens the oven to look at the lasagne. It's turned golden on top.

"You are the only thing I've produced in my life. A wretched person like me fathering a daughter like you."

She smiles her bashful smile once more.

"Help me now," he says. "You can lay the table. The meal will be ready soon."

They eat the hot lasagne in silence. Julie has a Coke with it, Charlo drinks water. He's going to drive Julie home, and he won't have any alcohol in his blood when he does. From now on he's not going to transgress in any way whatsoever. Not as long as he lives. This resolution makes him feel good, it's like an atonement.

Afterwards, they do the washing-up together. Standing side by side. Charlo enjoys the silence. He gets a bar of chocolate out of the cupboard, breaks it into pieces and puts them in a bowl. They take a chair each and watch the falling snow. Julie picks up the newspaper and starts leafing through it. And Charlo suddenly realises that she must have read about the Hamsund murder. That she has opinions about it. He's filled with a sudden curiosity. What kind of expression would she assume if he were to mention it? Quite at random, just in passing. Have you heard about that murder at Hamsund? He clenches his teeth. Hold your tongue! a voice inside him says. It's as if the murder is pressing inside him, and the pressure is rising in his chest, and all the way up to his mouth, where his tongue lies ready to form words. Julie skims on. Charlo sits watching her, she's so like Inga Lill, but her features are softer. Even so, she displays the same acuteness that her mother had, a need to get to the bottom of things. Suddenly she looks up at him.

"Have you seen this article?" she asks, holding the paper up. "This Inspector Sejer, the policeman who's leading the Hamsund murder case, hasn't had a single unsolved murder in his whole career. And he's over fifty. What about that?"

Charlo turns pale. He certainly hasn't read the article and he can't understand how he missed it.

"Oh, really?" he says doubtfully. She looks down at the text again, and he's glad she can't see his face because now it's as rigid as papier mâché.

"That would be funny," she says. "If the people who did it read the paper. Think of the panic. Not a single unsolved case."

Charlo slumps in his chair, searches for words, but they stick in his throat. Suddenly she looks up at him.

Takes a piece of chocolate, chews it with her sharp teeth.

"You're looking tired," she teases. "You're not used to real work, Dad."

Charlo runs a weary hand across his face. Yes, he's tired. He's got to watch out the whole time, forever guard his words. He clings to this smidgeon of tenderness, that she's noticed he's tired. Yes, he's tired: he feels a lot older than he actually is, it's like walking on thin ice, he hardly dares put his feet down, or make sudden movements, or raise his voice, for fear that someone might notice him, single him out in the crowd. Not a single unsolved case. It's disturbing. Julie puts the paper down.

"I must go back and do some homework," she says.

He nods, looks surreptitiously at the paper, thinks about getting ready to drive. She vanishes into the hallway and returns with her riding boots.

"You've got all that shoe polish and stuff in the kitchen. I'll just go over my boots before we go, then it'll be done. Is it still in the chest?"

He finds himself nodding, and hears her go out to the kitchen, hears her raise the lid of the chest. He gets up heavily from his chair, but his whole being is rigid with fear because he's remembered something, but he can't move quickly enough. At last he makes it out to the kitchen. Julie is looking at him in astonishment.

"This is my old gym bag, isn't it? Whatever have you got inside it?"

160

He makes no reply, he tries to think clearly, but his brain is foggy. She opens the bag and peers into it.

"Jewellery?" she says in surprise.

He starts nodding vigorously, still searching for words, for some kind of explanation, but no words come, there's only his thudding heart, the feeling of unreality, like in a film. She picks them up in turn, one by one, Harriet's bracelet and rings, the brooches and string of pearls. She places them on the table. Again, she looks at him uncertainly, as if she's suddenly been given a clue, it makes her face darker. Charlo twists his mouth into a stiff smile, his mind in an uproar.

"Yes, they were Grandma's," he says, and feels his head moving heavily up and down.

"But Grandma isn't dead," Julie says. She lifts the largest brooch, the cameo. Turns it this way and that in the light.

"Well, no. But she gave them to me. I got her old silverware, which I told you about, and which I sold. And these bits of jewellery."

"But I've never seen them before," she says probingly.

Charlo curses the physiological processes that are turning his cheeks red.

"They're things she's never worn," he explains in panic, "that's why you've never seen them. So she gave them to me. As an advance on her estate. They're not worth anything," he adds quickly.

"But why have you got them in the chest?" she asks. "In my gym bag?" In his confusion he shakes his head. He finds no explanation. He thinks he can hear the sound of cracking ice, that he really has fallen through badly. That the damage must be repaired, but he doesn't know how.

"Well, you know," he says, attempting a self-deprecatory laugh, "I've always been a scatterbrain." His laughter seems to reverberate around the room.

She nods in agreement. But something has made her uneasy, he can see that quite plainly. He doesn't know what to do about it, but he knows that he's got to smooth it over, make her forget.

"Here," he says, diving into the chest. His hand emerges clutching a tin. "This'll be good for your boots, I'll find you a cloth."

She sits down on the floor with the boots, still silent. The jewellery is on the table, on display. He can't bring himself to touch it. He feels he'd like to talk the entire thing away, as he rummages in the cupboard for something she can use as a cloth. He finds an old pair of worn out underpants and cuts them in half. Hands her the cotton material. She takes it hesitantly.

"It's a long time since I went to the nursing home," she says. "I feel bad about it. Perhaps I'll go and visit her."

"Don't mention the jewellery," he puts in quickly, "it'll only make her really confused."

"Will it?"

She dips the cloth in the polish.

"You know she can't remember things from one minute to the next. What she's said or done."

She's still taciturn. She polishes the boots until they shine, but there's a troubled furrow between her eyes.

Charlo tries to joke and laugh, without really succeeding. But she listens and responds. It'll all be fine now, no solemnity, no suspicions, no deceit.

CHAPTER
ELEVEN

He reads Julie's needs and desires before she can give them voice. He's always an instant ahead of her, watchful, ready. She rides, and he anticipates the precise moment when she begins to get too hot, and before she says anything, he runs out and takes her jacket. He notices when Crazy is tired or uncooperative, and then he'll scamper out with a whip, so she can ginger him up a bit. Whenever she's thirsty he knows, and brings her something to drink. He sits on a chair at the far end of the ring, with the yellow rug across his knees, like some faithful, aged crone. But he does his own work first. He repairs and renews and paints, he mends broken panes, he gets feed from the outbuilding, he removes loads of horse muck with the tractor. He does the feeding, he checks the water troughs and the lighting, changes light bulbs, sets mousetraps. He sweeps the stable passages and clears the snow away from the yard in front of the ring. He spreads a broad path of gravel from the stables, so the horses won't slip and break their legs.

Each day at three o'clock he's waiting outside the school. Julie comes in all weathers, she throws herself into her work, getting Crazy to master the difficult exercises. Coordinating the great, muscular body to obey her smallest instruction. Charlo puts up jumps for her and holds his breath as the horse canters towards them, his own body moving in sympathy, trying to will her over. The landing is thunderous, Julie clinging to the horse with her calves, jumping again and again. He's enjoying these days, he doesn't look back. The fact that he experiences a few happy days fills him with a deep contentment.

It's January and very cold. Julie rides in thermal overalls, Crazy's large body can't get properly warm, he's stubborn and stiff. Julie is tired. Charlo tries to slow her down.

"Put him back in his box," he suggests, "today we can just clean it out and leave things at that. And you can take a day off. It doesn't matter if he stays in for one day."

She shakes her head emphatically.

"That's out of the question. Horses have to have exercise every single day," she says categorically.

He praises and encourages, he comforts her when she complains. He makes up for all his sins. And she clings to him as she did when she was small. My daughter, he thinks, the lovely redhead, the veterinary surgeon.

It is on one of these icy January days that he suffers another strange episode. Frightening and incomprehensible. He's helping Julie to muck out. He throws himself into the task eagerly with the shavings fork, feels the muscles working in his arms. Now that he's got going, he mucks out the box next door as well. And the one next to that, too; he works so hard he makes the shavings fly. The barrow fills up and is heavy with horse muck. He wipes the sweat from his brow, his shirt feels cold down his back. He goes over and opens the hatch. Returns for the wheelbarrow, grips the handles and begins wheeling it down the passage. Just then, one of his legs gives way and he pitches violently forwards, his face is thrust into the damp droppings. The barrow tips over sideways, its contents spilling over his head. Confused, he lies there kicking, the acrid stench of muck in his nostrils. He wipes his face in bewilderment. The muck is everywhere, in his eyes and his mouth, and there's muck down the back of his neck.

Desperately, he attempts to gather his wits. Just then he hears Julie's laughter. He's never heard this laugh before, it cascades heartfelt and bright over his head, and he thinks how comic he must look, lying on the floor with the wheelbarrow over him. And Julie laughs, she just can't stop. For his part, he's dumb. Frantically, he tries to stand up, to right the wheelbarrow. Julie is unable to help him, she's clutching a broom and laughing so much it echoes round the stable. At last her laughter subsides into silence. Just a few little gasps of mirth. She stops because he's silent and struggling to get to his feet. She goes over to him, takes hold of the wheelbarrow with both hands, and turns it over.

"Oh, Dad," she says.

There are still some traces of laughter in her voice, but also something else, a note of anxiety. Because he's not laughing too.

"What happened to you?" she asks, drying her tears.

Charlo has stood up again, and is looking himself over, avoiding her eyes.

"Well," he says uncertainly. "One leg went all weak. It's odd."

She titters again, goes up to him and starts brushing his jacket, she's kindly now, soothing.

"I'll have to use the broom," she says, "it's stuck to your clothes, Dad, you'll have to go home and take a shower. My God, what a sight you are! Why did you stumble, was it slippery?"

He says nothing. The stench of dung fills his nose. Again, he thinks there's a flickering before his eyes, but he doesn't say anything. She uses the broom gently on his back, dries the last tears from her cheeks.

"Weak, how?" she asks, and now there's more concern in her voice.

"Well, I'm not sure," he says. "I probably just wasn't concentrating. You know how scatterbrained I am."

Deep down he knows there's something wrong. Again he had that feeling of weakness in his joints, first they seemed to go into spasm, then to lose all power. There's a deep throbbing in his breast, a rising disquiet, that something's wrong with him. It's strange, he thinks, he's never unwell. For as far back as he can remember he's never been ill, not since childhood measles and that sort of thing. But nothing since then.

He goes out of the stable, pulls off his jacket and shakes it as hard as he can. It does no good at all. As he stands outside in the cold and darkness, as he looks down at his own body, fear comes creeping over him. Something is about to overtake him. A punishment

167

because his sins are so great. He isn't going to escape. He stands shivering beneath the stars. It was too good to last, he thinks, what Julie and I found. Dear Lord, don't take it from me! Then he shakes his head in perplexity. Sighs and pulls himself together. He feels quite normal again, feels as if nothing has happened. No, really he's as fit as a fiddle. The wheelbarrow was too heavy, and perhaps it had more weight on the right side, and that made it impossible to control, that's how it happened. Maybe he slipped on some ice in the passage, it is very cold, there are lots of explanations. He's forced to go in again, but he doesn't know what he's going to say. The event has become so difficult to manage. Julie is grooming the horse. He shakes his head in resignation.

"I must be getting old," he says, and makes for the sink. He turns on the tap and splashes ice-cold water in his face.

She demurs and works on with her curry-comb, using long, powerful strokes. Crazy shines rubicund in the light and munches hay with imperturbable calm.

"Has it happened before?" she asks suddenly, watching him narrowly.

He doesn't want to answer. But they're together now and mustn't have secrets, no more than necessary.

"Yes," he admits. "A couple of times. But I didn't pay much attention to it, it's probably just a bad habit, that I don't look where I'm going."

She puts down the curry-comb and picks up the horse blanket, spreads it across the horse's back.

"I think you ought to see the doctor," she says.

He considers her suggestion. He never goes to the doctor, he's never ill. And what would he say? Sometimes I trip and fall? Surely everyone does that. But then there's this flickering vision. Are the two things connected? Are there other things going on in his system that he doesn't know about. Once again he peers down his body. The idea that it won't do what he asks is an impossible one for him. The notion fills him with righteous anger, he feels the indignation burning his cheeks.

"Yes," he replies, "I'll ring in the morning." He nods as if to emphasise the seriousness of the thing.

They close the box door and walk towards the exit, switching off the ceiling light. Julie opens the door, and Charlo feels the icy air creeping in everywhere. It cuts him like a knife. All the things that can attack human beings. Personally, he feels that he really doesn't want to know. He wants to live his life now, undisturbed by details. All the same, he phones the doctor the next day and makes an appointment.

Dr Graff takes his blood pressure and says it's excellent. Charlo sits on the edge of a chair, in nothing but his underwear. He feels horribly naked. He, a grown man, coming to the doctor because he's tripping over his own legs, it's pathetic. The doctor works away eagerly on his keyboard, writing everything up in his notes. Whether he smokes, and how much. If he sleeps well, if he eats well. If he's allergic to anything, if there are hereditary conditions in his family, things like that. Charlo answers dutifully and honestly.

169

"So you're not sure whether you tripped over something, or your knee gave way?"

"It might have been a patch of ice," Charlo says, because that's what he's hoping. "And then there's this flickering in front of my eyes. Maybe I need glasses. I'm at that sort of age."

"We'll do some blood tests," the doctor says. His voice is reassuring and neutral. "So that we can exclude a number of things."

Charlo nods and reaches for his shirt. He wonders what the doctor is trying to exclude, but he doesn't dare enquire. He's given a form, and told to sit down and wait outside the practice nurse's office. At the same time, a new appointment is made for him.

The nurse takes some blood. He watches the thin red stream and wonders what the blood will show. What it is he has too much or too little of. He wants to get out, go to the stables. He wants to pretend this isn't happening. Then he shakes it off. The body isn't a perfect organism, it goes wrong from time to time, it does with everybody. Once the nurse has finished helping herself liberally to his blood, he gets up from the chair. He straightens up and pulls down the sleeve of his shirt, stands there broad-shouldered, holding his stomach in. Showing off his fine physique. She isn't particularly interested.

Maybe he's being poisoned by his own crime? He can keep order of a kind inside his head, and try to put it behind him, but perhaps it's seeping out into his system and debilitating him? Remorse, guilt and panic distilled into some paralysing substance that's eating its

170

way into his joints, his muscles and nerves? He tries to laugh this fancy off. If he really is suffering from something, it must have been there right from the beginning, in his genes. Then he imagines that everything is coded, and that time unleashes it all, all diseases, all catastrophes. Was his crime also contained in his genes? Was he born with a predisposition, or was it just circumstances that turned him into a murderer? The fact that he has no answers troubles him. He needs to work through his own guilt, to place it somewhere outside himself. Not with his mother or father, he thinks, not with Inga Lill or Julie. Not within his own nature, he's not aggressive. He never flares up. Almost never. He doesn't go off the rails when he drinks. He did fairly well at school and got up to the usual boyish pranks. Now he's an honest man. He never parks illegally, he doesn't cheat with his income tax. He informs Social Security each time Møller pays him. He takes care of Julie, with gentleness, fatherliness and self-sacrifice. But things went wrong that once, in Harriet Krohn's house. She shouldn't have attacked him, she should have kept calm and let him do what he'd come to do in peace. She would have saved her own life, he thinks, and she'd be walking about now, sucking sweets in her ugly green dress.

The days pass slowly as he waits for the results of his blood tests.

He looks at the calendar and counts down, alternating between hope and anxiety. He wants to get the date behind him, to move on, there mustn't be any problems. Julie must be happy, and he must be there for her as long as she needs him. The day arrives, it's dull and wet, he's toyed with the notion that sunshine would be a good omen. There's no sunshine, only a keen wind that whips through the streets and blows his thinning hair around. His appointment is for three o'clock, and Julie says, then I'll come too. I can leave school a bit early, and we can go to the doctor together. Charlo is both touched and concerned because if there's bad news awaiting him, he won't be able to conceal it. She must be spared any worry. But he's really so fit. He can't believe that he's got anything the matter with him. Then he checks himself. Of course something can be the matter with him, it happens to everybody, it's only a question of time. Is it going to happen now, he wonders, has my time come? That wind is particularly sharp: a warning, icy blast that presages danger.

They sit together in the waiting room. Suddenly Julie takes his hand.

"Nervous?" she whispers.

He laughs and says he isn't. "No, sweetie, it's only a routine check-up. I've been overplaying it, and I feel a bit silly."

"So you're feeling quite all right?"

He looks down at his boots with their brown laces. His feet are firmly planted on the floor and he's got complete control over the pair of them.

"Yes," he says firmly. "And now I feel ridiculous. Going to the doctor just because I tripped over a wheelbarrow. What must he be thinking, Julie. Have you ever tripped over a wheelbarrow?"

She smiles and nods. "Yes. Or rather, it was worse than that. I'd got a full load and I'd opened the hatch. I tipped it up to empty all the droppings, and the whole barrow went through the hatch and got stuck. You know how heavy those wheelbarrows are. It took three of us to haul it out again."

"Yes," says Charlo, "and you didn't go to the doctor because of that. No, I'm probably just getting old," he remarks with a sad smile. "Old and anxious. There, now I'm being called. No flowers, please," he laughs, and gets up from his chair.

Dr Graff is waiting in the doorway, tall and dark and thin. He holds out a dry, white hand. It's the same ceremony as last time. They shake hands and go into his consulting room. The doctor closes the door. Points to a chair, and sits down at his desk. Charlo examines him carefully, but his face gives nothing away, it's a calm, pensive mask. First, he gets Charlo's records up on his computer. There, Charlo thinks, lie the answers. It's only a matter of seconds and the axe will fall. Leukaemia, he thinks. Diabetes.

"Well," the doctor says at last, looking at Charlo. "How have you been since we last met?"

"I'm feeling in great shape," says Charlo. "So if there is anything wrong with me, it can't be all that serious. No, I haven't noticed anything. My vision's been all right. My legs, too," he adds. Then he stops talking and waits.

The doctor looks at the blood test results, and scratches his chin.

"The symptoms you described to me last time haven't recurred? Is that right?"

Charlo nods fervently. He wants to go back out to Julie, to put this behind him.

"I think I must have been unlucky," he says, "I can't put my feet in the right place, I'm just clumsy. It's winter after all, with slush on the pavements. My boots haven't got much grip, I'll get some new footwear. I'm sorry about all this fuss, but I was worried there for a moment. You never quite know, but I feel fine."

The doctor listens and nods.

"Well," he says, looking at his screen, "we did a number of tests. And we haven't got any abnormal readings. But let me put it this way: come back if it happens again, and we'll investigate further. You're feeling perfectly well?"

"Absolutely," Charlo replies happily.

"What about your vision? Anything to report there?"

"Nothing serious. Presumably I need glasses."

"Yes, it might be an idea to visit an optician. Is there a family history of glaucoma?"

"Only cataracts. But I'm a bit young for them, aren't I?"

"Probably," says the doctor. "As things stand, I can't see any reason to start major investigations. Let's see how it goes. Don't hesitate to come back if you feel in doubt about anything. Just give us a call."

Charlo springs up from his chair. He's never felt better.

CHAPTER
TWELVE

Things are good now.

But they're fragile. He's skating on thin ice. He tiptoes through the days, looking over his shoulder, starting each time the phone rings. But nobody comes, nobody asks for him, there are no strange cars parked in the street.

It's the tail end of winter. Everything is lighter, easier, milder. The snow is melting on slopes and in ditches, puddles of ice water glitter in the sun, water trickles vernally. Huge, cotton wool cloud formations pile up in the blue sky, in a white, noiseless roar. Julie and Crazy work hard and purposefully. They're well acquainted by now, and the horse hasn't produced any unpleasant surprises. But he doesn't like wind. Trees and bushes move in a frightening way, and there's a nasty howling round the corners of the building. The occasional plastic bag comes flying in between his hooves, and he starts and rears, thrashing his forelegs angrily. Julie hangs on hard. She sticks to his neck like a burr. Apart from that, he's a great, friendly, copper-coloured giant.

Charlo prepares the outdoor ring. He drives the tractor slowly in circles, working the sand until it's as fine and even as a beach. He enjoys driving the tractor, it's almost like a toy to him, and it doesn't feel like work at all. He's at home on the large, green machine. There's always something to do at Møller's Riding Centre. He paints the fences white, he picks up litter, which he later burns in the incinerator by the car park. He hangs new rope around the paddocks, gathers up the biggest stones and the odd rusty horseshoe. He clears away the drinks bottles after the girls, he picks up clothing they've cast off in the indoor ring and places it in a box in the tack room.

Julie is riding out in the sunshine in just a T-shirt. The hair beneath her helmet is damp, her cheeks are red. Charlo runs to and fro, plying her with drinks, trying out his hand as a coach. He takes up position at the bottom of the ring, leaning against the fence. He stands in sunlight glittering from the melt water.

"A bit shorter on the reins," he calls, "be clear, stay a little ahead all the time. Don't forget his hindquarters, he's got to move with all four legs. His neck's too long, try to pull him in. That's it, yes. That's good. D'you want to try a jump?"

He takes a few steps into the ring.

"You want to try one thirty?"

She rides the horse in a volte. The horse is well collected, all four legs are there, working together in one great organism, a fabulous monster.

"Yes. Why not, I'll have a go."

Charlo walks to the jump in the middle of the ring. He moves the bar up, takes a few steps back, then realises just how high it is. He takes a quick glance at

Crazy, sees his long legs, his muscles and his strength. Presumably he'll fly over. But only if Julie is confident and determined, only if he trusts her. The balance must be perfect, the landing must be soft, and after the jump he has to turn to the right, towards the next jump, which is only one metre high, nothing for Crazy. Can they do it, is it safe? She wants to improve, so she's got to push herself. She's got to make Crazy do as she wants, she must dare. Charlo walks back, throws off his jacket and hangs it over the fence. Waits on tenterhooks. But then he can't keep silent, he begins shouting.

"Don't tense up, he'll sense that right away. Look at the jump, be with him, but don't let him go too far out!"

She puts him into an easy canter. Turns and finds the track, sits hunched up in the saddle, staring intently at the jump. Charlo sees the determination in her eyes. She must clear the jump, get both of them over, six hundred and fifty kilos, and they must clear it with style and elegance. Charlo's stomach muscles clench, he steels himself, trembles. She's never jumped so high. But Crazy has, he knows, and he hears his hooves thundering on the ground, sees the dust swirling about his legs, sees the yellowish-white foam at the horse's mouth. She closes in and shortens the stride, counts, measures the distance, and now they're taking off. It's a terrific take-off, and Charlo gasps as they fly over in one great leap, Crazy lifts his hooves and lands on his forelegs, Julie leaning against the horse's neck. They're over. Straight away she steers him to the right, the turn is too sharp, she's a bit on the back foot, but makes up

177

for it again. She takes him down to a trot, takes the next jump with an almost apathetic air. Charlo begins running. His shirt tails flapping around him.

"Perfect!" he shouts, coming up to her. Julie takes a deep breath, strokes the horse's neck.

"It certainly wasn't," she says, but her face is radiant. "I was a bit too frightened, and he sensed it, but he did what I asked him to."

"My God, Julie," he shouts "if only your mother had seen that! One metre thirty!"

She puts the horse into a walk again, peony red with pride.

"I'll do a little groundwork to finish off," she tells him coquettishly over her shoulder.

Charlo goes back to the fence. Leans against it, shuts his eyes. Stands there for a long while. He feels the sun warming his neck, he smells the scent of grass and animals, and tar softening in the warmth. The mild wind caresses his face. He stands in total tranquillity, his body safe and solid and completely well, he's sure of it. His thoughts turn to the past, flying waywardly from him like horses through an open gate, but he brings them under control and thinks forward. Of all the good things to come. He opens his eyes again and looks at Julie, she's practising pirouettes. It's a miracle to him what she can do with that big animal.

Into all this brightness and warmth, a shadow falls. He becomes aware of it in the corner of his right eye, a slow grey shadow. It's of no interest to him, he's looking straight ahead, watching the horse marking time on an incredibly small spot. The way it gathers all its weight into such a small area beggars belief. The shadow comes closer, it eats its way into his field of vision, he glances to the side, sees it's a car. It's a Volvo, a grey one. There's something familiar about it. It's moving very slowly, crawling hesitantly down the road. He watches the car until it stops; there's no reaction within him, he's only observing it, thinking no thoughts, only wanting to keep tabs on what's happening around him. Nobody gets out. So he turns to Julie again, she's reining back and walking forward, practising transitions. It's as if the horse is swaying over the ring, right, left, right, left, in some graceful ballet.

A car door slams. Charlo feels an impulse to turn and see who's coming, but he doesn't do it, he chooses to shut the world out. It'll just be a father coming to collect one of the girls, he has no idea who it is, he stands four-square on the sand, enjoying the sight before him in the ring. Soon he hears footsteps. There's the faint crunching of gravel. Only now does he feel the first prick, the first stab of fear that something's happening, something that could prove dangerous to him. But no, he thinks then, it doesn't happen like this. They'd come to the house, they'd be standing there on the doorstep, a couple of them probably, he's seen it in his mind's eye. He's dreamt about it at night. This is a lone man, he's only come to look at the horses, like many others. There, a shadow on his right, surprisingly tall. He doesn't want to turn his head, he leans heavily against the fence and folds his arms. It's no concern of his if the inquisitive want to drop in to take a look, is it?

179

He's interested in Julie, after all, she has his full attention.

He has the feeling, as he stands there, that the man's got a dog; he can hear whining. He heaves a sigh of relief. A walker with his dog, there are plenty of those at the centre. Charlo takes a clandestine look at the dog. It's a funny looking creature, small, the colour of lead and full of folds and wrinkles. Short legs, large paws. Deep-sunk eyes, ears thick and small, perhaps it's a puppy. Now it's seated itself next to its master, waiting for further commands. Although Charlo's watching Julie, he feels the man's eyes on him. But he carries on looking straight ahead, at the same time counting his own respirations without knowing why. Three, four, five, six.

"Charles Olav Torp?" The voice is very deep.

He nods mechanically by way of reply.

It's so muddy where he's standing, a few days of wind would do it good, dry it out, he thinks, and there's too much gravel on the lot after the winter's gritting, he ought to sweep it up. There are so many jobs to be done, he's become almost indispensable to Møller, which was what he wanted. Charlo can't control his thoughts, they're running in all directions. He sees the man hold out a hand, he really is very tall, perhaps just under two metres, broad-shouldered and neatly dressed in a leather jacket and black trousers.

"Sejer," he says. "Police."

It's as if Charlo has been sewn up too tightly. Now he unravels stitch by stitch. It's not supposed to be like this, not here with other people present. Not in front of

Julie. He puts his hands in his pockets. His face feels rigid.

"Yes?" he croaks hoarsely, his voice is already betraying him, and the landscape around him quickly recedes into the distance. He's jolted back in time, and all that's happened in recent months has been nothing but a glimpse into a future he's destined never to enjoy.

Sejer remains silent. Charlo pulls himself together. He must shake off this paralysis and behave politely.

"What's this about?" he asks with an attempt at a smile. He has to moisten his lips with his tongue. Møller's apple trees need pruning, he thinks, twigs are sprouting everywhere, presumably it hasn't been done for two or three years, and the grass hasn't been cut all that well. There really are so many things that need doing: if he wanted to, he could run about here from morning to night. A ticking has begun inside his head, small, sharp stabs.

"I'd be very grateful if you'd come to the station for a chat."

Charlo inhales. His head dips up and down without his willing it to. It doesn't occur to him to refuse, he must appear innocent. He must be cooperative and amicable, do his civic duty.

"What for?" he enquires weakly. He curses his feeble tone. Sejer holds back, considering.

"We're working on a difficult case," he says, "and various circumstances have led us to you. We're treating you merely as a witness, it's purely routine."

This last is said in a reassuring tone. Charlo realises that his mouth is open, but he can't bring himself to

181

close it. He can't get enough air, his eyes feel dry, his eyelashes seem to be sticking together, they cause him to stand there blinking like an idiot. He nods and listens to the words, places a hand on the fence. He's got to hold on to something.

"I've got to drive my daughter home," he explains, and nods in the direction of the ring. "But of course I'll drop in. I could stop by tomorrow." He attempts to emphasise his words, to seem willing and at the same time taking the initiative, making his own decisions. But he isn't making his own decisions, he's all over the place, he's running away like the dirty water beneath his feet.

Sejer's face is still impassive. Charlo sees the marked dent in the chin, the broad, determined jaw. He sees the sharp edge of the man's nose. His eyes are dark and scrutinising.

"It'll only take a couple of minutes," he says calmly. "I'll drive you back, of course."

It sounds like an order. The voice allows no room for protest, protest would be an admission. If he's going to deal with this, he must pay attention and be helpful. Charlo nods once more, he feels like a puppet on a string.

"Couldn't we do it in the car?" he suggests, nodding over his shoulder at the grey Volvo, and his own dented Honda. He rues the idea instantly. Sejer smiles patiently. He's got very strong features, his grey hair is cut very short. He is ten years older than Charlo. The nice leather jacket and pressed black trousers seem out of place in this environment where everyone goes about in riding breeches and long, mud-caked boots.

"Unfortunately, we have to follow certain procedures," he says, looking at him. Charlo gives way immediately, cursing himself and his own lack of composure, it is just routine. He's prepared. He thought he was prepared. He gives Julie a final glance, she hasn't noticed what's going on.

"Well," says Charlo, trying to seem magnanimous, "I'm sure I can spare a couple of minutes." Helplessly, he shrugs, a lump grows in his throat. Can no one save him now, can no one see what's taking place? Sejer begins to walk towards the Volvo with long, firm strides. Charlo follows. He's struggling with his legs a bit, they seem strange and wobbly. His feet are just appendages dangling from the ends of them.

Everything I say can, and presumably will, be used against me, he thinks.

Every movement of my face, every twitch of my mouth, every wavering gaze, will give me away. That special light in my eyes that signifies unspeakable guilt. No, for God's sake, he can't see my guilt, only words count now, what I actually say. I'll say no, no, that's not right, I can't remember, it's so long ago, and the days blend into one another, like drops of water. Try to take control. Try to remember all you say, he'll ask you to repeat things, maybe endlessly. Be friendly now, be calm. You mustn't lose your rag.

"I'm going to trample a whole lot of horse muck into your office."

He looks down at his boots, and gives a humiliated shrug. Sejer has opened the door. Charlo peers into the large room.

"Ah, I've had all sorts in this office," Sejer says with a sudden, charming smile. It makes Charlo relax. We're only going to have a little talk, he thinks, I'll make out all right, it's just a case of being strong. Sure and steady and determined. He enters and stands in the middle of the room. The office is light and airy, full of small, private things, pictures on the walls. Plants, which look well tended, on the window sill. A desk and a large window with a view of the river. A green filing cabinet and a fridge, perhaps containing cold drinks. A PC. Piles of documents and books on shelves.

"Sit down, Mr Torp," Sejer says, waving a hand.

He goes to the fridge and gets out a bottle of Farris mineral water. Charlo watches him furtively. Sejer moves about with serenity, there's nothing hurried in his manner. Now he owns both time and space. Charlo is on his guard. This isn't an interview, he thinks, just a chat. The dog has gone to lie down by the wall, and now resembles a grey coat with black buttons that someone has chucked in the corner. He is handed a glass, and Sejer uncaps the bottle and pours some water into it. Charlo tries to sit up in his chair, he braces himself, concentrating hard. Nothing must strike home. Nothing must get to him. What must Julie be thinking? He should have said something to her. No, she'd only be anxious, and Julie must be spared all worry. Julie must never be part of this, she must live out the whole of her life in blissful ignorance.

184

Sejer has returned to his chair. He takes off his leather jacket and hangs it meticulously over the back of the seat. There's a plastic blotting pad on the desktop. It's a map of the world, and Charlo automatically searches for Norway, which is reproduced in pink. He wishes he were far away. So, his gaze travels down Europe and arrives in Italy. From Italy he sets out for the port of Piraeus. And keeps on to one of the Greek islands.

Nothing is said. Perhaps he ought to gabble away, the way innocent people do, they speak without thinking, of this and that. But he can't break the silence. If he begins to say something, he may lose control, the words will come out helter-skelter and perhaps end in a trap. If this man is the sort who lays traps. Of course he is, it's his job, he's learnt a whole series of techniques. There's a rushing noise in his head as Charlo waits. Sejer looks at him gravely, leafs through a wad of papers. It's just the two of them now and the ticking seconds. Charlo crosses one leg over the other, then uncrosses it. There's a slight hiss in the silence, which slowly gets louder, he wonders if it's the sound of blood coursing through his brain.

"Obviously you've got a right to know why you're here," Sejer begins. He sits twiddling a pen. "I'm very grateful that you were prepared to cooperate, by the way."

Again, that deep voice, so pleasant to the ear, taking some of the edge off the gravity. Charlo begins to think. Maybe he should have refused. Is that how things stand, has he fallen straight into the first pitfall? No,

185

he's innocent after all, of course he wants to help. He doesn't know what would be wise. Should he be indignant, slightly exercised about being picked up like this, when he's actually got other things to do? He's a man who's working, he's got responsibilities.

"Of course," he says, and adjusts himself in his seat. "Please explain. You see, I've got to fetch my daughter, she'll be finished fairly soon."

Sejer glances at his wristwatch.

"I quite understand. We'll get going, then. First, just for the record. Your name is Charles Olav Torp, born the second of April, nineteen sixty-three?"

"Yes."

"Address, Blomsgate number twenty?"

"That's right."

Sejer looks at his papers.

"And you've got a daughter, Julie Torp, born the twenty-seventh of May, nineteen eighty-eight?"

Charlo's alarmed. He doesn't like this mention of Julie, she mustn't get involved with this at any price.

"Correct," he answers loudly. His eyes are wavering already, he searches for some fixed point and chooses the dog by the wall. It's asleep.

"And she lives in the student flats at Oscarsgate 2. A pupil at Allsaker Sixth-form College?"

"Yes."

Sejer makes notes, glances up. "Have you got any form of ID? It's just a formality."

Charlo hesitates, finding this incomprehensible. But he gets out his wallet, his tattered, brown wallet. He almost feels ashamed of its poor condition, its broken

186

zip and worn leather. The blood donor sticker is yellow with age, he doesn't give blood any more, since they stopped paying. He takes out his driving licence and pushes it across the desk. Sejer examines it carefully, then he looks at the wallet. Charlo feels ill at ease. The smell of the stables clings to his clothes and starts to suffuse the room. The licence is handed back, and he replaces his wallet in his inside pocket.

"I want to go back to the month of November."

Sejer puts down his pen. Clasps his hands in front of him on the desk.

"And I know it's not easy remembering exactly where you were or what you were doing on any particular date. I know it's hard to remember times. It's human to forget. But I've got reasons to believe that there are certain things you will remember. That's why you're here. I believe you can help us with a difficult case. Do you understand?"

"Yes."

The inspector pauses.

"We have good reason to believe that you were involved in a car accident, on exactly the seventh of November, in the vicinity of Hamsund."

Charlo chews his lip as if he's trying to recall. He screws up his eyes and finally starts nodding slowly.

"Yes," he says reflectively. "I did have an accident in the car. In the autumn sometime," he says, "but I can't remember the date. It was indeed at Hamsund. That's right, it was an exasperating incident." He nods once more. Looks Sejer in the eyes, which takes a certain amount of effort. He hopes to God his pupils look normal.

"This collision interests me," says Sejer. "So I'd like to go through it point by point."

Charlo shakes his head, bemused.

"There's not much to tell." He feels the sweat in his armpits. "It was a youth who didn't observe the right of way. He was driving a small Toyota. I was on a priority road," he explains, "he hit my right front wing."

Sejer leans back. He stretches his long body, looking comfortable and relaxed.

Charlo can't help himself. "How did you know I was involved?"

Sejer keeps silent, just looks at him, with those grey eyes. He ignores the question. Charlo has the sneaking feeling that he's lost control already. He has no authority in here, he's just some poor sod, and the man on the other side of the desk has the whip hand in everything.

"This junction," Sejer says, "let's take a close look at it." He gets up and rummages amongst some documents on a shelf, and returns with a map. Charlo can see that markings have been made on it with a felt-tip pen.

"D'you recognise this junction?"

He pushes the map over to him. Charlo studies the roads, the arrows.

"Yes, just about," he says. He doesn't want to go back there, the thought of it is repellent.

"There's the railway station," Sejer says pointing. "Can you show me where you came from?"

"It's difficult to remember after all this time."

188

"I realise." He nods, understanding and patient. "But it's important to us that you try."

This is like banging his head on a brick wall. He's captive in here, he's got to answer. Could he ask for a lawyer? No, that's ridiculous, he hasn't been charged with anything, he's just a witness.

"It's possible I came from over here," he says, and points. He doesn't dare lie about it. The truth, he thinks, for as long as possible.

Sejer looks at the map.

"Fredboesgate," he says distinctly, and looks up. "You came from Fredboesgate?"

Charlo nods. Panic seizes him because everything's moving so quickly, he's already placed himself in the vicinity of Harriet's house.

"Yes," he says and nods submissively. He doesn't look at Sejer, but studies the map with feigned interest.

"And the other car?"

"It was a Toyota," Charlo says. "A Yaris, I think. He came from here."

He points, notices that the street is called Holtegate. Satisfied, Sejer nods.

"Could it have been the seventh of November?"

Charlo leans across the desk, trying to gain the initiative. Again he looks at the dog resting by the wall. It doesn't move. Like a toy animal that a child has slung there.

"It could quite possibly have been in November," he says, "but I can't be more precise than that. I was unemployed then," he adds, and gets carried away in a stream of words, can't stop himself, "and the days just became a blur, I couldn't tell them apart, that's why I can't be sure of dates. Now I've found work at the riding centre," he adds, "not full-time work, but it helps. I can be useful, do something with my hands, and suchlike. I've told the Social Security, too, so they cut my Unemployment Benefit accordingly. I'm an honest man," he concludes, with a defiant look at the inspector.

Sejer remains silent after this tirade. Charlo senses the redness of his cheeks. He regains control of himself, he'll just answer questions, that's all, not go off like that. But there's a pressure inside him, a defence, he didn't want that, didn't mean it, he was just a prisoner of the situation and his own fear. Of his own, desperate need.

"But it could have been the seventh?" Sejer repeats.

Charlo shrugs. "Quite possibly. Well," he says getting exasperated, "I suppose it was the teenager in the Toyota who led you to me. I don't know if he took my registration number or what, but if he says it was the seventh, then it must have been!"

He regrets his outburst immediately.

"It was the seventh," Sejer remarks quietly.

He makes notes on his paper again. Then he folds his hands on the desk. Charlo's blood runs cold. He can't see any end to this. This is the start, he thinks. Of the nightmare. They've picked me out from the crowd. He has no idea how they managed it.

"Yes, he got part of your registration number. Have you any thoughts about why he might have done that?"

190

Charlo is mute. He looks at the dog again, he likes watching the sleeping animal.

"No," he says with a shrug. Sejer leans across the desk, suddenly very close.

"Didn't you get rather worked up about this collision?"

His voice has assumed a note of sympathy. Charlo rubs his chin.

"Yes, I got worked up. I assume you've been given a full account. I lost my temper. I thought he was driving like an idiot, and I probably got quite angry. Almost anyone would have, in my shoes. But what did he actually say? Did he feel threatened? I never threatened him, but I did totally lose my rag. My life wasn't easy just then," he admits, with a touch of self-pity, "I was probably on a bit of a short fuse. That's only human, it's not a crime."

The word pops out his mouth. He leans back, wants to take control of the conversation, but it won't be controlled.

"Your life wasn't easy," Sejer says. "Can you elaborate a little?"

"I don't quite see what my life has got to do with this," he replies quickly. "You say I'm only a witness. You keep going on about this collision and things. What is it you really want?"

Sejer picks up his pen again. Holds it between his fingers.

"I can understand that you don't see the point. But there is a point."

Charlo hesitates. He doesn't dare argue. The chances of letting something slip are greater then, it's best to cooperate. He sees that the truth would be best.

"I've already told you," he says. "I was unemployed. No work to go to. Short of money. Things like that. It's soul-destroying not having a job, you lose all your self-esteem. Dignity, self-respect. You avoid people, can't be bothered to answer questions. The days are a living hell, you don't sleep at night and then lie in bed late. Just making food is a chore. You feel like you've fallen off a merry-go-round, and you're standing there watching the others who're still on it. It's like being a spectator of life."

"But things are better now? That's right, isn't it?"

Charlo nods silently. Compresses his lips.

Sejer drinks some Farris.

"Let's take it from the beginning," he says. "You were driving out of Fredboesgate." As he says the word "Fredboesgate", he looks up at Charlo. "You approached the junction. The weather was bad on the seventh of November, sleet, very slippery."

"That's right."

"What time of night was this?"

"Well, it was about ten. Or maybe half past, possibly, I'm not quite sure."

"Did you see the car coming?"

"Yes. But I was immersed in my own thoughts, I was sure he'd seen the sign telling him to give way, and of course he braked, but the car skidded straight on in those road conditions. A Toyota Yaris, I ask you. Without winter tyres. People shouldn't be allowed to drive that sort of car in winter weather. Shouldn't be allowed to drive them at all. They're just sardine tins on wheels."

"So," Sejer says. "There was a crash. Then what did you do?"

"I remained at the wheel for a little while, dazed. I looked into the other car, there was a teenager, he seemed terrified."

"Go on," Sejer says.

"I opened my door and got out. Yanked open his door and began yelling. It was all extremely childish, but I couldn't stop myself."

"How did the young man respond?"

"I expect you've asked him about that," says Charlo, wanting to retreat again. He'd like to go home. He doesn't think he's doing very well. Nonsense, he's doing brilliantly, he's telling the truth, and that's easy. Up to a certain point.

"Yes, but I need your take on it, you know?"

It's as if Charlo suddenly wakes up. He's up to his waist in the freezing torrent.

"But why do you keep on about this collision?" he asks, looking at Sejer.

The inspector returns his gaze.

"We don't need to go into our motives for asking the questions we ask," he says. "What's interesting from our point of view is that you were in Hamsund at a time that's critical to my investigation."

"And what kind of investigation is that?" Charlo asks, and holds his breath waiting for the reply.

193

"A murder case," Sejer says calmly. He looks into Charlo's eyes.

"So I may have seen something? Is that what you think?"

"Yes."

Charlo takes courage. Looks straight at Sejer.

"In that case, I'm afraid I'll have to disappoint you. I wasn't particularly observant that evening, and I can't remember anything about cars or people. I only recall the crash and the young bloke. Afterwards I drove home. I tried to beat out the damned thing with a hammer. I mean, the dent. Repainted it a bit. That sort of thing."

Sejer holds his gaze. "I'm sorry, but there's something I don't understand. It was the Toyota driver's fault. You could have had the dent repaired in a body shop at his expense. But you wouldn't fill in the claim form. Why not, Mr Torp?"

Charlo isn't getting sufficient oxygen, his cheeks are hollow.

"But I've already tried to explain that I wasn't myself that evening," he says, and he can hear from the tone of his voice that his temper is rising.

"Let's go into this a bit," Sejer coaxes. "You weren't yourself. In what way?"

Charlo takes a drink of Farris. Tries to gather his thoughts.

"I had a lot to contend with," he confesses, because now he can see the situation for what it is. He must provide a proper and compelling explanation for why he fled the scene of the accident. "I've already

194

mentioned that I was unemployed. There were also debts I couldn't pay. I had a gambling addiction that ruined my whole life. My daughter didn't want to see me. I'd been forced into a corner. And the collision was too much for me. I just lost it, and that's only human, really."

"Absolutely," Sejer agrees. "So, you had debts?"

"I'd borrowed money from friends and the like. Gambled at Bjerke and Øvrevoll. And fruit machines. I've always been keen on horses. It all mounted up to quite a large debt. It worried me sick. People were after me, nothing was secure."

"I see. You *had* gambling debts, you say. But not any more? Have they been paid off?"

Charlo is unsure of what to say. "Yes, I won some money," he blurts out.

"Ah, your luck was in?"

"People wouldn't get addicted to gambling if they never won," Charlo retorts.

"Of course not," Sejer says, smiling. He rises from his chair and walks to the window. The wrinkled dog gets up and pads after him, stations itself next to its master. Sejer stands gazing out for a while.

Charlo gets a break. He shifts a little in his chair, looks nervously at the time, thinking about Julie. Can't understand why Sejer is just staring out of the window like this.

"I've got a little question," Sejer says. "What took you to Fredboesgate?"

Charlo shakes his head vehemently.

"Nothing at all. I only drove through it."

195

"Where had you come from?"

Sejer has turned, he's leaning against the wall.

Charlo thinks frantically. "Well, I came from Kongsberg."

"I see. You came from Kongsberg. And what were you doing in Kongsberg?"

Charlo becomes confused. He realises that he hasn't prepared any of this, hasn't spent time reshaping the evening. I'm a bloody amateur, he thinks miserably.

"I just drove about," he says at last. "It was one of those evenings when I was very down. I drove about at random. Went to various places."

"You left your house in Blomsgate at what time?"

"Er, about six p.m. But really . . ."

"And when did you get back home?"

Charlo remembers that his neighbour, Erlandson, saw him from his window. They may have interviewed him. He's filled with uncertainty. Tells the truth anyway.

"It was probably eleven o'clock or thereabouts."

"So," says Sejer, coming across to the desk. "You drove round without any plan from six in the evening until eleven o'clock?"

"I must have done."

"That's a long time. That's a lot of fuel. Could you afford it?"

"Yes."

He crumples a little in his chair, sees the ludicrousness of his explanation.

"I walked around the town for a while," he adds.

"In that awful weather?" Sejer smiles. His smile is wide and always arrives unexpectedly.

196

"It was a bad day," Charlo declares. And it's true, too. The worst day of his life.

"Do you know Hamsund?" Sejer enquires.

"Not at all."

"They've got a lovely church there. You ought to go and take a look at it sometime."

Charlo blinks in terror.

"Yes, I've seen it in the distance," he says. "I've driven past." Then he recalls the woman he met in the churchyard. Have they been keeping him under surveillance the whole time, following his every move? The grey Volvo shadowing him through the streets without his knowledge? He clasps his hands in his lap. Glances surreptitiously at his wrist-watch again. Sejer folds his arms, he looks indefatigable. Charlo retreats into himself. How has he done? He's managed well, he hasn't admitted anything, apart from his own wretchedness.

"Let's try to plot your movements that evening," Sejer suggests, planting his elbows on the desktop.

"There's no point. I don't even remember it that well. I drove about, as I've already explained. From my house to the middle of town. Then I walked about a bit looking in shop windows. At all the things I couldn't afford," he says bitterly. "After a while I was pretty wet because of the sleet. Got in the car again and drove out to Kongsberg. I wandered about there for quite a while. Looked at people. That sort of thing."

Sejer nods.

"OK. You drove from Blomsgate to the town centre. Roughly how long did you walk about there?"

"Maybe an hour or two."

"Could you be a bit more precise?"

"More like two hours."

"That takes us to eight o'clock," Sejer says. "Then you drove to Kongsberg. That would take about forty-five minutes. Say an hour because of the poor weather?"

"Yes."

"That's nine o'clock. How long did you stroll around Kongsberg?"

"Um, perhaps an hour," says Charlo, doing feverish calculations in his head.

"So, that's ten o'clock. Then you turned for home and arrived about eleven. That's good. We've got that straight. But you made a detour through Hamsund. And spent some time berating that young man?"

"Yes."

"And there were no witnesses to the accident?"

"No," Charlo replies truthfully.

Once more Sejer takes a break. It lasts a long time. Charlo presses his lips together, prepares himself for an attack, can't seem to breathe properly. This calm, he thinks, is getting on my nerves. Sejer is like an iceberg, there is something imposing and cold about him.

"As you passed along Fredboesgate," he says suddenly, "did you notice anything in particular?"

Charlo shakes his head.

"Did you meet any other cars?"

"Not that I remember."

"What about pedestrians?"

"Don't think so."

198

"Did you see any cars parked at the kerb, for instance?"

"No. It's too narrow."

"You passed the old hotel?"

"Hotel? Don't know."

"The Fredly. It's disused. You don't know it?"

"I don't know Hamsund. I've already said."

Sejer pushes his documents away.

"OK. We'll call it a day," he says. "Just one last, small thing. Do you read the papers?"

"Yes, of course."

"Which ones?"

"Well, it varies a bit. *Dagbladet* and *VG*. Sometimes *Aftenposten*, sometimes the local paper."

"Every day?"

"Yes."

"But you didn't see our press release?"

"Which press release?" Charlo queries, trying desperately to remember.

"We advertised in all the papers, and on radio and television, for the person involved in the road traffic accident at Hamsund."

"You did?"

"You never came forward."

"It must have passed me by. You can't take in everything."

Sejer nods.

"What about the case itself?" he asks. "Did you read about that?"

"The case?"

"The murder at Hamsund, which I'm investigating. The murder of Harriet Krohn."

"Oh yes, of course. I've read about that. Yes, that was terrible."

He raises his eyes and looks at Sejer, trying to keep them steady. Sejer turns to the dog. "Come along, Frank. We've got to drive the man back." Frank comes padding up. Charlo rises from his chair, dazed.

"I'm sorry I wasn't more help."

Sejer gives him a penetrating look.

"I dare say you'll get another opportunity," he says. "We've only just begun."

Julie is sitting by the door of the box, munching a carrot. She gets up, dusts wood shavings from her backside and sends him a challenging look.

"Where on earth have you been?"

Charlo shrugs in resignation. He glances at his watch.

"Ugh," he says with an irritated gesture, "it was just a load of nonsense. That chap was a policeman. It was all about the collision I told you about, long ago, that I was involved in. At Hamsund. Some problem with the insurance."

Julie looks at him doubtfully. "A problem with the insurance?" She doesn't understand, isn't happy with his answer and continues to pin him with her gaze.

Charlo sighs heavily. "Oh, it's too complicated to explain." He waves it away with his hand. "But it's been sorted out now. You know, bureaucracy," he says rolling his eyes, "there's no end to the amount of trouble they can cause poor sods like me. Evidently, there were some bits that hadn't been filled in, I just had to answer some questions, about how it happened."

"But, the police?" she repeats uncertainly. "Surely they don't have anything to do with insurance?"

"They seem to have. I don't understand such things."

Julie turns and goes into Crazy's box, pats his neck. An iota of suspicion lingers in her eyes. Charlo tries to smooth things over.

"Let's go and get a pizza, Julie," he suggests, "it's easy to heat up, we can do it in the microwave. Are you as hungry as I am?"

She nods, closes the box door, picks up her bag and walks resolutely down the passage. He can't tell if she believes him, he can't read her now, she has withdrawn into herself and is thinking her own thoughts. He follows. The door bangs shut heavily behind them, the timber giving a long drawn-out creak.

"But," she says when they're sitting in the car, "that collision took place ages ago. Why are they going on about it now?"

Charlo turns on to the main road, accelerates and changes up.

"The wheels turn so slowly," he explains. "It doesn't matter to me, of course, I've already had the money. It was just formalities, God knows what they were going on about. But there's no point in arguing with them, so I gave them what they wanted."

She nods, falls silent again. He asks if she wants pizza with pepperoni, and she does. She sits in the car while he shops. He's troubled. He rushes about the aisles feeling irritable. Julie is suspicious, always on her guard, she doesn't trust him, not absolutely and completely, as he wants her to. Because now he can be trusted, now he's turned over a new leaf. If they just leave him alone. What's the point of digging up the past? He can't bring Harriet back to life again. He puts a pizza and a couple of Cokes on the checkout conveyor belt, pays and goes out again. The car is ticking over in neutral. Julie has pulled her red hair over her shoulder, and plaits it with nimble fingers before slipping a scrunchie round it.

"I could eat a horse," Charlo says.

She gives him a mock hurt look, and they both laugh. At last they're laughing, and he relaxes, and thinks, it went well. I did all right, they know nothing, it was just a shot in the dark. Things must be proved beyond all reasonable doubt, and there's a lot of bloody doubt there. Even so, it's quieter than usual between them while he's driving. He thinks that maybe she's tired, it's hard work dealing with a horse, and she's got her homework as well. No, it's more than that. The silence is palpable, he has the feeling that she's mulling something over, but doesn't dare ask the question. Well, it'll come out sooner or later. If she has questions, he'll answer them.

Later on, they're having their meal in Charlo's kitchen. Julie is seated on the green chest, chewing, Charlo lifts his glass of Coke and proposes a toast.

"To the new record," he says "one metre thirty. Congratulations, Julie, you're a real star."

She raises her glass, too, and they look into each other's eyes as they drink. Julie takes a new slice of pizza, bites into it and chews. She seems distracted. Charlo thinks, our conversation isn't flowing like it usually does. What's coming between us? Why do I feel on edge? Julie's green eyes seem so dark, so anxious. It's as if she's keeping something back. Charlo puts his piece of pizza down on his plate, leans forward and looks straight at her. Attack is the best form of defence, he thinks.

"So," he says, and smiles. "You're very thoughtful today. Tell Dad all about it."

She swallows. Gives her head a slight shake.

"You're so quiet," he goes on. "Have you got a lot on your mind?"

She nods and pushes her plate away. Leans back against the wall. Her shoulders are tense, her white neck is so thin, he can see the veins, the fine blue lines.

"Come on, tell Dad," he repeats. She peers up at him, purses her mouth.

"I'm thinking about Grandma," she says at last.

She lowers her gaze immediately, tosses her head. Charlo's heart misses a beat.

"About Grandma?"

He looks at her in surprise, tries to understand. Licks his mouth, his lips are so dry.

"I went to visit Grandma yesterday."

She shoots little glances in his direction the whole time, as if gauging his reaction.

"She must have been pleased to see you," he says hastily, helping himself in his confusion to another piece of pizza that he definitely doesn't want. "I mean, even though she's very muddled, she'd have been glad of your visit."

Julie puts her elbows on the table. She looks at him hard.

"Grandma's only muddled sometimes," she says now. "In between, she's quite lucid. Then she can remember everything."

"Really?" Charlo says. He takes a bite of his pizza, chews for a long time.

"I asked about those bits of old jewellery," Julie says. "But she's never given you any pieces of jewellery. She's never had a cameo. Or any silver."

Charlo manages a smile. He shakes his head with forbearance.

"I'm sorry to have to say it, but I'm afraid she's lost her grip on reality, Julie." He leans forward, not knowing where he gets the strength from. "Something's troubling you. Tell me what it is now."

Suddenly she looks tormented.

"It's just that I'm so scared. I find bits of old jewellery in your chest, and I don't know where they come from. And today, you're picked up by the police. I don't know what to think."

Charlo gives her a horrified look.

"But," he exclaims, "are you sitting there worrying about me, my darling?"

She makes no reply, only stares at him.

"I've told you what that was all about, Julie."

He pushes his plate away and summons all his powers of persuasion.

"What is it that you're scared of really?" he asks.

She squirms slightly, feels awkward.

"I'm scared you'll get caught up in something."

Charlo grins.

"There. But I can put your mind at ease. Now listen to me. This is important, this is something you've got to believe. For the first time in my life I'm in control. For the first time in a long time I'm doing things right." He clutches his glass and gulps at his Coke. "I've kicked my bad habits. I'm working hard for Møller, I'm looking after you and managing fine. The last thing I want is for you to start worrying about me. Because now I'm really on top of it all. And God knows but I've wasted half my life in madness and bad habits. But I've thrown all that off. I'm the world's most respectable man now. I don't fiddle my taxes, I don't drink, I'm not violent. But I understand that you find that hard to believe because you're not used to it. You're used to looking for relapses. But there's no more backsliding, I've finished with that. D'you understand?"

She lifts her head and looks at him, gives him a shamefaced smile.

"Sorry," she says faintly. "But it's all a bit much for me. The way you suddenly turn up with everything ironed out, just like that. Paid your debts and bought me a horse. It's almost too good to be true."

He's sitting with both his hands wrapped around his glass, and now he assumes a sympathetic expression. He's lying, lying through his teeth, laying it on with a trowel, and it's as easy as winking. He thanks God for his special talent for dissimulation, people have to feign things or they wouldn't survive, and he's good at it because he has to be. She relaxes once more, sighs heavily, shakes her head.

"Grandma's very old," he says softly. "She's lost the thread completely."

"I know," says Julie.

"She still thinks I'm twenty-two. She still believes that Mum's alive."

"Yes."

"Old people are so frightened," he explains. "And fear creates confusion."

"But occasionally her mind is crystal clear."

"For a few, short moments. But you mustn't be taken in. Did she recognise you straight away?"

"Not until I said something."

"There. That's what I mean. She recognises voices. Have I managed to put your mind at rest? Tell me."

She smiles bravely, looking ashamed.

"It's only because I'm scared," she says. "I'm scared of losing what I've finally got."

He looks at her hard. "That's never going to happen!" he says, wringing his hands in his lap all the while. He feels like a bull charging towards a cliff. He's running straight ahead, refusing to look to the side, running as far as he can. They sit there for a long time, fingering their glasses.

CHAPTER
THIRTEEN

Gradually she's comforted by his assurances. She leans on him trustingly once more and concentrates on the present. On all the work that must be done. She receives his support and help and comfort, and she begins to believe that it will last.

Time passes and nothing happens. Charlo hears no more from the police. But he looks over his shoulder continually, he trawls through all the papers for any news. Peace slowly returns to his life. He knows what he has to do hour by hour, and the days pass rapidly. He gets fitter. He lifts and carries and toils, the blood pumps through his body, he's always so warm, so strong. He eats well and sleeps well. His nights are dreamless, or rather, he can't remember his dreams at all, he wakes with a sense of bewilderment at the fact that he's been given yet another day. That it's lying there before him to do with as he pleases, that he's still a free man. He's managing financially, he has no expensive tastes, he buys food and a little tobacco now and then, he no longer drinks. This is how things should be for ever, he thinks, Julie and me together. Hard work and harmony. He's out of the shadows now, his turn has come at last.

In March, Julie takes part in her first competition with Crazy. She enters Intermediate B and comes in second. Charlo is in the stand with tears in his eyes. He's so proud he almost bursts out of his shirt. She rides in white tie and tails, with a small, black top hat and white gloves. She has plaited Crazy's mane and sprayed him with coat shine, none of the other horses glows like he does. This was what we were aiming for, Charlo thinks. We deserve this. But sometimes he gets irritated because his sight falters. Everything gradually goes hazy, or he starts seeing double. Then he has to blink a few times, and after a while his sight returns to normal. Oh well, he thinks, maybe it's time for glasses. Everyone has them, even small children, so why should I be any different? Time is passing and I'm gradually deteriorating. It doesn't feel frightening, just a little irksome.

Eventually he gets round to booking an appointment with an optician. Goes along at the appointed time, sits down and does everything he's told. The optician is a young woman, she's sitting on a chair with wheels and comes right up close, into his lap. She is awesomely near, he can smell the scent of her skin. He begins reading from the board. But today his sight is fine, he can see everything, quite clearly. He's annoyed and relieved at the same time.

"It comes and goes," he explains.

"Yes," she says pushing her chair back again, "sight is often variable from day to day, or hour to hour. That's completely normal. But as things stand, I don't think you need glasses."

He looks at her and steels himself. "But apart from that," he asks, "do my eyes look normal?"

She hesitates. "Do they look normal? Yes, I would have said so. Are you unhappy about them?"

She sends him a bemused smile. He laughs it off, shakes his head. He leaves and feels relieved. Presumably it's nerves, he thinks, I've begun listening to my body in a different way now.

He's sitting at the kitchen table distractedly fiddling with a pepper mill. He's keeping an eye on the traffic outside, to see if anyone comes. On a sudden whim, he unscrews the top of the mill and shakes the peppercorns out on to the table, they're as brown and dry as mouse shit and scatter in all directions. He gathers them into a little pile. He thinks back over his life, and all the things he's done. Suppose these peppercorns stand for his deeds, both the bad and the good, and that there were some scales on the table; could he get them to balance? He thinks of the years with Inga Lill, of the time when he was in control. Of the time when he could support her, when he still had a job. Aren't those years worth a few peppercorns? He counts out ten, places them in an imaginary scale on the left, for the good things. Then there was the embezzlement at work. It wasn't a large amount, but he's forced to place ten peppercorns on the right, for the bad deeds. He stops for a moment and considers. His big deceit with Julie, gambling her money away, was unpardonable, and must be worth ten peppercorns. The scales are out of balance already. But then he remembers that he's just bought her a horse. Pleased, he places ten peppercorns on the left. That looks better. But the worst thing of all remains. The murder, how much does that weigh? Is thirty enough? Forty?

He starts counting peppercorns. He wants to be truthful when it comes to his crime. So he takes forty peppercorns and places them on the right. He sits there for a long time, staring at the two piles. Is there any chance at all of righting this, of living with it? Yes, time will take care of everything. Much of his life is still before him. Maybe forty years, maybe more. If he does good every day for the rest of his life, couldn't he earn forty peppercorns to go on the left, and pay his debt? Immediately he begins to count peppercorns again. You can't judge a man's life before it's over. He pushes the peppercorns over to the left and leans back contentedly. Time will work in his favour, and his pupils are perfectly fine.

He sleeps well that night. Curled up in bed like a child, with his hands beneath his cheek. He drops into a light, shimmering sleep and dreams about Julie and Crazy. They're galloping along a beach, the water flies around the horse's hooves, the great body glints in the sun, Julie's gorgeous hair billows like a red pennant in the wind. Fast, graceful and unconquerable, they're on their way to an adventure. He wakes with his head completely clear. For a while he lies staring up at the ceiling, again he follows the flex with his eyes, from the globe and down to the plug on the wall. He throws the duvet aside, puts his feet on the ground, and stands up. He's unprepared for what happens next. Both his legs buckle under him, and he pitches forward with all his weight, bashes his head on the bedside table with tremendous force and falls flat. He feels a stab of pain, and a moment later the cold floor against his cheek. He lies there for a while groping like a blind man, his temples hammering. He can't believe this; it's past surely, there's nothing the matter with him, the doctor said so, his blood said so. His blood is as pure as spring water, all the readings are normal. He tries to rise but can't control his legs. This is more than he can bear, a great fury grows within him, and he hauls himself up awkwardly in a mixture of anger and tears, sits on his bed again, punches the mattress, cursing quietly and bitterly.

He looks at his kneecaps. What the hell is wrong with them? he thinks. He stays like this for a long time. He bends his knees, wiggles his toes. His fingers, too, they're working fine, they're so sensitive, he's never felt them so sensitive before. His vision is blurred again, he can see only the vague outlines of furniture and other objects in the bedroom. He blinks repeatedly, it makes no difference at all. He sits there immobile, not knowing what to do. Filled with anxiety, his feet planted on the cold floor. Help me, Julie, I'm fading away! But she's not there, he's a lone man on the edge of his bed, and he's helpless.

Finally, he gets to his feet again, his legs just about able to carry him, and walks haltingly across the room, no longer capable of trusting his own body. It's seven-thirty, no one will answer if he phones the medical centre now, he'll have to wait. He finds an old dressing gown. Sits in a chair by the window and listens to the ticking of the wall clock. There's an Opel driving past, and shortly after a BMW. He keeps massaging his thighs the whole time, wants to rub some strength back into them, make them his own legs, the ones he's always had, legs that do as he wants. Fear tingles down his spine, he bites his lip hard and recognises the taste of blood in his mouth. I must phone the doctor, he thinks, must get help with this. What is lurking inside his body? He curls his fingers again, there's nothing wrong with his fine control and his vision has almost returned to normal. Could it just be that he's careless, not concentrating? Did he get up too quickly, was he giddy? No, that couldn't be right, because he lost all strength, it hit him suddenly. He leans on the table. The idea of a virus crosses his mind. It could be that, he's heard so much about it, heard of people who wake up paralysed, and a week later they can walk again. Most probably it's harmless, and the doctor will find it. Something microscopic which is affecting him, certainly not dangerous.

At eight he rings the medical centre, but there's no answer. This means that they don't open until nine, and he spends a long hour waiting. He loiters, filling in the time, eats a slice of bread, eats it slowly, washed down with a cup of coffee. His eyes are always moving to the street to check for unfamiliar cars. At five past nine he phones the medical centre for the second time. Briefly he explains what has happened. It's quiet for a few moments at the other end, as if she's sitting reading something. He waits. Then the receptionist is back on the line. He's told to come in at once.

He considers this as he sits in the waiting room, the fact that he was told to come in immediately. As if he really is in a mess and there isn't a second to lose. What have they written in his notes that's given him such easy access, what do they think? He speculates about bone cancer, he wonders if something has attacked his joints, an infection maybe, a tumour. He looks at the other people waiting, but he can't meet their eyes, he feels too uneasy. He clutches a magazine, but can't concentrate on the royal family. The doctor appears at his surgery door and calls Charlo's name. He's being seen before everyone else. He studies the doctor's face, but it is impassive as always, his smile is the usual calm one, his voice pleasant. Charlo sits down, perched on the very edge of his chair.

"So," the doctor says earnestly. "Your symptoms have returned?"

"Yes," Charlo replies. He looks at the computer screen, but can't read what's written there. "I got up this morning and fell flat on the floor. To be honest, it's really beginning to annoy me." He feels bitter sitting there, he feels afflicted. But the enemy is invisible, it's like shadow-boxing, and he feels a trifle exhausted.

The doctor reads his notes and nods.

"I think we'd better have you admitted for tests."

Charlo gapes. "Admitted?"

"To the Department of Neurology at the Central Hospital," the doctor continues steadily. "It'll only take a couple of days. Not all diseases can be diagnosed with blood samples, so you'll probably have some other tests. Mainly just to exclude things."

"But, hospital?" Charlo stammers. He's filled with anxiety again, he's got a thousand questions. He's never been in hospital before, never had anything wrong with him, never injured himself.

"We need some specialist help," the doctor says. "You mustn't alarm yourself unduly."

"But," says a fraught Charlo, "I've got a daughter, and I've got to collect her from school. She's got to go to the stables, we've got a horse. It needs tending daily. I work at the riding centre myself as a handyman. I'm needed there every day."

The doctor nods evenly. "I'll give you a sick note, of course. As I say it'll take a couple of days. I think we ought to get to the bottom of this now. Don't you agree?"

Charlo nods disconsolately. "Yes, of course. But what more can you tell me, have you got any theories? I mean, do you recognise this?"

The doctor is silent for a few moments. He takes his eyes off the screen and looks at Charlo. "It wouldn't be right for me to start speculating," he says. "I'll leave that to the specialists. You'll be in the best of hands."

"But neurology?" Charlo blurts out. "Why there, exactly?"

"We can't be certain it's neurological," he says quickly, "but we've got to begin somewhere. Try to keep calm. You're doing the sensible thing."

214

Charlo waits while the doctor writes out a referral. He sits studying his hands, now and then glancing round the consulting room. He catches sight of a wall chart of the human body, with all the bones and muscles and sinews depicted. It's quite a machine, he thinks, it's a wonder it works as well as it does, year after year. Hardly surprising that once in a while something goes a little wonky. Perhaps it won't be serious. But the idea of going into hospital is an impossible one for him. He feels small. He thinks about Inga Lill, and of all that she had to endure. The doctor finishes. He asks if Charlo is in any pain, if he needs any medication. He says he doesn't. They shake hands. The doctor wishes him the best of luck. Charlo steals out of the surgery and stands in the street breathing in the fresh air. It all seems unreal to him. He walks, and feels as fit as a fiddle. All his muscles are working, his skeleton thoroughly up to the job. At three o'clock he picks Julie up outside the school.

She looks at him with troubled eyes.

"Neurological?"

She's frightened by the word, too. Medical would have been better, Charlo thinks, less ominous.

"Can you get a bus to the stables?" he asks. "It's just for a couple of days, and then I promise I'll be back again."

She nods and looks at him solemnly. "You needn't worry about me," she says calmly, "I'll find a way."

He drives, thoughts buzzing in his head. Now, he thinks, when everything was working out so well. Now, when there's order and happiness and work, this threatening cloud appears and throws a dark shadow over it all. He tries to shake it off, his hands clutching the steering wheel hard, once again he has the feeling of being perfectly healthy.

"We'll miss you," Julie says, "even if it is only for a couple of days. Møller is so used to you doing everything for him. He sings your praises, d'you realise that?"

Charlo nods contentedly. "You know what?" he says, "I love that feeling of being indispensable. I'd forgotten how good it is."

After that they say no more. The landscape glides past, he sees the apple trees blossoming white and pink, and that the grass is bright green between the patches of wet snow. Could it be that all this will be taken away from him? He doesn't often think about death. Now he sees everything in vivid relief, the lofty sun, the deep blue sky. The hum of the engine, Julie's breathing. He feels so alive. Yes, it will be taken from me, he realises, because all people die. But it won't happen yet. I've earned some good years with Julie. He gives her a sidelong glance. It's us two against the rest, he thinks, we are strong. We'll make out.

A week later he's standing outside the hospital, a small overnight bag in his hand. The bag contains pyjamas, a toothbrush and slippers. Washing things, some underwear and a book. He feels a little cold. He's confused, it's a bit like standing at the frontier of a foreign country, a country whose customs and language

216

you don't know. He can see the outline of a wheelchair inside the door. People are going in and out of the building. He steps through the wide entrance, asks his way to the Department of Neurology. Even saying the word makes him go cold. The term is redolent of mystery and horror. The woman at the desk gives him directions, and he moves off towards the lift. Is there pain and indignity in store? Lack of experience makes him feel uncomfortable. Eventually, he finds the place he's supposed to be and seats himself in a comfortable chair.

First, he has to answer a whole host of questions. They're put to him by an experienced nurse. No, he's never been in hospital. No, he isn't allergic to anything and doesn't take any medicine. No, he isn't aware of any special hereditary conditions in his family. The nurse takes her time, there's no end to the things she needs to know. He answers as best he can, racks his brain, tells the truth. Then she shows him to his bed, which is in a double room. Both beds are unoccupied. He puts his bag down and goes to the window. He's on the tenth floor and has a panorama of the whole town. He turns and looks at his bed again. Are they expecting him to get into it? He's only just got up. He sits in a chair by the window and takes in the view, it's magnificent.

The room is large and there's a whole lot of equipment above the beds, equipment he can't even begin to understand. Eventually he goes to his bed anyway, pulls off his clothes, puts on his pyjamas. Creeps in under the crisply folded duvet. It feels

217

strange lying there like that, he's well after all, nothing troubling him now. Only his thoughts. He lets them wander freely, can't be bothered to channel them.

An hour later he's fetched by a nurse. He follows her, half-clothed. It's been a long time since he's displayed his body to anyone, and he's no spring chicken any more. He feels terribly embarrassed. Feels that everything about him is wrong, the balding head, the hanging stomach. But the nurse is young and pretty. She's courteous and friendly. Yet he's well aware that he's only one of many. She's certainly not interested in him or his destiny, not really; she's careful and vigilant and pleasant, she's doing her duty. In the end, he withdraws into himself, just wants the time to pass, so that he can get it over with and go home again, to Julie. To that fragile, free life of his. They say nothing as they work except, there, that's done, now you're finished Mr Torp. You can go back to your room.

He goes back to his room, gets into bed again. Registers that an elderly man is sleeping in the other bed. He picks up his book and starts reading, realises that he's hungry. Presumably now they're in the office looking at my results, he thinks. Standing there with furrowed brows as they nod at each other and agree. He doesn't know what they're agreeing about. He can't concentrate on his book, so he lays it aside. He lies there looking out of the window at the cloud formations.

They keep it up for three days.

He goes from room to room, lies down for them on couches. He closes his eyes and holds his breath. He follows instructions, he cooperates. Answers everything truthfully. He puts himself in their hands, it's like falling, he doesn't know where he's going to end up, what kind of accident awaits him. The feeling of helplessness is overwhelming. They talk amongst themselves and he can't understand what they're saying. The various machines put the fear of God into him, but none of them hurt. Not until he's given a lumbar puncture. Out of sheer fright he concentrates hard on what they ask him to do. Breathe calmly, in and out, it'll soon be over, it's going fine, Mr Torp.

Now they've been through everything. He lies in bed waiting, feeling himself at their mercy. Afterwards he'll recall this moment. The doctor appears in the door, accompanied by a female nurse. He's carrying a sheaf of papers. Charlo sits up in bed, there's a slight rushing in his head. He's going home at last. His body has been examined in every possible way. Julie is waiting, they're going out to eat. Everything will be as before, he hopes. His back is sweating.

"Mr Torp," the doctor begins. "We need to have a little chat."

He comes over to the bed, bringing a chair with him. Charlo doesn't know whether his seating himself comfortably like this is a good sign or not. Perhaps he's simply grabbing the opportunity to take the weight off his feet for a bit, or perhaps what he has to say will take a long time. Or, he's sitting down to emphasise something serious. For there is a sense of gravity in the room now. Charlo glances at the sheaf of documents: that's his future, that's his sentence. The nurse remains

219

standing at the foot of the bed. Charlo raises the support and adjusts his pillow. His heart is beating hard under his pyjamas.

"We've carried out a number of investigations, and from the results we can say a bit about your problems."

"Right."

He nods solemnly, clasps his hands, sits in his bed like an old man.

"Some diseases are diagnosed primarily by their symptoms. In other words, we don't always have physical findings."

Charlo sits, nodding. He can hear that rushing again, it's louder now.

"In your case, we have some findings, and together with other observations, and the symptoms you've described yourself, we're fairly certain about what we're dealing with. I mean, we have the criteria for a definite diagnosis."

Charlo is so nervous that he sits there gaping. He sees the doctor steeling himself, his mouth tightening.

"Let me put it this way. You're suffering from a disease of the central nervous system. It's chronic. I'll try and explain it so that you'll understand, because this is quite complicated."

Charlo nods and waits.

"It concerns the myelin sheaths surrounding your nerves. You see, your nerves are covered by something like an insulating material. Or a lining, if you will. And this lining can, in certain cases, be attacked by what we call a sclerosis. Over time, this sclerosis will destroy the lining, and small holes will appear in the tissue.

220

Gradually the tissue will turn hard, rather like scar tissue. We can see this on X-rays. In your case the myelin sheaths are slightly frayed. This in turn causes the impulses to be delayed. The impulses that cause your arms and legs to move, in the manner and at the speed you're used to."

"I see."

Charlo drinks in the information, tries to keep up, but feels himself flagging. He can't see clearly. His head feels dizzy.

"The results from your spinal fluid also support this theory. You say that you've had several clinical attacks, and localisation of these also corroborates the theory. You often suffered from colds as a child. And you've also had some problems with your sight, that's right, isn't it?"

"Yes."

He has to strain to form the little word. He feels paralysed sitting there in bed.

"Clinical neurological examination has revealed reduced sensitivity in various parts of your body. Only a small amount so far, but this, too, fits in with the pattern of disease we've built up. There's also an indication of reduced neurotransmission. Unfortunately, we can do nothing about the tissue that's already been attacked. It's impossible to mend. But we can curtail the attacks with medication. If that's appropriate. It depends on the development of the disease."

"The development?"

Charlo's mouth goes dry. He doesn't know what the doctor's talking about, or driving at.

"This disease is very variable. Just how badly you'll be affected is impossible to predict. Some people manage extremely well. In fact, only a third or, I should say, a quarter of all patients experience major problems. The prognosis isn't necessarily that bad. We just have to hope that yours will be a less severe case, and such cases do exist."

"But what happens if I get worse? Will I keep falling down?"

"As I said, I don't want to make predictions," the doctor says. "We need time, we must see how it develops."

"But could I become paralysed? Is that what you're saying?"

"Only in the very worst case. Let's be positive, there's no reason for it to happen to you."

"But it *could* happen?"

"In the worst case, yes. But the odds that you'll avoid it are considerable."

Charlo sweeps a hand over his balding head.

"So, is there a name for this thing? What is this disease we're talking about?"

The doctor lowers his eyes and looks at his papers.

"The disease is named after what is actually happening to you. Sclerosis in the tissue surrounding the nerves."

"Yes?"

The doctor looks at him earnestly.

"Multiple sclerosis."

Charlo falls back on to his pillow. His eyes dart about the room; it seems to be swimming in front of him. No, he thinks, they're wrong. People with multiple sclerosis become paralysed, they end up in wheelchairs. They don't live all that long. I must get home, he thinks, Julie and I are going out to eat, I can't just lie here listening to this nonsense.

"Do you want to call somebody?" the doctor says quietly. He nods towards the phone. It looks as if he wants to leave the room. He has nothing more to say.

"Multiple sclerosis?" Charlo whispers. "Are you absolutely sure?"

The doctor glances at the nurse.

"We're fairly certain. Your symptoms are typical of the disease. Try to be calm. For all we know, you may have many good years ahead of you."

Yes, that's what he's always believed. Many good years with Julie and Crazy. His mouth is so dry. He wants to get out of bed. He wants to stand and prove to himself, and to the two people in white, that he's well and can use his legs. And as long as he's well, his legs will work. His hands begin to shake uncontrollably. In desperation, he clasps them beneath the duvet.

"As things are," the doctor says, "you can go straight home. You must stay in contact with your medical practitioner. He'll discuss medication and suchlike more closely with you, should you begin to need it."

Charlo nods feebly. This must be a bad dream, and he'll wake up soon. Then they just go, and he's left lying there alone. The room feels large and cold, he pulls up the duvet, he wants to hide away from everything. This isn't happening, he thinks. Why do catastrophes always head my way? He's so shaken that he feels nauseous. Suddenly, he pushes the duvet aside, gets up and goes across to the mirror. He stands staring at himself, his broad face, his grey eyes. Fear has made them lighter. For a while he stands there immobile, his hands propped on the washbasin. Then he goes back to his bed, packs his few belongings, and dresses. A nurse appears and asks if he needs a taxi. He gives a slight shake of his head. No, he's got his own car, he doesn't need help of any kind. He clenches his fists. Feels that he's on the verge of tears, there's a pressing at his throat, a stinging under his eyelids. Even so, she stands there watching him with a mild expression. So that he can blurt out his despair if he wants to. Lay his head against her uniform and sob like a child. But he doesn't do it. He turns his back and hunches his shoulders. Hears her leaving and closing the door. He puts his quilted jacket on, looks around the room. Then, with rapid steps, he makes for the door.

He gets home and collapses into a chair.

His bag thumps to the floor. He can't be bothered to unpack, it can stand there with his slippers and pyjamas reminding him of this awful day. Multiple sclerosis. The words are like a big, slimy insect inside his mouth, and suddenly he retches. There are tears in his eyes. He sits crumpled and despairing in his chair, as he remembers the doctor's words. Those damned sheaths, decaying, it's unbearable. He imagines his nerves as a network of brittle, worn out wires which can no longer conduct electricity. From now on he'll get slower and weaker. From now on he'll find that his legs won't obey him, that his brain will send messages that never arrive. He tells his feet to drum on the floor. They do so, without difficulty, and he's not slow, either. Take it easy now, don't cry. The prognosis isn't that bad, of course he'll be one of those who'll manage the disease well, he's sure of it. He gets up and takes a few turns around the room. Talking sternly to himself. There are two voices inside him now, arguing.

Why should you get off more lightly than other people, d'you think you're invincible?

Haven't I been through enough in my miserable life as it is, this is completely unfair, I don't deserve it.

You're forgetting something important. Think about what you've done. Consider that.

So I must be punished now, is that what you mean?

You'll have to atone in some way or other. It's your reckoning we're talking about, and it doesn't balance.

I do Harriet Krohn no good by sitting in a wheelchair.

Don't say that. One day you'll die. The debt must be repaid before then.

I don't owe anything, I've been unlucky, damn you!

On an impulse he goes to the bookcase. He looks at the encyclopaedia, pulls out volume eight. He finds the letter M and begins to search. Multiple, multiple personality, and here, multiple sclerosis. His eyes move down the page. Disseminated sclerosis, from the Greek *skleros*, hard, and Latin *disseminare*, scatter. A chronic disease of the nervous system, the cause of which, despite intense research, remains obscure. Examination of the brains and spinal cords of patients who have died of multiple sclerosis show a decrease in the myelin layer that surrounds the nerve fibres. There is also an increase in the connective tissue in the brain and spinal cord. This causes scar tissue which is harder than the normal tissue of the central nervous system, and the name of the disease derives from this. These changes are often spread out in the brain and spinal cord, and the term "multiple" refers to this phenomenon. Many hypotheses have been advanced for the cause of the disease, but none have yet been proven. Infection, especially viral infection, poisoning, lack of certain elements in the diet, allergies and many other causes have been blamed. The two major theories are that either the disease is caused by a viral infection with a very long latent period that takes years to manifest itself, and which also develops very slowly; the other is that the disease is linked to autoimmunity, in other words, that the organism has a reaction to its own tissue.

So, is he allergic to himself? He shakes his head and reads on.

The symptoms are muscle stiffness, and poor control of movement, especially in the legs. Impaired or double vision is also very common. Muscle tightening and reflex twitching can be very troublesome. As yet there is no treatment that can cure the disease. Hormone treatment, especially with ACTH and similar products, appears to shorten the acute attacks of the illness. There are multiple sclerosis associations in countries right across the world, including Norway.

He slams the book shut.

No, he's not joining any association, he's not acknowledging this, he doesn't want to know about other people who are suffering from the same thing, he doesn't want to talk to them. He goes to the window and stands there with his hand in front of his mouth. Lays his brow against the cool glass. It's happening now, inside his body, his nerve coverings are being eaten up, and he can't prevent it. It's happening as he stands here, breathing into his hand, and it will go on for the rest of his life. Oh, God, now he'll have to pay. He glances quickly up at the sky, it's just the same bloody blue. Terrifying images appear in his mind's eye. Him, sitting in a chair with a rug across his knees. A urine flask partly hidden beneath the rug; useless, white uncoordinated feet. His face and body distorted by cortisone, an unpleasant whiff of disease, a vanishing physique. An on-looker on life. Watching while others live, do and work. Or even worse, he's bedridden. One morning he wakes and can't get up. He must go to a nursing home and wither away in a corner with a bunch of geriatrics, pale, dry people with distant, glassy eyes. Drinking red juice through a straw, and not allowed to smoke. He can't tear himself away from the window, from this position. His mouth is dry as sandpaper. He's vibrating like a cymbal, someone has struck him hard, there's a singing in his ears. Here comes his neighbour Erlandson, who raises a hand and waves. He can't wave back. He can't make any decision, the next step is impossible. Calmly does it. Go into the shower. You must get air into your lungs, Charlo, there's plenty of time left. Maybe.

He goes into the bathroom. Stands there for a long time under the stream of water, soaping his sick body. He looks down over his thighs, his arms and hands and feet. He sees everything in a different light. Are there more secrets inside his body? Is there more lying in wait, soon to break out and knock him to the ground? Inga Lill, you don't know it, but I'll have to go through hell. Why you and me? What about Julie? What horrors are lurking in her genes? Are we a blighted family? What's the point of living an honest life, when everything's ordained from the start and can't be altered? What's the point of sweating for Møller, when I may end up in a wheelchair? He steps out of the shower, feeling his diagnosis like a severe increase in weight. It lies particularly over his shoulders and breast. The diagnosis clings to him like something clammy, that can't be washed away, the minutes spent in the shower give him no sensation of being cleansed. He dries himself hard with his towel, his movements are defiant, but the rage, which is beginning to smoulder inside him, finds no vent. He takes a few quick breaths in the steamy room.

He'll have to ring Julie. But first he must prepare himself, he can't tell her the truth, he'll have to sidestep it and come up with something that sounds harmless. Something curable, that can't be inherited, isn't contagious. He goes to the phone and dials her number. The voice at the other end makes tears come to his eyes, and for an instant he wants to blurt out the whole thing. Find some care and comfort and sympathy. Everything he needs so badly. But he pulls himself together, gets back on track and is strong once more.

"Well," he says, "it's all over now, I'm back at home again, thank goodness.

"What did they say? Well, there's not a great deal to tell. Some sort of virus, that's all, inside some nerves. It'll get better by itself, presumably, and if it doesn't, I'll get some medicine.

"No, I'm not off sick now, I'm ready for work, no restrictions at all. Just keep on working.

"No, they don't know how I got it, it's a mystery, they say, but people manage fine for years, there's nothing to worry about. It could have been worse. You know, I'm feeling great, not at all downcast."

"Will you pick me up?" she asks now.

"Yes, I'll fetch you. Where would you like to eat? Shall we go to Hannah's Kitchen?"

"But it's so expensive."

"I couldn't care less about that," he blusters.

She laughs. He relaxes a bit. Perhaps with willpower he can keep the disease at bay. He's heard of such things, he believes that anything's possible. He can steel himself, force the illness to retreat. Make himself immune.

"I'll be with you in half an hour," he says into the receiver, "just got to change my clothes." He puts down the phone and goes into the bathroom. Stands before the mirror buttoning a shirt. He finds a pair of grey trousers and examines himself. He looks good. He doesn't look like a sick man, so he needn't behave like one, either. But even so. Pain, decay. Helplessness. In and out of hospital. What sort of life can he expect? Help with everything. A body that gradually goes downhill and ultimately becomes useless. The remainder of his life on Social Security. He bustles about the house, wrestling with a jumble of thoughts, then starts at the sound of the doorbell.

Sejer is standing on the doorstep, dressed in a newly pressed light blue shirt, suave and authoritative.

"Good to see you again, Mr Torp."

His grey gaze is sharp. Charlo backs into the hallway, defiance swelling in his breast. Why can't they leave him in peace! He's got so much else to worry about now, he's a sick man, he's got to meet Julie. He glowers at Sejer.

"What's the problem?" Charlo snaps.

He fills the doorway, his eyes hard. He's not available today, not at any price. His mind is already full of catastrophes, of putative outcomes for what has befallen him. He gasps for breath and plucks up courage.

"I'm busy."

Sejer holds his gaze.

"We'd like you to accompany us to the station, Mr Torp."

He glances in the direction of the road. Charlo comes to the doorstep again. Now he glimpses the patrol car. A uniformed officer is at the wheel.

"No," he says angrily, "you'll have to excuse me, it's just not convenient!"

Sejer produces a thin smile.

"I see, but I'm afraid it is convenient for us."

230

He's standing there as firmly as ever, just as powerful and authoritative. Charlo shakes his head determinedly, moves back a couple of paces.

"The thing is," he says impetuously, "that I was discharged from hospital an hour ago. I've had a lot going on, and on top of that I've got an appointment. In fact, I'm running late." He looks at his watch demonstratively. He's simmering, quivering. He's frightened he'll lose his temper and shout.

"We know you've been at the hospital, Mr Torp. I'm sorry if we've turned up at an inconvenient moment," Sejer says, "but you've got no option this time. We want to interview you down at the station. Now."

An interview. Not a chat. Charlo folds his arms and gives the policeman a bitter look. He remembers that he must appear innocent. This isn't happening, he thinks, this is just one of my dreams, it seems familiar.

"Surely it's possible to do it another day," he says, waving his hand irritably. "My daughter is waiting for me, we're going out to dinner, I'm just leaving."

Sejer takes a step forward. "Phone your daughter straight away and cancel the engagement."

His voice is now a resonant command.

"How long will it take? I could ring and postpone it for an hour or two. Would that do?"

"No. You must ring and cancel, and then come with us."

Charlo gasps for breath. This persecution infuriates him so much that sweat beads on his brow. He turns on his heel and goes into the living room, lifts the handset and dials Julie's number. He crushes the spiral of telephone cord between his fingers.

"Hi there, it's Dad again. I'm going to be a little late. Something's cropped up that I'll have to deal with first. Yes, I will explain, just wait for me and I'll be along in a while. No, you don't need to worry, it's just some stupid detail, but it can't wait. I could phone when I'm ready to leave if you want. I've got to go now, someone's waiting. No, he's not a friend of mine, it's just some mess from long ago that I've got to clear up. Straight away. I'll call as soon as I'm finished. See you soon."

He cradles the phone, and stays there brooding. He feels he's standing beside himself, that everything is unreal. But he knows this is no dream. The blow has fallen, they've come for him.

He gets into the back of the patrol car.

He thinks about the thing that's stricken him. His central nervous system will slowly let him down. Everything outside the windows seems distant, he's a tourist in his own street, in his own life. He's lived in this street for years, now he sees it all for the first time: the low, brown timber houses, the neat hedges, the occasional ornamental shrub by a house wall, soon to flower and decorate the whole street. A young officer with curly hair is driving the car. Charlo meets his gaze in the mirror and looks away resentfully. He won't give them anything, not a thought, not a word. They don't know what he's made of, how composed he can be. He lowers his head and contemplates the zip of his jacket.

232

He curls his toes, they feel spry. My God, what toes he's got, they obey his smallest command! The doctor has made a mistake. Sejer is taking a shot in the dark. He's gambling everything now, and he's going to lose. I won't break, he thinks, I must just keep a clear head, I mustn't give myself away.

The officer drives slowly, the car is a Ford Mondeo. The short drive to the police station takes an eternity. He has the constant feeling that he's seeing the town for the first time, in a sort of sudden attack of clear-sightedness. There's Cash & Carry, there's Tina's Flowers. There's the model on the hoarding in her skimpy, lace underwear, smiling prettily as always. There's the church on the hill above the town and the fire station with its splendid towers. He sees the courthouse looming up on the right.

Sejer opens the door for him and Charlo steps out. He straightens up in the sunshine, fills his lungs with air. He's struggling with a kind of numbness, he mustn't let it take hold, he must tense every muscle in his body and be alert. Stay ahead. Like playing chess, he thinks, and he was a good player at one time. He stands there a while, drinking it in, the sun glittering on the windows, a beautiful tree with bare branches, people strolling in the streets. This is what they want to take away from him. But it'll cost them dear, he thinks as he walks through the door. The reception is dim. The building envelops him.

CHAPTER
FOURTEEN

His irritation and nervousness act as a strong curb on his body. They make his movements abrupt and irascible, he can't help it, even though he'd like to be leisurely, lithe and aloof. He'd like to saunter into the office, seat himself with exquisite languor, be confident and secure and on top of things. He isn't confident. He jerks the chair out from the desk, causing it to make a loud scraping noise. He pushes his illness out of his mind, plants his feet firmly on the floor and concentrates on his innocence. It's the thing he must put across during the interview, he feels entitled to it because he didn't want events to turn out so, it just happened, and he must make the man with greying hair understand this.

He notices the dog, Frank. He's been lying near the wall, now he comes ambling over on his large paws to say hello. Charlo can't resist the temptation to bend and stroke the wrinkled dog. His fingers vanish in his coat, which feels peculiar, like sandpaper. He looks into his black eyes. One moment he thinks there's the reflection of a gentle soul; the next, he sees nothing, they just shine, like buttons. Sejer walks about the room, Charlo looks at him sideways on, he appears purposeful, comfortable. He retrieves some documents from a shelf, glances swiftly at his watch, and takes his place in his chair. It's all accomplished with slow movements, a tardiness that irritates Charlo.

"Well, I think you owe me a good explanation at least," Charlo says severely.

He tries to sound determined, but doesn't quite pull it off. Sejer glances up at him. His eyes are at first deadly earnest, but then they soften.

"Well," he says, resting his elbows on the desk, "there are a number of things I need to clarify. You know how it is, we work slowly and methodically. Investigation takes time. Occasionally, we have to pester people with questions about what they've been up to. I'm sorry you feel hounded, but it's very important work."

He looks at Charlo across the desk.

"Let's make a start. Let's take the seventh of November again, from the beginning."

Charlo meets his eyes.

"I've said all I have to say about that day, and you've made notes. I've said a lot more than I needed to, I can't be bothered to beat about the bush any more, you must ask definite questions, and I'll answer to the best of my ability!"

His outburst resonates in the room. Sejer nods seriously.

"In that case I'll simply ask you to repeat what you've previously said."

"But what is all this fuss about the seventh of November?"

"It concerns the murder of Harriet Krohn. We're building up a picture of the traffic, it's important for us. Every small movement in the area."

"Really?"

Sejer glances at his documents.

"I've got a suggestion. Let's talk about that trip to Kongsberg, Mr Torp. It interests me."

"There's nothing interesting about it."

"Quite the opposite. According to your previous explanation, you went to Kongsberg. You walked around the town for an hour. Tell me about that hour."

Charlo shakes his head uncertainly.

"Are you joking?"

"I never joke. This is deadly serious, Mr Torp, I want you to be clear about that."

Charlo feels a wave of resignation. He clutches the arms of his chair.

"There's not much to say about that hour. I walked around looking at shop windows. My feet were frozen."

"What did you see in those windows?"

Again Charlo shakes his head. "What a ridiculous question. And you wonder why you need a long time to solve a murder?"

"Can you name anything, Mr Torp?"

"Name what I saw? In the shop windows? What's the point of that?"

He folds his arms and sticks his jaw out.

"I need an outline of that hour. Those sixty minutes spent at Kongsberg. We can talk about the reason later. What did you see in the windows?"

Charlo wonders if he's being serious. It certainly looks like it.

"Most of it was probably clothes and stuff. But to be honest . . ."

"Clothes. OK. I'm making a note. What else did you look at?"

"Well, there was some sports equipment. I can't remember that well, I wasn't paying much attention, I was just mooching about."

Sejer nods. "You were mooching about for sixty minutes. You looked at shop windows, but you weren't paying much attention. And your feet were cold. So why did you keep walking for an hour?"

"I had nothing else to do. Surely a man can walk about the town without it signifying anything untoward?"

"Where did you park the Honda?"

He shrugs helplessly. "At the railway station," he says quickly. It just pops out. He knows nothing about Kongsberg, he's only been there a couple of times. He realises that he'll have to conjure up an entire city out of lies. Lie about streets he doesn't know, thoughts he hasn't thought, people he hasn't seen.

"And you went from the railway station and into town on foot?"

"That's right."

"Were there many people about?"

"No. The weather was too bad."

"Did you go in anywhere? To a cafe?"

"No."

"Why did you want to go to Kongsberg?"

"It was just a whim. As I said, I was quite down at that point, I drove about to kill time; you've got so much spare time when you're unemployed. I can't sit watching television all day, and I enjoy driving. Being on the move. My God, things were hard sometimes."

He speaks tensely, clenching his teeth. Disease is waiting out there in the shadows, threatening him, he moves his feet beneath the desk, tries to collect himself.

"Did you walk over the whole town, or just in the streets of the town centre?"

"I stayed mainly in the town centre."

"Kongsberg's a small place. Didn't you walk round the same streets several times?"

"Quite possibly, I can't remember."

"So, it's somewhat hazy in your memory, this hour spent in Kongsberg?"

"Yes, I suppose it is."

"It's hazy because you weren't feeling good?"

"Presumably."

"Did you buy any fuel on the way?"

"No, I had a full tank."

"Did you speak to anyone at all that evening?"

"No, I didn't meet anyone I knew. I hardly ever do, I mostly keep myself to myself."

"So, that entire evening, from the time you left Blomsgate at six o'clock, until the time you returned at eleven, you didn't speak to anyone. Apart from the young man who collided with you?"

"That's right."

Sejer looks down at his papers again.

"Do you think you're temperamental by nature?"

"I thought you wanted to chart the traffic?"

"Yes. And you were a part of that traffic. Let me repeat the question. Are you an excitable man, Mr Torp?"

"Not at all. I'm actually quite placid. Ask Julie."

"But you weren't that evening. You say it's rare for you. So why did you lose control on the seventh of November at half past ten?"

"I've explained all that."

"I want to hear it again."

"I was out of sorts, as I said. For many reasons."

"Tell me what they were again."

Charlo props his head on his hands.

"I told you that I had debts. That people were after me. I wasn't sleeping at night and I couldn't make ends meet."

"But now the debts are paid?"

Charlo bites his lip.

"Yes."

"How did you manage that, Mr Torp?"

"As I said before, I won some money."

Sejer nods slowly.

"What sort of gambling?"

Charlo's brain tries to work rapidly.

"On the lottery," he blurts out. And regrets it immediately. He can't think fast enough. Reduced neurotransmission is affecting me already, he suddenly realises, and it'll get worse.

"So, you got lucky?"

"I do actually get lucky sometimes. But it isn't the norm. God knows, I've had my fair share of misery."

"And you rushed off and paid your debts, got a job at the riding centre and were reconciled with your daughter?"

"Yes, things are much better now."

He moistens his lips, tries to parry Sejer's words, get a bit of perspective. He's uncertain about where all this is leading.

"How much did you win, Mr Torp?"

"It was a tidy sum."

"Is the amount a secret?"

A chill runs through Charlo. He tries to cling on, but realises that he's sliding into confusion.

"I just can't see the point of all these questions. Surely, what I win on the lottery is my own business."

"That's all right, Mr Torp," Sejer says brusquely. "We can get that information ourselves, it's the least of our worries."

His heart sinks.

"It was a syndicate," he interjects. "Which divided up a large win."

Sejer leans back comfortably. "And I suppose you can't remember the name of the person who bought the ticket?"

"No, I bet through a friend, it was an impulse."

"Well that's all right, then. I'm sure you know the name of your friend?"

"I don't go round shopping my friends. You people will only start plaguing him with questions."

"But it's entirely innocent, Mr Torp. A lottery win. A name, a date and an amount is all we require. I'm sure he'll help us if we ask him nicely."

"No. Let's get to the point now. What's all this about? My daughter Julie is waiting for me, we're going out."

"It's about the seventh of November, as I've already explained. It concerns a murder, and I need a murderer."

"Yes, you said that the last time I was here. But that's got nothing to do with me."

"You were in Fredboesgate at a very interesting moment."

"No, I wasn't. I was just driving through. It only took a few seconds."

"You have to leave the main road to drive through Hamsund. Why did you want to go to Hamsund?"

"No special reason. I've explained why: I like driving."

"Even when the road conditions are appalling?"

"The road conditions don't matter."

"Were you dressed for that sort of weather?"

"I was as a matter of fact."

"What were you wearing?"

"I can't remember, I've got several jackets."

"Could it have been a green parka?"

"It could have been. Don't ask me questions when you already know the answers."

"So you have got one?"

"I had one."

"You've got rid of it? Why, Mr Torp?"

"Because it was old and worn out."

"What did you do with it?"

"I chucked it in a rubbish skip. The seams were coming apart. The pockets had worn through and several buttons were missing."

Sejer begins making notes again, Charlo tries to read them, but can't. He's not seeing too well either, his vision is blurred. He blinks in bewilderment. He looks at his watch, feels the despair growing as he thinks of Julie waiting. He's not doing that well. Lying to Julie is easy. This feels impossible. He rubs his face with tired hands. Sits there with his eyes hidden behind his palms. Surely they aren't allowed to send sick people to prison, he thinks. Automatically, he reaches for his back pocket, where he keeps his tobacco.

"May I smoke here?"

Sejer nods. "Of course. I'll get you an ashtray. Are you thirsty, Mr Torp?"

"Yes."

He gets out a bottle of Farris mineral water. Charlo attempts to roll a cigarette, his fingers are trembling slightly.

"Are you feeling threatened, Mr Torp?"

"Threatened? By you? No. But I don't like the way this conversation is going."

"Then let's go another way. There's a lot to choose from, an entire evening, several hours. Let's stay here in town."

He pours out some water and sits down again.

"Before you left for Kongsberg you walked around the town here. For about two hours. According to your first account. Tell me about those two hours."

Charlo lights his cigarette, inhales greedily.

242

"Christ, you're fond of repetitions. I walked about looking at shop windows. I looked at underwear and shoes and furniture. I looked at people, I looked at advertisement hoardings, at women and at cars. I looked at the boats on the river. I looked at one of your cars, out on patrol."

"For two hours?"

"Yes. And then I went on the jetty."

"What did you do on the jetty?"

Charlo looks at him across the desk.

"I thought about jumping in."

"Jumping into the river? Drowning yourself?"

"Yes. That's it. The truth is what you want, isn't it? That's the truth."

"So you weren't just out of sorts. You were practically suicidal?"

"You could say that."

"So on the evening of the seventh of November you didn't just feel a bit down. You were mentally unstable?"

"If that's the way you want it, it's fine by me. Unstable. That's right. It was like being put through a mangle."

Charlo draws the ashtray towards him and taps the ash off his cigarette. He drains half his glass of Farris and dries his mouth.

"Hardly surprising you got so worked up about the collision," says Sejer.

"Yes, I went completely berserk. I was wound up to breaking point. There's a limit to what you can put up with in one evening."

"That young man, was he frightened?"

"He sat there shaking like a leaf. His face was as white as chalk. I regret behaving so badly."

"Back to that long stroll of yours. Did you go in anywhere?"

"No."

"With all that bad weather, you didn't succumb to the temptation of going into a shop and warming yourself up?"

"No, I stayed outdoors."

"Were you wet?"

"I think we can safely say I was pretty damp. My boots were letting in water."

"Even so, despite all this, you drove to Kongsberg and continued to wander the streets there? While the sleet fell on you?"

"Yes, strangely enough."

"So you think it was strange?"

"When I think back on it now, or rather, when I have to explain it, it does sound rather pathetic."

"Did you feel pathetic?"

"That too. I think I can safely say I went through most emotions that evening. The entire gamut."

"So, even though you weren't especially concerned about what you could see in the shop windows, your thoughts were in high gear?"

"They were. My head was about to burst, searching for a solution."

"A solution to your financial problems?"

"Yes. I considered robbing a bank."

At this, he sends Sejer a challenging look.

"And why didn't you turn this idea into action?"

"I'm not a criminal," he says curtly, and fixes his eyes on the detective.

"What are your thoughts on this Hamsund murder we're investigating?"

Charlo places his hands on the desk, clasps them and twiddles his thumbs.

"I haven't given it all that much consideration. But it's made an impression, naturally. She was elderly, lonely and ill. Not that age makes any difference, murder is still murder, I mean, legally. But for some reason people get so worked up when it's an old person. Well, in a way they're more vulnerable than someone younger, that's probably why we think it's so bad. But nobody knows what really happened in that kitchen."

Sejer glances up at him.

"So it took place in the kitchen, Mr Torp?"

Charlo catches his breath.

"That was what it said in the papers. She was found there, everyone knows that."

"Sorry to disappoint you. That detail has never been in the newspapers."

"Then it was on the radio. I know I've heard it!"

Sejer doesn't reply. For a long time he makes notes, and Charlo starts sweating at his hairline. He can't afford mistakes like that. Think, a voice inside him says, think before you answer!

"What did you mean when you said 'what really happened'?"

"The details. The lead up. What caused her to die."

245

"That's why we're searching for the culprit. And if we don't find him, he won't be able to explain or defend himself."

"Quite so," says Charlo. "The question is whether he thinks it's worth the trouble. There's always a chance that he won't be believed. Won't be understood. If you know what I mean."

"You haven't got a very high opinion of our legal system, have you?"

"No, not really."

"But your record is clean. You've never been in contact with the police before."

"No, but I read the papers. And if the perpetrator really believed that a confession would be in his best interests he'd turn up, naturally."

"What about you?" Sejer says. "Do you think a confession would benefit the culprit in any way?"

"That depends on how he's placed. What sort of man he is. If he's got family, or others around him who are important to him, he'll get separated from them. For a long time."

"Most people who're in prison get visits. Post and email. Telephone calls."

"Well, that sounds nice."

"No, not nice, but reasonable."

Just as he relaxes, he feels the proximity of disease in his body. It seems instantly paralysing. He attempts to concentrate on the murder, which he did commit, but not with intent or premeditation or malice. He finds it hard to believe that he's still sitting there, that he hasn't run out in frustration. He's caught up in this conversation, this duel. He rolls himself another cigarette and drinks some Farris. Opens a button on his shirt. The dog is sleeping by the wall.

"What about you, Mr Torp? Did you grow up here?"

"Yes, I was born over on the east side of town. Never lived anywhere else. I grew up close to the Methodist church. We used to muck about down by the river. I know this town like the back of my hand. A lovely town — a bit of a mess, perhaps, unplanned. But you have to put up with that. Have you ever stood by the railway line at night and looked across to the brewery? All those bridge spans and glittering lights. It's fantastic."

Sejer nods. Charlo glances at the pictures on his wall.

"Is that your beautiful young wife?"

Sejer follows his gaze. "That's my daughter, Ingrid. And my grandson, Matteus."

"He's black. Adopted?"

"From Somalia."

Charlo scrutinises the photos.

"The civil war, eh?"

"Yes, there are lots of orphans there. What about you. You've got a daughter."

"She'll be seventeen soon. A clever young woman. She keeps me on the straight and narrow."

"You need that? You need someone to keep you on the straight and narrow?"

Charlo nods wearily. "I was a gambling addict in the past. She's frightened I'll revert to my old ways. She hasn't had an easy time, I brought a great deal of shame on my family."

"But it's not going to happen again?"

"No, that I'm certain of. I feel deep down that it's over."

"A lottery win and, hey presto, you're hooked on gambling again?"

"I'd long decided to kick the habit. It was no good any more, I was a nervous wreck. There were rumours that someone would be coming to get me. I couldn't sleep at night, it was totally impossible to relax. Life was hell, to be brutally honest."

Charlo coaxes the dog. It walks over to him and sits down by his chair.

"How long have I got to sit here? Time's getting on. Julie's waiting."

"We don't need to hurry, Mr Torp. We'll take whatever time we need. It's not in my interests to keep you sitting here feeling nervous or mistreated."

Charlo lets go of Frank. The dog sits there a little despondently, looking at him, then he returns to his place by the wall.

"Let's move on," says Sejer. "Perhaps now it's time to establish what you actually wanted to do in Hamsund. What errand you had there."

Charlo sits up in his chair.

"As I said before. I didn't have any errand. Turning off the main road was an impulse. I remember seeing the floodlit church and turning off automatically. I just wanted to pass the time, so that I could go home and turn in. That's what it was all about. Making the days pass."

248

"What was the time when you turned off towards Hamsund?"

"It was probably almost ten-thirty."

"I see. And then you drove round a bit?"

"Yes, I passed the railway station, and drove up the street there."

"Up Fredboesgate?"

"Yes. I just drove through it, looked at the nice old houses, they're really quite charming, I've heard they're listed. I drove to the end of the street, and then turned around."

"What made you park the car and get out?"

"I didn't."

Sejer bends over his documents.

"Didn't you park your red Honda Accord behind the old hotel?"

"Not that I recall."

"No, but someone else noticed, and recalled it."

"It must have been a different car. No, I never got out of the car, I'm quite certain of that."

"You weren't going to visit someone?"

"I don't know anyone in Hamsund."

"So, it was after your little trip through Fredboesgate that you had your accident?"

"Yes."

"You were mentally unstable, intermittently suicidal, soaking wet, worried about the future, but despite all this you still wanted to look at some listed buildings?"

"Yes. You see, I was a bit up and down, slightly confused. But as I said, it was all about trying to pass the time."

"Perhaps you sat in your car, behind the old hotel, and had a rest?"

"I really can't remember about the hotel. That I parked there."

"If you were down in the dumps as you say, it may be hard to remember details. But I'm sure they'll gradually return. That's why we're sitting here. And the time, Mr Torp? Are you quite sure it was ten-thirty when you got to Hamsund?

"I remember that I looked at the time."

"But your car was parked behind the hotel at ten o'clock."

"That can't be right."

"It's right according to my documents. Perhaps you're mistaken?"

"It was dark and all that, and filthy weather. If someone saw a car similar to mine behind the hotel, I don't think that means much. People get things wrong all the time. And I'm not the only person who drives a Honda."

"Its reliability will appear in the long run. I'm sure you're wrong about the time. That's hardly a crime, but I need to have it exactly. Did you sit there, perhaps, wondering if you ought to visit someone?"

"I've already said that I don't know anyone there."

"But the flowers, Mr Torp. Who were they for? You had a large bunch of flowers with you."

Charlo slowly blanches. He clenches his teeth.

"Now you're completely on the wrong track," he says.

"A large, mixed bouquet. Really nice. A lot of work had been put into it."

"I never buy flowers. This is all nonsense."

"Try to think back, Mr Torp. To the flower shop."

"Which flower shop?"

"Tina's Flowers, next to Cash & Carry."

"I've never been there."

"The seventh of November, just before eight in the evening. They close at eight, you only just made it. Who were the flowers for?"

"I'm telling you, you're on the wrong track!"

"They were for a woman, weren't they?"

"I don't know any women in Hamsund."

Silence. Sit there, feel the other's strength, weigh your words, think. Plan the next move, remember. Save your skin, get out of this room. Oh, God! He's not going to get out. Sejer interrupts his thoughts.

"The bouquet cost two hundred and fifty kroner. You spent a lot of money, it must have been important to you."

Charlo lowers his head and is silent, drums his fingers on the desk.

"You'll have to find another angle because I can't go with this one." He stares doggedly at the desktop.

"Mr Torp," Sejer says quietly. "It's not our belief or suspicion that you bought flowers on the seventh of November. It's something we know. So, let's take them with us to Hamsund and have done with it. We want to move on, don't we?"

"My mind's really tired. I've been in hospital the past few days. Can we take a break?"

CHAPTER
FIFTEEN

"What are you thinking about?" Sejer asks.

"I'm thinking that you're going to start giving me a hard time."

"You think I'm going to put you through it?"

"Obviously."

"Only if it's necessary. So what did you do before the riding centre? I mean, before you were unemployed?"

"I worked in a car showroom. I was a pretty good salesman. Honda and Subaru. New and used."

"Liked it?"

"Yes. I had a great time. Before I really began to mess things up."

"Why did you give it up? Did it close?"

"No," he says candidly. "I was sacked on the spot. I embezzled a small sum because of my gambling debts. They never reported me. But, you know, I was on my uppers. And that was the biggest misdeed of my life." He looks straight at Sejer. "It was done on the spur of the moment, though, it wasn't anything I planned to do. The temptation was too great. I had debts even then."

"So what's your opinion of something that's planned? Does that make it a worse crime?"

"Yes, don't you think so?"

Sejer drinks his Farris.

"Obviously, we use many different terms. Premeditated, wilful and involuntary. And there are reasons for that. And then there are mitigating circumstances. These are actually quite a new concept in judicial terms. In the past they didn't exist. A murder was a murder, and was punished in the same way. But your embezzlement probably had some extenuating circumstances. Presumably you were desperate?"

"I was desperate," Charlo nods, "and I was also ashamed. I was unable to look after my family, and that was a huge, unbearable humiliation."

"That's not difficult to understand."

"Luckily, we managed to keep it from Julie, she wasn't all that old at the time. But now I've bared my soul to her. I've told her everything."

"There are no secrets between you any more?"

"No. No big ones at least."

He drains his glass.

"Except for the fact that you're sitting here," says Sejer, "haven't you got to explain that to her as well?"

"Naturally. In one way or another."

"What will you tell her?"

"The truth, of course. That I'm only being questioned as a witness."

"You think that's what you are?"

"Am I a suspect? If that's the case, I assume you've got a duty to inform me."

Sejer nods gravely. "Well," he says, "we have reasonable grounds for suspicion. That's why you're here."

"Is that so," says Charlo. "You've come out with it at last. You couldn't exactly be accused of jumping the gun."

"Let's tidy things up a bit," Sejer says. "Certain things are getting in the way. Unimportant things."

"Such as what?"

"Your trip to Kongsberg. Can we sweep that out of the way?"

"Why?"

"You were never there. You're simply trying to fill up the evening."

"Of course I went to Kongsberg. Why should that be a problem?"

"I believe you drove straight to Hamsund. And there was a large bunch of flowers on the seat next to you. You parked behind the old hotel, and got out with the flowers."

"You've obviously got it all worked out. So, what did I do next?"

"You went to number four Fredboesgate. The green house. And rang Harriet Krohn's bell."

Now it's been said. It's out in the open. But there isn't such a roaring in his ears as he'd anticipated. He says: "No. No, I didn't go to her house, I don't even know who she is."

"I don't believe that either. I think she was selected fairly randomly. But armed with a bouquet of flowers it was easy to gain access."

"I never bought any flowers!"

"Easy now, Mr Torp. Listen to me. We ought to try to tidy things up here, and not spend time on trivialities. We know that you had flowers."

254

"I bought them for Julie."

"So, they were for her? But back then, in November, when she wouldn't see you? You've already explained about that."

"I was trying to get her to forgive me."

"But it didn't work?"

"I knocked on the door of her room, but she wasn't there."

"So what did you do with the flowers?"

"I threw them away."

"Where?"

"Just in a dustbin, somewhere in town. I was upset."

"You had very little money. But you splashed out on expensive flowers?"

"When it comes to Julie, nothing is too much."

"So this visit to her digs is something you've only just remembered now?"

"Yes, I'd forgotten it. But it's coming back slowly."

"In other words, there could be other things you've forgotten?"

"I don't think so. I'd probably suppressed the memory of the flowers, it was a setback."

"You didn't have other setbacks in the course of the evening?"

"Oh yes, the collision, you could call that a setback."

"But that wasn't your fault, you had the right of way."

"Yes. But it was a miserable end to a miserable evening."

Sejer nods and makes notes. "Is that the way you'd characterise the evening? Miserable?"

"Yes. I got home completely exhausted. I felt as if I'd been put through a mill."

"So it was pretty bad. But is it your instability you're talking about now? You were exhausted by it?"

"Yes. I remember sitting in a chair in my living room, and finding my wits slowly returning. As if I'd been far away."

"Had you been?"

"What?"

"Had you been far away? Out of yourself?"

"Yes, I think you could say that. As if my body and soul had lost contact with each other. Have you ever experienced that?"

"Yes, I have indeed. You feel like a robot."

"Exactly," nods Charlo.

"Did you feel like a robot?"

"You could put it that way."

"What sort of injuries did you sustain in the collision?"

"Injuries? Oh, nothing at all. I got off with a bad shock. And I strained both wrists because I was clutching the wheel so hard."

"So you escaped completely uninjured?"

"Yes, we both did. Or did he injure himself? He said nothing about it. But then he didn't get the chance because I was so mad."

"No, he hasn't said anything about it. He was actually talking about you."

"I suffered no injuries, as I've said."

Sejer sits back in his chair and looks appraisingly at him.

"There was blood on the lower part of your parka. Where did it come from?"

"No, you're on a wild goose chase again. There was no blood anywhere."

"On the right side of your parka. Obvious bloodstains."

"I think I know what he was referring to. That parka did have some bad stains, and he possibly thought they were blood. I was changing the engine oil on one occasion, and I made a mess. That was why I threw it away, as I've already said."

"You dumped it because it was worn out."

"And because it was stained."

"Once again, you've left out a detail. Let's look at some others."

"No, there's no point. There's nothing more to say."

"You weren't involved in a brawl with anyone in the locality?"

"Certainly not, I'm a peaceable man. And I certainly would have remembered that."

"Yes, I believe you when you say you're peaceable. But we have in fact established that you do occasionally lose control."

"Only very rarely."

"And the seventh of November was one of those rare occasions. I believe you'd had just about as much as you could take that evening. I believe that's why you keep forgetting things. Let's try again. You drove round to the back of the hotel and parked. A man walking a dog observed the car. This isn't something I suspect or suggest, it's something I know for a fact."

Charlo closes his eyes. I'm ill, he thinks, gradually I'll get weaker and weaker. I mustn't think about that now. He says: "All right. I must have forgotten that as well. I sat there and had a cigarette, then I drove out again."

"Out again and where?"

"Past the railway station to this celebrated junction."

"You drove straight from the hotel and had a collision?"

"That's right."

"So, you needed a cigarette?"

"Yes."

"Did you have to drive to the back of a hotel to roll a cigarette?"

"No. Not really. I could have stopped along the road, there wasn't any traffic."

"So why this manoeuvre?"

"I don't know. Perhaps I wanted to hide. I was feeling pretty desperate."

"You say you were desperate. Tell me about that feeling of desperation. Did it come over you slowly? Or in a sudden rush?"

"I can't remember that well. No, I think it came on slowly. I don't know, I had so many emotions. I badly needed a way out. A way out of all my difficulties."

"Was that what you were thinking when you drove out of town? That you needed a way out?"

"Yes, I was thinking about that a lot."

"You'd given up the idea of robbing a bank. Did you have any other ideas?"

"The bank job was a joke. I never gave it serious consideration."

"OK. Perhaps you thought of something else?"

"No, everything looked bleak."

"But still you drove to Hamsund? Taking the E134 along the river, and then on to the R35?"

"I was hoping something would turn up."

"A miracle?"

"I don't believe in miracles."

"You had a more tangible plan?"

Charlo wrings his hands, reaches for his tobacco. Tears it out of the pouch and lays it on a cigarette paper.

"Only vague thoughts."

"Can you let me in on them?"

"No. I'm not taking that chance, you could get the wrong idea."

"What sort of wrong idea?"

"About what I've done and haven't done."

"So you're worried about that? About what I think?"

"I know what you're after, I'm not that stupid."

"Tell me."

"You don't need me to do that."

"I don't. But I think it's good to put things into words. It's not as dangerous as you think."

"I've got my own thoughts about that."

"That's your prerogative."

A pause. Each falls silent. Sejer thinks his own thoughts. Charlo tries to rest a bit, restore himself. He curls his toes in his trainers, no problem.

"So, you drove up Fredboesgate. You parked behind the old hotel, then you left the car. Where did you go?"

"I didn't go anywhere. I just sat in the car smoking."

"You've forgotten something important again, Mr Torp. The witness who spotted your car said it was empty. You weren't in it. Where had you gone?"

"Maybe I took a stroll along the street, I can't quite remember."

"Can you remember Harriet's house?"

"I've no idea where she lived."

"In the green house, number four."

"No, I can't remember that."

"But you looked at the lovely listed buildings?"

"I admired them, but not in great detail."

"Tell me where you went."

"Well, I might have walked to the end of the street, and then possibly I turned and came back again."

"Did you meet anyone?"

"Not a soul."

"This is very important, Mr Torp. What time was it when you took your stroll in Fredboesgate?"

He forgets to think, and answers straight out.

"It must have been ten or thereabouts."

"In other words, whatever you did in Fredboesgate, took half an hour? Your car accident occurred at ten-thirty."

"Well, it took half an hour then. To walk up and down the street."

"You went up and down several times?"

"You're making it sound as if I did. I can't think properly any more."

"That's because we're going in circles. Perhaps we ought to get right to the heart of the case?"

"What case?"

260

"The murder of Harriet Krohn. That's why you're here, you do realise that?"

"Naturally. Unfortunately I was in the same area, and you people have got no one else to bring in. That's why I'm here. But driving about the roads is no crime."

"Of course not. Even so I find it strange. Up and down Fredboesgate for half an hour. Desperate and depressed, in a wet parka?"

"Yes, I was at rock bottom."

"You felt yourself to be of unsound mind?"

"No, I wouldn't say that. That's putting it too strongly."

"Were you thinking about the solution? The one you needed so badly?"

"I suppose I was. But I found no solution. I went back to the car, drove away and let all my despair rain down over the lad in the Toyota. That's all there is to say about it. I'm sorry, you wanted something else, I'm sure. But that's all you're getting."

Sejer checks his papers again.

"Some minutes ago you said that it was ten-thirty when you turned off towards Hamsund. Now you've changed your statement. You walked up Fredboesgate at ten o'clock. Any comment about that?"

"Not really. My brain's a bit weary."

There's a silence. The dog gets up suddenly and whines, giving his master a doleful look.

"Let's go outside for a minute, Mr Torp, and stretch our legs. Frank needs to go anyway."

The dog heads for a flowerbed outside the courthouse. He rummages amongst ornamental shrubs and emerging perennials for a good spot. Then he crouches awkwardly and does his business. Sejer pulls a plastic bag from his pocket.

"What sort of age will he live to?" Charlo asks.

"Quite a considerable one, probably. For a dog at least. Frank is a Chinese fighting dog. A Shar Pei. I hope he'll be with me a long time."

He places the bag in a litter bin. Charlo breathes in the fresh air. He is grateful for the break, he's regained control. It's important to keep a check on oneself, not make a slip of the tongue. It's like walking a tightrope.

"Are you a religious man, Mr Torp?"

"Not really. But there's some sort of God out there. He's got his back turned, though."

"I'm not religious either," says Sejer. "But I've got a lot of time for Roman Catholic confession."

Charlo rolls up his sleeves.

"Why so?" he asks and stops as the dog pauses. It's sniffing at a sweet wrapper.

"Confession is a type of discipline. You have to express things out loud, you have to find the words. So, at the end of your life, you'll be glad you're not full of unpleasant secrets. Because you've confessed them bit by bit."

"You're an investigator," Charlo says. "I can see why you'd appreciate confessions."

"Yes, but it isn't just that I like them. I mean, at the time it can be hard to see how any good can come out of a confession. But in the long run. For the remainder of your life."

262

"I'm unconvinced," Charlo says, "I imagine a sin getting bigger when one shows it to others. That it grows and brings with it a whole load of reproach."

"In the short term, yes. But I'm talking about the rest of our lives," says Sejer. "I'm thinking about how we've got to die sometime. How we'll be lying there in a bed knowing that the end is near. To manage that, we must be able to let go of life. If we don't confide, we have to take all our misery to the grave with us. I shouldn't like to do that."

Charlo thinks about what he's said.

"We don't take anything to the grave with us."

"No. But we carry it with us during the process of dying. And the process must be hard enough without that. Don't you think?"

Charlo reaches for his tobacco again. The dog vanishes into a shrubbery once more and begins digging enthusiastically with its puppy paws, making the earth fly out behind it.

"I prefer cats," Charlo says.

"Why?"

"They don't demand things of us like dogs do. Dogs are so intimate, so intense. They make their presence felt all the time. Panting. Begging. Cats are more on the periphery, they jump on your lap if they feel like it, and leave when they can't be bothered any more. They don't impinge on your thoughts."

"You don't like that? Having your thoughts disturbed?"

"No, it makes me bad-tempered. I'm rather childish that way."

"So the Toyota that crashed into you disturbed your thoughts?"

"Yes. I was concentrating deeply just then, on other things."

"Tell me."

"The day had been long and hard. At last I was going home. To my chair and my bed. In my mind I was already at home, I was longing to be there. So I wasn't paying attention."

He lights his cigarette and inhales.

"Because the evening had been an ordeal?"

"Yes. It was an ordeal. I felt as if I was clinging to a cliff-edge, only a void beneath me. I couldn't see any future, only darkness and despair."

"Wasn't there anyone you could phone?"

"No. I've only got Julie. And she has to be spared at all costs, she mustn't get mixed up in my problems."

"You think you can prevent that? They grow up, you know. And they understand a great deal."

"Yes, yes. You're right of course. And she certainly is a smart cookie. But I can't bear the thought of her being worried about me. Children shouldn't worry about adults."

"But she isn't a child. She's seventeen. What do you think she'll be doing now? She knows where you are. She's sitting alone with her thoughts. Waiting. Looking at the clock. Her imagination running riot."

"Well, I'll explain to her. I'll explain," he says again, and takes a pull at his roll-up. Determination written on his face.

"So, you've got an explanation?"

264

"Of course."

"Is it a good one?"

"I think so."

Sejer makes for a bench. He lowers himself on to it and Charlo follows his example.

"Will I think it's good?" Sejer's eyes settle on him.

"I don't know. Don't think so."

"Don't underestimate me."

"No. But you've never been in my shoes."

"I've had plenty of problems of my own."

They fall quiet, raise their faces to the sun.

"You don't look like a harassed man," Charlo says after the silence. "You're doing well. A good job and a nice office. Responsibility. Authority. I've got none of those, I've never had them."

"Did you want them?"

"Naturally. But I got completely sucked into gambling. It ruined things for me. For my family."

"Yes, we become obsessed by things, affected by things. But there is always a choice."

"I've never felt that. I've always felt driven."

"Driven to gambling addiction and embezzlement?"

"Yes. You talk like all the rest of them. The ones that say you can just choose, and stop doing all those destructive things. It points to a lack of imagination, and knowledge of what a human being is."

"And what is a human being?"

Charlo shuts his eyes. "There are probably as many answers as there are human beings. And I hate all that guff about free will."

"Because you feel you haven't got it. But many people would maintain that they do have it. You're envious, and so you dismiss the term."

"You're very psychological."

"It's part of my job. But really, I'm genuinely curious about all types of people."

"I'm not particularly interesting."

"You must let others be the judges of that. You can't know how others perceive you."

Suddenly, Frank comes bouncing up with something in his mouth.

"Well, my goodness," Sejer says bending down. "This rascal's found a bone!"

"It looks rotten," Charlo says.

"It doesn't matter. Look how proud he is."

"Yes, their lives are simple."

"And yours is more complicated?"

"As things stand," Charlo says, "the rest of my life is a blur. I can't make anything out clearly."

"That sounds a bit dramatic."

"Yes. There's a lot you don't know."

"Feel free to tell me. I'm sitting here."

"I'm just trying to retain a little dignity."

"I've no plans to rob you of it, it wouldn't be in my interest. Dignity is an important thing."

"I don't think I've ever had much."

"Now you really do sound pessimistic. You've paid your debts, got yourself a job etcetera. Made it up to Julie."

"Yes, but it'll be a long road. And I may not even be able to walk."

266

"What's this you're saying?"

"Nothing."

Sejer falls silent again, reaches down and steals the dog's bone. It growls at once and begins scratching at his trouser leg. They sit there for twenty minutes. Charlo drinks in the sun's warmth. Now and again he moves his legs carefully, feels that they're there. They seem healthy, he can twiddle his foot. At the moment.

Sejer asks questions.

Always in that calm tone, there's nothing threatening about him. Charlo answers. He's always got to think first; gradually a weariness settles over his mind, a lack of awareness of what he's already said. A degree of confusion. He becomes nervous. He feels an overpowering urge to tell all, to move on. To lie down on a bed, close his eyes, empty his head. No, says a voice inside him, keep quiet!

"What were you thinking about as you sat in your car behind the hotel?"

"I'm not sure. I was thinking about everything and nothing. My thoughts were all over the place, I wasn't concentrating. That's probably why I crashed. Normally, I'd have realised that the Toyota wasn't going to stop."

"But things weren't normal?"

"I was in a tight corner. And the collision jarred me out of my reverie. I'm actually very sorry about it. Sometimes I think I should try to get hold of him, explain, and apologise. He was very upset when I began shouting and swearing. I mean, I'm usually polite. My parents were very hot on that, they taught me to behave properly, and I do."

"I don't doubt it."

"When I was young and dating Inga Lill, I did everything by the book. I had a job and a house. Plenty to offer. It's funny to think of that now."

"But then you lost it all? Tell me how it all started."

"It was like being caught in an undertow. The gambling. The wins. The losses were merely a necessary part of it, each win made up for everything. Have you ever tried it?"

"No, I never gamble. No pools, no lottery. I don't play board games, either. I've got a grandson, and I've looked after him all through his childhood. I've read to him, taken him to the cinema, played football, run through the forest with him, taken him on trips. But I've never played a game with him."

"Why not?"

"I'm scared he might win."

Charlo looks at him across the desk.

"So, in fact, you're scared as well. You haven't left any case unsolved in your entire police career."

"So you read that article?"

"Julie found it in the paper."

"Does it make you nervous?"

"No. I'm impressed, of course. But that record will be broken sometime. Perhaps it will be broken this year. Because you can't find the Hamsund murderer."

"I haven't given up hope. I'm tenacious."

"Certainly. But perhaps he is, too. Have you considered that?"

"Frequently."

Once more, Charlo glances over at Frank.

"You really have trained that dog well. Even though he's still a puppy. How did you manage it?"

"It's a mystery to me as well. But Frank does what I tell him. It's a gift that's fallen into my lap. I deserve no credit for it. What about you and horses? Have you got a good rapport with them?"

"Yes, I find it as easy as pie. I just react to them naturally. It's a matter of reading them. They send out a mass of signals which have to be read."

"But how did you learn to do it?"

"It's just a natural talent, I think. Nothing I deserve any credit for."

Sejer clasps his hands behind his head and stretches in his chair.

"But you deserve credit for something, surely?"

"I really don't know what for. Well, yes, I do work hard for Møller. And I look after Julie. That's good, if a little belated, if you know what I mean."

"Has she got any other adults she can turn to?"

"No, only friends of her own age. Why d'you ask?"

"I just wondered. You said that the rest of your life is a blur. Perhaps it's a good thing she's almost grown up?"

"It is good."

"Let's return to Fredboesgate."

"I don't particularly want to."

"I understand that, Mr Torp. But we must."

"I'm not going to go back to it at all, I find it obnoxious. I think I've said enough."

"Did something happen there that you don't want to talk about?"

"I think I've said what there is to say. I'm sorry, but I've nothing more to give."

"Not even a few small details?"

"Especially not details."

"D'you find them unpleasant?"

"I'm beginning to wonder if I shouldn't have a solicitor."

Sejer nods. "It's up to you. Do you need one?"

"No, I haven't done anything."

"In that case you can tell it just the way it was. You bought a bunch of flowers to gain access to Harriet Krohn's kitchen. They were on her kitchen worktop, Mr Torp. A lily, roses and anemones."

"Yes, I remember the bouquet, but they were for Julie."

"Describe the bouquet you bought."

"For Christ's sake. There were several sorts of flowers, I don't know the names of any of them."

"But you said you remembered it. Maybe you remember the colours?"

"Well, there was some pink and blue. I didn't ask for anything in particular, I just asked her to make up a mixed bouquet."

"And it ended up in a rubbish bin where?"

"Possibly it was at the Shell services at the top of Oscarsgate. I stopped there after I'd been to Julie's."

"Why?"

"Er, I went into the shop."

"Yet another visit you've forgotten. You said you didn't go in anywhere."

"Yes, but I'm starting to get tired. It's hardly surprising I'm getting muddled."

"Absolutely, I quite see that. It's why I'm continuing to ask questions. Because it's my belief that, sooner or later, we'll get to the important matters."

"And what are those?"

"The murder of Harriet Krohn. Answer me this, Mr Torp: what kind of weapon did you have with you?"

"I didn't have any weapon."

"A baseball bat?"

"No."

"A hammer, perhaps?"

"Didn't you hear? I said no. I didn't have any weapon!"

"Just flowers?"

"Yes. I mean, no. Now I'm getting confused. Can't you go a bit more slowly?"

"I'm sorry."

Sejer leans back defensively.

"So, you walked to Miss Krohn's house, armed only with flowers?"

Charlo keeps silent. What was it he just admitted?

"No, I didn't go to Miss Krohn's house."

Sejer leans forward once more.

"Come on, Mr Torp, don't start going up a blind alley again, or we're never going to get anywhere."

"And where are we supposed to get to?"

"To the truth. We're going to get to the truth."

"And what is the truth according to you? That I killed Harriet Krohn?"

"You're the one with the answers here. The explanations. I'm not going to second-guess. But I can be plain and ask you directly. Did you kill Harriet Krohn?"

"No."

"She was alive when you left the house, is that what you're saying?"

"Yes."

He puts his hands to his head. Expels the air from his lungs, tries to twist away. "She was lying on the floor. In the kitchen."

He hunches in his chair and hides his face in his hands. He's fallen over the precipice.

"Why?"

"I gave her a little push."

He looks up at Sejer again, wishing to save what he can.

"That's how you'd describe it? A push?"

"Yes. But she was quite thin and fragile, and she may have struck the kitchen unit as she fell. She may have passed out."

"And you left her there, lying by the kitchen unit?"

"Yes. I got panicky, you know, I thought perhaps she'd injured herself."

"You can do better than that, Mr Torp. There was a great deal of blood in the kitchen. You knew for a fact she was injured. And you panicked?"

"Yes."

272

"But not enough to leave the silver behind. Did you find some cash, too?"

Charlo grimaces. "Yes, I found a few kroner in her bedroom."

He looks past Sejer and out of the window, at the clouds.

"Can you be a little more exact about the amount?"

"Well, several thousand-krone notes."

Sejer nods to himself.

"So there was no lottery win?"

"No, I just made it up."

"Why did you push her?"

"Because she went mad when I opened her sideboard. She attacked me from behind and began screaming and scratching. I became desperate, I admit it; you see, I get like that sometimes. I couldn't understand why she was getting so worked up about her silver."

"So you pushed her hard?"

"Not especially hard. She came at me again and carried on, and I remember thinking how greedy she was for that silver, as if it was the most precious thing she had. She could have let me take it without a fuss, and she'd have fared better."

"She's dead, Mr Torp. She was killed."

"Well, I just can't understand that because, as I said, I only gave her a push. She ran out into the kitchen, and I ran after her, and pushed her again, and of course it was just my luck that her forehead hit the edge of the metal draining board, but that was what happened. And

I don't regard it as murder, I mean, it was an accident. Not something I'd planned in advance."

Sejer makes notes and says nothing. Charlo's mouth is dry, but his glass is empty. He waits, his mind in turmoil.

"Mr Torp," Sejer says slowly. "You've come a long way, and I'm grateful for that. But you're leaving out certain important facts. Your explanation isn't quite full enough."

"It happened just the way I said. I was only interested in her silver, I got agitated and gave her a shove."

"But we've examined the victim carefully. And her injuries don't concur with your account. In other words, we've got a problem. I must ask you to go into more detail."

"I've already said that I don't like going into details. I think I've given you a lot now, I've bent over backwards."

"You're to be commended for that. We're definitely getting somewhere. But if Miss Krohn had fallen and struck the unit, she would have had a lump on her forehead. The fact is that the victim sustained severe injuries. What did you hit her with?"

"I didn't hit her. I sort of pushed her away from me, because she was clinging on to me like a leech. She was really irritating me."

"According to our experts the weapon was probably metal, with some kind of sharp edge. Have you got any suggestions?"

"It must have been the edge of the draining board."

274

"It's not sharp, it has more of a rounded profile, I saw that for myself when I was in the house."

"I haven't got anything more to contribute, nothing more to say."

"When did you arrive at her house?"

"At about ten o'clock."

"Tell me what happened."

"I was at my wits' end, as I said. I rang the bell, and she came to the door. I said I had a flower delivery, and that I needed a signature. So she went back into the house to fetch her glasses, and I followed her. I caught sight of the sideboard at once, and thought that the valuables would be inside it. I opened it and pulled the drawers out. There was a lot of silver, and it was old. But then she got really irate. She flew at me, and I hit out as best I could to keep her off me. I suppose it seems ridiculous, she looked so frail, but just then she was strong and totally beside herself. I thought that was stupid. I wasn't going to do anything to her. She rushed out into the kitchen, and I followed. Then I pushed her against the unit. She collapsed on the floor. And I was very concerned about that, obviously, but I was worried about getting away."

"How did you transport the silver?"

"I put it in a cotton bag I had with me."

"And the money?"

"I found it in her bedroom, inside a wardrobe."

"And then?"

"Then I left the house. I got into the car. Naturally I was a bit shaky. But it was all over quite quickly. I smoked a roll-up and started the car. Drove down to the railway station. And had the collision. That was when I really brimmed over, as I've already explained."

"What did you do with the weapon?"

"I didn't have a weapon, I'm just a common burglar, you can't get me for anything else."

"You'll be charged with murder and aggravated burglary. That's quite a different matter."

"Ask the pathologist to check in case she had a stroke or a haemorrhage from the shock. Because I didn't kill anyone. I'm not like that."

Sejer leans back in his chair, seeming to relax a bit, and for an instant he closes his eyes.

"She had multiple skull fractures," he says at length. "Thirteen in all."

"Old people have brittle bones, they can't take much."

"When did you decide to go to Harriet Krohn's?"

"When I was wandering about the town frantically seeking a solution."

"You said you hadn't planned it."

"Yes, it was done on impulse."

"But you'd brought along a cotton bag for the silver. Did you bring it from home?"

Charlo bites his lip. "Can I have some Farris?"

Sejer nods and gets up, goes and fetches a bottle from the fridge.

"No, the bag was already in the car, it's Julie's old gym bag, it was just lying in the back seat."

"How convenient, Mr Torp."

"Yes."

"Let me explain. There was a great deal of blood in the kitchen. And a big pool round the corpse. You don't get that amount of blood when someone falls and strikes their head on a sharp edge."

"You people will have to work out the blood thing, it's not my job to explain it."

"What will explain it is the weapon you used. Tell me now, don't waste time. You've got a daughter who's waiting to hear from you, and we all need to get on with our lives."

Charlo takes a drink of Farris.

"I can't see how it matters. She's dead, tragically, everything else is just detail, and it won't bring her back to life again."

"Think again. You'll have to defend yourself, and then everything will have to be right. If you stand up in court and lie, the jury will use it against you."

"But, for Christ's sake . . ."

"For his sake, certainly, but most of all for your own. What did you hit her with?"

Charlo squeezes his eyes shut and opens them again. Oh, God. He'd better go the last mile as well; he needs rest, he needs sleep. He needs to come to himself again.

"The butt of a revolver."

Sejer lets out a contented sigh.

"Well, that's out in the open. What kind of revolver was it?"

"An old Husqvarna from the war. It belonged to my father. And for the record, it wasn't loaded. I didn't want to hurt anyone, only scare them."

"Instead you used it as a club?"

"Yes, she was so determined. God, I didn't know what to do. I hit her once on the head. The thing about the kitchen unit wasn't true, but I didn't want to look like a cold-blooded murderer, because I'm not. But you're pushing me so hard, I can't take any more. We've got to end now, I've made a clean breast of everything."

"How many times did you hit her?"

"Only once. Or, well, it might have been twice."

"Mr Torp, I repeat: she had thirteen skull fractures."

"That can't be right. That's not the way I remember it."

"Her skull was smashed. And some of her blood spattered on to your parka."

Charlo hangs his head. "How did you track me down?" he asks suddenly. "After all this time. I can't understand it."

"Straightforward, methodical investigation. Time-consuming work. Countless conversations with lots of people about every minute observation. I'm not giving you more detail than that. But I want to ask you this. Why did you choose Harriet Krohn?"

"Pure chance, really. I sometimes used the same cafe that she went to with a friend. It's popular with the elderly. I noticed her at once. She was so plainly dressed, a person who spent little money on herself. Who just saved and saved over the years. She was also very frail, and she wore a thick, gold bracelet on her wrist. It was a kind of promise that she was prosperous. I followed her to the green house and saw that she lived alone."

"So you planned this over time?"

278

"Not really. I simply felt impelled."

"Are you ready to make a full statement?"

"Do we have to go through it all over again? I don't know if I can."

"I know it's been an effort, Mr Torp. The more frank and precise you are, the sooner we'll be finished. Afterwards, you can rest."

"Whatever you do, don't take the horse away from Julie! I don't think she'd get over it."

"You should have thought of that before."

"But she lives for that horse! And surely she shouldn't be allowed to suffer for what I've done?"

"Did you pay for it with Harriet Krohn's money?"

"Yes. I sold the silver."

"To whom?"

"No, I don't want to shop anyone."

"As things stand, I think you ought to concentrate on yourself and your own situation. And excuse my curiosity, but before we start from the beginning again, there's one small detail that's nagging me."

"Yes?"

"How did you damage that front tooth of yours?"

Charlo puts a hand up to his mouth. Thinks back.

"It happened about five years ago. At the pub. I'd had a bit too much to drink, and was paying a visit to the loo. On the way out I tripped, and my mouth hit the edge of the washbasin. I tripped," he repeats, and suddenly something dawns on him. He's always blamed the drink. Perhaps, in reality, his legs gave way under him. Even then. He falls silent.

"What are you thinking about, Mr Torp?"

279

"That I should have had it fixed, but I didn't have the money. It doesn't look very nice, does it?"

"Not at all," Sejer says smiling. "It's one of those charming little details. That people notice, and remember."

CHAPTER
SIXTEEN

He spends four weeks on remand.

Then a further four weeks, and all the time he isn't allowed any letters or visitors. He passes much of his time dozing on the narrow bunk beneath the window, he glides away and forgets everything, until he's rudely awoken by keys jangling in the lock. The days are uniform, they blend into one another, uneventfully. He often sits by the window staring out. Not much happens out there, a woman on a bicycle is a real treat, he notes all the details, the bike's shiny paint, the flapping skirt, the glimpses of naked, golden calves. A couple of youngsters messing about with a skateboard. Little things. The cloud formations, the trees moving in the wind, their great crowns swaying. A flock of birds crossing the sky.

He likes the food and he eats well. In the evenings he's allowed to go into the yard for a smoke. He tells them about his illness, informs them in subdued tones of his possible fate in a few years' time. They listen and nod, but they don't show him the sympathy he'd hoped for. So far he's been able to manage, but at times he finds himself waiting for the big deterioration. The disease is like a dormant volcano, frequently he lies on his bunk sensing his body. Nothing that happens in it escapes him, or his questioning anxiety. A stitch in his side, a sensation in his leg, it's all analysed.

At last he's allowed visitors. He lets Julie know and settles down to wait. He walks in a tight circle in his cell, to get his body warm. There's so much he wants to say. She has the right to an explanation. He knows he's got the words. He's been through everything so often in his thoughts, and latterly with his lawyer. He knows that he can explain his panic. When she attacked him, from behind, and began screaming. He looks at the time, he glances out of the window. Straightens the blanket on the bunk slightly, nervously adjusts his shirt collar. Julie is so wise, so sensible. He believes it will be all right. He runs his hand through his hair, looks at the time again and waits. His ears are tuned to the noises in the corridor, he listens for sounds of footsteps and keys. Soon they'll stand in the door saying, you've got a visitor, Torp. It only takes five minutes to walk up from Oscarsgate to the courthouse, she'll be on time for sure. No doubt she'll be pleased to see him, he does another round of the floor. He prepares himself, feels that he's in control. He ends up standing by the window. The traffic outside is intermittent. The odd car, the occasional woman with a pram, the weather is warm and sunny. It doesn't occur to him that he'll spend years within these four walls, it's incomprehensible to him. It doesn't occur to him that he'll do time: after all, he's ill. And so he's buoyant and light-hearted, and only focused on Julie who'll soon be here.

He's quite certain she'll be here.

CHAPTER
SEVENTEEN

The town is in constant flux and resembles a building site with its heavy plant and cranes. People, both good and bad, walk about its streets. The strong and the weak. Those who've never been tested. Those who live in blissful ignorance of what really lurks within them, in the dark corners of their minds. The ordinary people live on the east side, the wealthy on the west, and the higher up the hillside you go, the larger and more expensive are the dwellings. At the foot of the hill stands the courthouse. A gently curving, dirty grey building of iron and glass and concrete. The county jail is on the fifth floor. The low sun strikes a window, throwing a rectangle of sunlight on the green floor. The cell measures eight square metres and contains a desk and a bunk. A man lies on the bunk. He lies quite still with his hands cupped behind his head, flexing his toes inside his socks. Time flows through him, just as the river outside flows past, even and inexorable. He lies waiting for his lunch, feels his stomach rumbling. He decides to write a letter. Writing is pleasant, and he can use it to fill the remaining hour. He gets up and goes over to the desk, pulls out the chair. He opens a lined pad of paper. He takes a deep breath and puts pen to paper, he writes:

Dearest Julie,

It's Dad here again, I'm sorry to pester you, but we've got so much to talk about now, you know, that I'll carry on writing until you answer. You will answer, won't you? I assume you got my message, that now I can have visitors, so just come along, they're pretty good here, but it would be an idea if you rang first so that I can get myself ready. I must admit to being a little nervous, but after all, we do know each other, and I'm sure we can work it out, I'm sure we can. So just come one day when it's convenient, I won't be going anywhere, and I need to explain things so badly. You've got a right to an explanation. Now that you know everything. Now that you know how things stand, how ill I am, how uncertain my future is; if the worst comes to the worst I could become dependent, I'm sure you understand how serious this is, that we've got to keep in contact, I have no one else, after all. I've only got myself to blame, I know that, but that doesn't make it any the less painful to be as alone as I am now, it's unbearable. I see the others getting visits, and it's hard to be the only one sitting alone in my cell all day long. Presumably you're hard at it with exams and suchlike, I know that you're clever and single-minded, and of course I'm glad that you're putting school first, education is important, and if you want to get to veterinary college you'll need good marks. So, just get stuck into your work and keep at it, but don't forget that I'm here waiting. I'm hoping for a bit of understanding. You're astute and practically grown up now, perhaps you need time, perhaps you're in shock, but it'll pass.

284

We're still working hard, my lawyer and me, to get a pardon on grounds of ill health, but that's not the only avenue we're looking into. When I think back to that terrible day, 7 November, many things become clear to me, because in here I've got plenty of time, and I've delved into myself and analysed the situation and what actually happened. I walked the streets as if delirious, I moved with a fever in my body, as if on greased rails. Before me an abyss, behind me only wretchedness, it was like having a pack of mongrels snapping at my heels, a situation so extreme that it threatened my very sanity, if you know what I mean. All this proved too much for me; I realise now that I was probably psychotic. I dimly recall an argument raging inside my head, which is one of the symptoms and, I'm sure you know, mental illness must lead to acquittal. There's plenty of documentation from similar cases. I've at last realised that I probably wasn't of sound mind. If they make me serve time for this, it should be in a hospital; it's true I've confessed, but I haven't admitted criminal liability, according to my excellent counsel, whose name is Friis. Now you know how the matter stands.

The disease continues to develop, I often fall on the way to the exercise yard, in the corridor, and the prison officers converge from all directions to try to get me back on my feet again. I don't know whether to laugh or cry, and sometimes I hear witty comments, I try to laugh them off. I try to understand why this has happened to me. In the evenings I lie on my bunk and think about the future, it doesn't look bright, but even so I've settled down, I don't complain, just daydream a lot about the good times with you and Crazy. I've made no friends, I don't feel any affinity with the others who are locked up here.

Dearest Julie, you mustn't worry about Crazy, I'll find a way out and, if necessary, I'll sell the house, so that you'll be able to pay for him with honest money. My lawyer will help me, at least there's someone on my side. I never wanted this to happen, and I think you know that, but it would be nice if you said it out loud, I don't think that's too much to ask. Can't you search within yourself and come up with a little forbearance? Something that would make my days a bit easier?

The legal system is merciless, it's a mill that goes grinding on and on. I often feel exhausted, drained of all strength, but I'm impressed with the prison officers, they're not bothered about what the inmates have done, they do their jobs and are friendly, and I should add: far more understanding than other people.

Are you looking after yourself? The worst thing of all is that I can't help you any more, but I'm always with you in thought, and even though you've turned your back on me now, we're bound together by unbreakable ties. I won't give up hoping that maybe you'll write back, or come here one day, to visit. This letter isn't a long one because it's lunchtime now, you see, and I'm hungry, I haven't lost my appetite, I need food, I try to enjoy the small things, try to carry on. And then they bring reading material into my cell, that's so good, that makes the time pass quickly. I'll write again next week. Don't believe what you read in the newspapers, they don't tell the whole story, they're bland and sensationalist, trying to portray me as a cold-blooded killer, and you can't get further from the truth than that, as you'll realise because you understand me. But I'm the only one who knows the real

286

truth, no one else saw what happened, and it can all be explained. If only you'll give me the chance.

I'm not a wicked man!

For the love of God, Julie, you must believe me!

DARK AS MY HEART

Antti Tuomainen

Aleski lost his mother on a rainy October day when he was thirteen years old. Twenty years later, he is certain that he knows who's responsible. Everything points to millionaire Henrik Saarinen. But the police don't agree. So Aleski has only one option: to get close to Saarinen and find out, on his own, the truth about his mother's fate. But as he soon discovers, delving into Saarinen and his alluring daughter's family secrets is a confusing and dangerous enterprise . . .

BITTER FRUITS

Alice Clark-Platts

The murder of a first-year university student shocks the city of Durham. The victim, Emily Brabents, was from the privileged and popular set at Joyce College, a cradle for the country's future elite. As Detective Inspector Erica Martin investigates the college, she finds a close-knit community fuelled by jealousy, obsession and secrets. The very last thing she expects is an instant confession . . . The picture of Emily that begins to emerge is that of a girl wanted by everyone, but not truly known by anyone — that is, except for Daniel Shepherd: her fellow student and ever-faithful friend, and the only one who cares. The only one who would do *anything* for her . . .